John Stuart Blackie, Archibald Stodart Walker

Selected Poems

Of John Stuart Blackie

John Stuart Blackie, Archibald Stodart Walker

Selected Poems
Of John Stuart Blackie

ISBN/EAN: 9783744770880

Printed in Europe, USA, Canada, Australia, Japan

Cover: Foto ©Raphael Reischuk / pixelio.de

More available books at **www.hansebooks.com**

The Selected Poems

OF

John Stuart Blackie

EDITED WITH AN APPRECIATION

BY

ARCHIBALD STODART WALKER

WITH A PORTRAIT
After the Painting by J. H. Lorimer, A.R.S.A.

LONDON

JOHN MACQUEEN

HASTINGS HOUSE, NORFOLK STREET, STRAND

1896

So I will sing on—fast as fancies come
Rudely—the verse being as the mood it paints.

.   .   .   .

I am made up of an intensest life.'

ROBERT BROWNING.

Forsitan et nostrum nomen miscebitur istis:
Nec mea Lethæis scripta dabuntur aquis.

OVIDIUS.

Dedicated

WITH DEEP AFFECTION

TO

TWO GOOD WOMEN

HIS WIFE—MY AUNT

HIS SISTER—MY MOTHER

INTRODUCTORY NOTE

IN compiling this volume of selections from the poems of John Stuart Blackie, I am but carrying out a wish which he expressed to me shortly before he died. This holiday task I have taken as a work of love. My uncle never troubled himself as to the question of whether he was a major or minor poet, and in presenting this volume I prefer merely to announce it in the words of the sub-title of his 'Messis Vitae,' namely as 'Gleanings of Song from a Happy Life.' Many of the lays, lyrics and ballads included, are familiar to Scots throughout the world, and it is my hope that this selection will be as welcome to them as to a wider public not so familiar with these joyous effusions of a healthy soul.

In placing the selections under various headings, my division has necessarily been more or less arbitrary, and for a palpable reason I offer no apology for including certain lays, as, for instance, 'The Lay

of the Brave Cameron,' under the heading of
' Ballads.'

With the exception of a few hitherto unpublished
poems, the selection is made from 'The Lays and
Legends of Ancient Greece,' 'Lyrical Poems,' 'Lays
of the Highlands and Islands,' 'Musa Burschicosa,'
'Messis Vitae,' 'Songs of Religion and Life,' 'The
War Songs of the Germans,' and 'The Language
and Literature of the Scottish Highlands,' to the
publishers of which, Messrs William Blackwood &
Sons, Messrs Macmillan & Co., Mr David Douglas
and Mr Walter Scott, I have to express my gratitude
for their gracious consent to quote from works of
which they hold the copyright, or part copyright.

It is only necessary for me to add, that if any
poem is omitted from the volume, which anyone, acquainted with the poems of my uncle, deems worthy
of inclusion in such a selection, I can only plead the
excuses for neglecting such an inclusion, of the limit
of my space and the limit of my judgment.

A. S. W.

30 WALKER STREET, EDINBURGH,
    March 1896.

CONTENTS

SONNETS

CONTENTS

BALLADS, LEGENDS AND NARRATIVE POEMS

TRANSLATIONS FROM THE GAELIC

CONTENTS

TRANSLATIONS FROM THE GERMAN

Selected Poems of John Stuart Blackie

AN APPRECIATION

' If Love will serve, lo ! how I love my friend,
If Reverence, lo ! how I reverence him,
If Faith be asked in something beautiful,
Lo ! what a splendour is my faith in him.'
ROBERT BUCHANAN.

IT is not for me to attempt to sketch the life history of John Stuart Blackie. That has already been done in an intelligent and sympathetic way by Miss Anna Stoddart, and my readers will turn to her pages for most that is worthy of record and preservation in the story of his rich and active life. All I can hope to attempt is, to lay a small stone upon his cairn ; to give, in attempting to estimate the character of the man, a small tribute of esteem to one, whom from close personal intercourse I learned to love, and I hope, understand well.

If, as I firmly believe, that man can estimate best who loves best, then I can offer no apology for my estimation. I do not presume a criticism, though that is much easier, as Vauvenarques says, than an estimation, and if what I write may savour more of a eulogy than an appreciation, I would only ask that my presentation be judged in the light of my intimate acquaintance and of my affection.

I have many memories of him, some very real, very

A

living, some in a degree less so; some more sacred
are like spectres creeping up from the God's-acre
of my heart. Of these memories some are 'roses
blowing along the pathway I pursue'; in brooding
over others, I seem to catch the echo of a martial
note. I like to think of him (to use a dear friend's
words) as 'The Happy Warrior;' but I think of him
more, when gathered round the fire of an evening, we
talked together, and he poured out to me words of
wisdom, the outcome of a life of thought, action and
moral triumph. Only those few who came near to
his heart in this way, really had a full appreciation of
the simple sweetness and saintly nobleness of his
character. In such a way one received a better
picture of the man than could be obtained from the
apparently strange contradictions of his public appearances. The picture of his life, however well-drawn,
will always have a certain want of perspective, for he
was not a man easy to understand; outspoken on
some subjects, he was extremely reticent on others,
and it was difficult always to make a philosophical
balance. It is this feeling that weighed with me
when I read the many notices and biographies which
appeared after his death, some even by near friends.
There was, of course, always half the truth, and that,
as my uncle used to say, is sometimes worse than a
lie. There is one great exception, that is the work of
Miss Anna Stoddart, to whom I must express my
personal gratitude, for painting such a living picture of
him whose departure has made my life more shadowy
and my living less joyful.

My memories of him are chiefly those connected

with his home life in his latter years. Oh, that a Boswell could have sat at the festal boards of Altna Craig, Hill Street, and Douglas Crescent, 'when we gathered and ate with much disputing hum,' and chronicled the flashes of wisdom and wit which poured incessantly from his lips, the ready servants of his brain and heart ! There was no pedantry to damp the soul there, no clogging formalism to block the living streams which flowed in those physically and morally healthy veins. A comparatively insignificant illusion here, a trivial remark there, was readily caught by those marvellous ears of his, and turned into the channels of wisdom, from which one returned morally and mentally stimulated. However boisterous the sally, however dramatic the action, it was merely the froth on a well of virile wisdom, deep insight, catholic comparison and lovable charity. It might be a playful dig at the ribs of an Oxford don, a hard knock on the head of a 'Radical infallible,' or it might be the instilling of the wisdom of Goethe, or the 'quit-you-like-men' doctrine of St Paul, but all came from a heart that bore ill to no man, from one who 'found a kiss in every cross,' and couched in language that made the heart beat stronger at the time, and which left much that on meditation made the brain grow bigger.

At other times I found him not the teacher, but the taught. Seeking in—I must grant—a terribly searching way, to find out what you knew, and applying it to the general philosophy of life. When I recall him now, I always have in my memory the impression of a wise man. There was nothing ordinary about him, and the least ordinary was the unique richness and moral glow of his language. I speak of him, of course, as I knew him at home, and I do not stand as judge for the experiences of other men. He was of all things broadly human, and all the philosophy that really interested him, was the philosophy that came down to the very hearth, if I may so put it, of man. Life, and the practical problems of life, were the 'trade-marks,' of all his teaching. He recognised the value of 'digging into the dead guts of things,' but he recognised the limits of such research and gave it its due place in the educational economy. Wisdom, not mere knowledge, love, reverence, moderation, were for him the cardinal virtues with which to reach to the highest of all attainable virtues, truth.

Of other memories, I have that of the first letter he wrote to me, in which he said,—'I know you will have the good sense not to be offended with the rough and unceremonious way in which I have sometimes contradicted your propositions. Contradiction is useful for all, and those who cannot learn from contradiction will remain mere special pleaders for their own point of view all their lives, and never know what wisdom means. The grand thing is to start in life with a deep conviction of the vastness of the world and the smallness of man, and to fling out broad arms of loving appreciation and reverential regard to all the phases of the true, the good, and the beautiful, which make up this eternal divine miracle called the world, which is in very deed the living architecture, poetry, sculpture, painting, and music of the one self-existent, plastic, all-embracing *logos* of which the biggest man is only a small fraction.   Above all things, avoid the temptation of wishing to appear clever and smart ; cleverness is only valuable as an unconscious accompaniment of an honest reality, such as the bicker of a mountain tarn or the flashing of a trout in a stream.   Read the Sermon on the Mount, or the twelfth of Romans, or 1 Cor. xiii., at least once a week, and act them out every day of the week and every hour of the day. Know above all things what Goethe preaches as emphatically as St Paul, that *love is the fulfilling of the law ;* it is the regular steam power of the soul, or electricity—if you please—of the moral world, "knowledge puffeth up, but charity edifieth."   There is no constructive, no shaping power, in mere knowledge, it merely supplies materials for the motive power, and the regulative reason to use for the realisation of a noble ideal divinely rooted in the nature of a noble soul.'

Many years ago Thomas Carlyle wrote of John Stuart Blackie :   ' A man of lively intellectual faculties, of ardent friendly character, and of wide speculation and acquirement, very fearless, very kindly, without ill-humour and without guile.'   A very kindly estimation, coming as it does from the Sage of Chelsea, remembering how severe were many of the judgments he passed on those even with whom he was in the closest personal relationship ; a much more charitable estimation of the man than the previous one from the letter of Carlyle to Emerson, in which the 'notable monster,' looking only at the time upon Blackie's exuberant presentation, and not troubling to get down to the soul of the man, spoke of him as 'a man of more sail than ballast.'

John Stuart Blackie, indeed, had plenty of sail. His barque was always in good working order, to sail 'away, away down the stream,' but at the same time it was always well-braced, and the hand that guided was never off the rudder. Too many candid critics, in their notices of his life, have failed in the want of mental perspective to grasp the fact, that Professor Blackie's many exuberant outbursts in public were simply the outcome of a vast amount of animal spirit, and a resultant of the fact, that with the exception of these public appearances, he had few other means of mental detraction. At home, accustomed to a hard and persistent intellectual life, serious, thoughtful, and ascetic, he sought in the catholic sphere of the popular platform a relief from 'sitting with moody pains and anxious peering looks, clogging the veins of laden brains with the dust of maundering books.' No longer tied down by philosophic consecutiveness and scientific accuracy, he found, in the less exacting, but more humanising atmosphere of the popular platform an outcome for his bright presentation of the beauties, physical and ethical, of this beautiful world. It is not true that these lectures were delivered off-hand without preparation. Down to the smallest action of life, that was not Blackie's method. However unimportant the occasion, however comparatively unimportant in the economy of things, the subject, yet it demanded, and received from him, the most earnest investigation and meditation. The facts, and the matured consideration of the facts, were there, however much, in the joy and healthy exuberance of the moment, he omitted reference to his manuscript, left the more limited fields of the specific subject on hand, and wandered into the richer growths of Socrates, Goethe, Aristotle, and St Paul. And even when on occasion something more than usually extravagant was hurled at the heads of a sympathetic audience, on consideration of this, perhaps, humorous aphorism, it would lend one more and more to the belief in a popular dictum, that 'there is generally more in Blackie's nonsense, than in most people's sense.'

Unless this aspect of the question is carefully borne in mind, and an attempt at estimation be founded on the knowledge of how earnest, persistent and scientific a student he was, and how much important work was evolved in his life-time, one will be apt to arrive at that false conclusion which some critics of the man have arrived at. I grant it was difficult to picture in the jovial, lively, often very eccentric, figure of the platform, the quiet, serious methodical man of the library, the eager and reverential searcher after truth. Dr Whyte's metaphor was a happy one when he said, 'Like Socrates, he was not unlike those Athenian busts of Silenus, which had pipes and flutes in their mouths, but open them and there was the image of a God.'

And in this connection I might tell my only Blackie 'story.' Not long ago he paid a visit to the sanctum of an Edinburgh publisher, and mentioned that he had lectured the previous night on Scottish

Home Rule. The publisher said, 'I am astonished at your fondness for making an exhibition of yourself.' Professor Blackie, without another word, turned on his heel and went away, slamming the door. Presently he came back, opened the door, thrust in his head and said, 'Do you know that's just what my wife tells me!'

Certain it is that the popularity and affection which he enjoyed in his native land as a professor, increased in volume and geographical extent when he became a public lecturer. And it was no mean gift which enabled the close student of philology and philosophy to so re-cook his academic dishes, as to satisfy the appetites of the extra-mural world. And that he succeeded in doing so is testified by all. His studies in German literature and philosophy gave him ample scope to lecture on the practical philosophy of Goethe, to preach to them of 'the three reverences,' and the practical and far-seeing maxium, 'that the world is governed by wisdom, by authority and by show;' his classical attainments and his intimate acquaintance with the wise men of Greece gave him the foundation for his popular re-dressing of the Socratic, Platonic and Aristotelean philosophies.

Writing to Dr Walter Smith on the 9th of March last, a few days after the Scottish people had laid him with kingly honours in the Dean Cemetery, Sir Theodore Martin wrote of his old friend: 'It was impossible not to love him—not only for his fiery energy and determination to work out for good whatever power God had given him, but for the truly original purity of his nature.' And this 'determination to work out for good whatever power God had given him,' was evinced in every step he took towards work. The knowledge of the most fruitful source for the ultilisation of his powers came slow at first. Trammelled by the limitations of his early northern environment, and ungifted in his youth with any particular inspiration to recognise the superior merits of any particular profession, a brief sojourn, in the attempt to grapple with the lower branches of the law in Aberdeen, was soon dispelled by an accidental occurrence of a depressing kind, acting on a nature yet untrained to treat such fatalities philosophically. He became troubled about his 'inner life,' and we find him attempting to get some breath into the lungs of his moral nature by a nearly fatal course of morbid introspection. But there was a wise man of Aberdeen, called Forbes, and his timely remark that Blackie 'wanted his jacket widening,' had the desired result of dragging him from the narrowing influences of the theology of his own native Universities, and planting him among the philosophers of Germany and of Italy. All these influences, all these environments at Aberdeen, at Edinburgh, in Germany, in Italy, and afterwards in Greece, and again while studying for the Bar in Edinburgh, had important bearings upon his character, upon his moral and intellectual aspect. No doubt, from his early training, he received that tendency to see so much that was to be admired in the religious history and systems of his forefathers, and no doubt, too, in these early days the influence of a wise father first stimulated him with a love, to become a passion in its intensity, for the romantic traditions and associations of his beloved Scotland.

To his German environment can be traced that influence which lead him to grasp with a firm hand, a philosophical interpretation of the history of the world, to obtain for the first time a clear conception of the philosophic attitude which should always be found in the academic teacher; and also to his German influences can be traced most of those broad, Catholic tendencies which were to be found in after years in whatever he wrote or spoke on questions of a theological, moral and social nature.

The general influence of his theological training in Aberdeen, Edinburgh and Germany, found expression from time to time in his warm interest in the methods of different theological and ecclesiastical systems and in the interpretations of them, of the fundamental points of the foundations of Christian Church Government.

From Italy, no doubt, came his interest in architecture, art and archæology, especially the latter ; in fact, it was by the merest chance that he escaped taking up the subject as the chief element in his life work.

And of his Hellenistic environment it is only necessary to say, that it was the source of all his vigorous pursuit of the question treating of the philological connection between what are called ancient and modern Greek.

To this must he added his training for the Bar, which, considered purely abstractly, must have had a considerable influence in adding an analytical as well as a synthetical power to his estimation of all questions, and which certainly made of him a cautious and a systematic man in all the more practical concerns of life.

Accordingly, in an analysis of his complex personality, we would have to trace the various sources of this and that characteristic and find out the remnants of Blackie the introspective student of theology, Blackie the German, Blackie the archæologist, Blackie the lawyer, Blackie the Hellenist, and lastly, Blackie the philologist, all tending to the Blackie as we knew him —Blackie the philosopher and seer.

But up to the time when we find him admitted a member of the Scottish Bar, we trace no definite evidence of that intense love for the beauties and the inspirations of Nature, which became so evident in his later years, and from which sprang most that was eloquent not only in his verse, but in all his interpretation of the meanings of God's creation. It was at the time when he first caught the glamour from the hills, 'his glorious Bens,' as he called them, that we find him pouring forth his best utterances in verse. The genesis of his poetry, the poetry of religion and life in their broadest meanings, dates from a time after the genesis of his broad Catholic philosophy in Germany, and when once the glory of the hills was upon him, the influence of this new light never left him. Hereafter he sought Nature as the fountain head of his philosophy ; hereafter Nature became the important word in his vocabulary. Nature in teaching —Nature in song—Nature in religion—and although in most of his poetical works 'the æsthetical,' as Miss

Stoddart says, 'was subservient to the ethical,' yet much of his best work in this direction is to be found in those poems which speak of the beauties of Nature in its unpeopled nakedness. Nature, as representing the revelations of the brown heath and shaggy wood, the mountain and the flood. True, again, in all his pictures of the presentations and changes of Nature, he never caught the glamour and mystery of Nature itself, as for instance it was caught by Robert Buchanan in his 'Coruisken Sonnets.' Both Blackie and Buchanan came under the influence of similar spells in the Western Highlands, and it is curious to compare the mystic interpretations of Buchanan with the ethical interpretation of Blackie.

It would be as impossible for me in the space I have at my disposal, as it would be idle at this early hour, to attempt to form a true estimate of Blackie's literary work. It is a long cry from the translation of 'Faust' in 1833 to his 'Christianity and The Ideal of Humanity' in 1893, and during those years some 40 volumes saw the light of day. Of this work it would be impossible to say that it all rises to an equal standard of comparative excellence, and to judge correctly of the value of his contribution to literature, one must not lose sight of the fact, that much of it was intended only to be of a comparatively ephemeral nature, rather to act as a stimulus at the moment, than to remain a permanent monument on the question or questions concerned. Under this category must be placed several of his volumes of essays; many of them full of sound sense, keen judgment and rare discrimination, and all written in that nervous, forcible

English so characteristic of the man. In fact, there are or were few of his contemporaries who possessed in such a marked degree that power to rouse. It was the mightiest gift of Carlyle, in a less degree it is one of the powers of Ruskin, and, in John Stuart Blackie's case, it assured for him that great influence on a people which was evidenced over and over again, not the least remarkably, on March 2d last.

Excluding, then, this work of a comparatively ephemeral nature, we are left with some very important contributions, which critics of standing have accorded no mean place in the niche of literature. His translations of 'Homer,' 'Æschylus,' 'Faust,' have called forth the praise of those entitled to judge, and if his 'Homer' never received that recognition in the classical world which its 'profound scholarship and research, clear insight, healthy feeling and great literary power' (to quote a contemporary criticism) deserved, the secret might be found in the fact that it emanated from a Scottish University. In connection with this translation, a learned German remarks, that 'it was a happy thought of Blackie's to render the great "Volks Epos" (people's poem) of Greece into the metre familiar to his countrymen in their own folk songs.' In concluding an exhaustive criticism of the work at the time, a leading critic said, 'the work is a proof of the vitality and high aims of Scottish scholarship, and reflects the greatest honour on the university and country in which it has been produced.'

The following two passages of a somewhat different

nature will give some idea of the metre and spirit of
the translation :—

'Thus he ; and stretched his arm to clasp his infant son so
    dear,
But on the breast of his well-ezoned nurse the babe shrunk back
    with fear,
Scared at the gleam of the barnished brass which cased that
    warrior dread,
And screamed to see the horse-hair crest high nodding o'er his
    head.
The father laughed, the mother smiled ; then Hector brave
    unbound
The helmet from his head, and laid it glittering on the ground,
And kissed his son, and dandled him aloft with fondest joy ;
Then to greet Jove and all the gods, thus prayed to bless the
    boy :
Jove, and ye mighty gods, grant this my son, one day, may be
As I am now to Trojan men— the bulwark of the free ;
Ruling o'er Troy by valorous might ; then from the hostile fray
Shall some one see him home return, and thus shall proudly
    say :—
From a good sire a better son hath rescued Troy to-day !
And when he bears proud trophies through the sounding streets
    of Troy,
His mother shall behold her son, and her heart shall leap for
    joy !
He spake : and to his dear wife's hands he gave the lovely
    child ;
She took him to her balmy breast, and, through her weeping,
    smiled.'

' But now the hosts together rushed, and each did each assail,
And buckler upon buckler rang, and hurtled mail on mail,
And might of man did might oppose, flashed spear to spear and
    rang
The war-cry loud and shrill, and shield met shield with brassy
    clang ;
And many a shout and many a yell to heaven commingled
    goeth
From men who struck and men who fell ; the field with crimson
    floweth.
As when fierce wintry torrents down some grey hill's deep-
    scarred side
Pour to the glen the headlong force of their foamy-hissing tide

Sheer through the black ravine, with fountains ever fresh
    supplied ;
While perched on some high crag the swain hears the shrill
    tempest's rattle ;
So swelled from host to host the din, and rang the yell of battle.'

And from a host of congratulatory letters from scholars and others, I offer no apology for quoting these words of a poet. Writing on 7th November 1866, Robert Buchanan said, 'My learning goes far enough to allow me to apply the *poetic* test to your work. So far as I have read, no Homer has so delighted me since Chapman, but Chapman was quite guiltless of the fine Ionian flavour which you give so admirably.'

But more important, perhaps, than the mere translation itself are the Dissertations and Notes prefixed, and much as I personally feel as to the importance of these, I prefer again to quote my critic.

'They form an essential part of the purpose of the whole work—the presentation of the real Homer to modern readers. So completely has Professor Blackie had his eye fixed on this his main object, that he has omitted to discuss the authorship of the *Odyssey*, and the vexed questions connected with it. This is the one serious omission in the Dissertations. With this one exception, they form by far the best and ablest exposition of Homeric questions in English. As we have said already, English scholars have shamefully neglected this part of philology. The only important works on the subject are the works of men who are not professionally scholars—Gladstone, Grote, and Mure. Gladstone's is the work of a great intellect, but it is written under very heavy disadvantages. He was unacquainted with almost the entire history of Homeric discussions on the Continent within the last fifty years, and with the books published during that period on the subject. In fact, he seems to have prejudged the whole matter, and therefore kept his eyes shut. Grote was well acquainted with the recent discussions, but it did not fall within his province to take up many of the Homeric questions. Mure, on the other hand, had both full knowledge of the literature and ought to have handled all the questions; and in many respects his discussion is of great value. But he took up an entirely false position : he criticised Homer very much from the point of view of the last century. He regarded Homer evidently as a man of profound reflection; he treats him as if he were a cultivated and widely-read poetic artist—in fact, he deals with him very much as he might deal with Milton; and, therefore, he saw no necessity for discussing some of the most important Homeric questions. Professor Blackie has thus had a comparatively unoccupied field ; and he certainly has done his work admirably. Every page teems with learning; but this learning is thoroughly under control. He shows a complete acquaintance with all the important works on Homer. He has gone in every case to the sources ; and he has discussed some of the questions—such as that on the amount of truth contained in tradition—with originality and insight. He has also compressed the results of his research into comparatively small compass. Some of the chapters—such as those on the state of the text and the labours of Zenodotus

and Aristarchus and the Alexandrian critics generally
—contain information that can be got nowhere else,
except in monographs by German scholars, and now
partially in Hayman. And these Dissertations have
the merit of being very readable. Professor Blackie
has managed to throw life and interest about many a
dry point. Throughout all his discussions, Professor
Blackie is conservative. He believes strongly in the
unity of the *Iliad*, in a real Homer, in a real Trojan
war, in a real Achilles and Agamemnon. He has
contrived most skilfully to deepen this impression of
reality as he goes on ; and somehow one gets to think
that he knows more of Homer and the Trojan war
from Professor Blackie's book than from any other
author's whatever.'

'The mythological notes are in some respects the
most important in the volume. The scientific treat-
ment of mythology, as exhibited in the writings of
Otfried Müller, Gerhard, Preller, Welcker, Schwartz,
and others, is not represented by a single book in
English ; and the student will find the results of
these, so far as they pertain to Homer, stated for the
first time in these notes. Professor Blackie deserves
more than the credit of stating results. He has not
merely exhibited the thoughts of others, but he has
given the results of his own much-matured thought
and original investigation.'

'The archæological notes are very curious. They
show, perhaps more than anything else, the thorough-
ness with which Professor Blackie has mastered his
subject. He has got hold of all the out-of-the-way
discussions on Homeric zoology, botany, metallurgy,

B

archery, armour, and other such matters; and the reader will find information in these notes on the history of the arts and sciences at once interesting and rare.'

In danger of losing the perspective of my appreciation, I have allowed myself to dwell further on this work than may seem advisable, but I am convinced that insufficient justice has been done by the reading world to these Dissertations and Notes, and I am also convinced that a separate re-publication of this part of the work would be acceptable to many scholars interested in these vexed questions.

Of his translation of 'Faust,' I can add nothing to the high praise accorded by such men as Thomas Carlyle and George Henry Lewes, and for his masterly translation of Æschylus, in which work Professor Blackie was seen at his best as a translator, it is sufficient to say that it eventually procured for him the Greek Chair in the University of Edinburgh.

But, in my humble opinion, my uncle's best work is not to be found either in his 'Homer' or his 'Æschylus' or in his 'Faust,' but firstly, in his contributions to *Blackwood* and *Tait* and the *Foreign Quarterly* on German history and literature, and secondly, in his volume entitled 'The Wise Men of Greece.' It is impossible to speak too highly of the intimate knowledge of the German language, literature and spirit which enabled him to contribute so much that was important to our knowledge of that important sphere of the world's history and literature, and the highest tribute there could be paid him,—tribute higher than even the praise of Carlyle, — was the praise and gratitude of many of the German critics. Writing shortly after his death, a contemporary said, ' Dr Kirchner writes for the *Illustrirte Zeitung* a notice of his career, full of appreciative criticism of his work, and of the sympathy with those who are mourning his loss. Written by a foreigner, the sketch is of special interest, as affording striking proof of the wide influence which, by his writings, Blackie acquired outside his own country, and also because it lays stress on a phase of his literary activity which we in Scotland have perhaps hardly realised at its true value. "We in Germany," says Dr Kirchner, "owe grateful recognition to those who, by study and translation of our literature, use their best endeavours to win for it the appreciation of their countrymen. Among these John Stuart Blackie has a foremost place. Blackie has, in fact, done more than most men, as much as any one man except Thomas Carlyle, to bridge over the gap which unquestionably exists between the English and German mind, to clear away the thick atmosphere of misconception and prejudice which even Englishmen of wide culture find it difficult to ignore." '

The contributions to German literature and history include not only his ' Faust,' and the articles above mentioned, but also his ' Wisdom of Goethe,' a volume of precious gems translated from the works of the greatest of German poets. ' Having in my personal experience,' he says, ' had reason to thank God that at an early period of my life I became acquainted with the writings of this great man, it occurred to me that I could not do better service to the intelligent youth of this generation, for whom it has been my duty and pleasure to work through a long life, than to lay before them in a systematic form the most significant *dicta* on the important problems of sound thinking and noble living.   As Dr Kirchner says, "In these reflections, maxims and verses, it is not difficult to trace the master-mind that inspired Blackie's 'Self-Culture.'"'

Important also are Professor Blackie's numerous translations of the Studentenlieder, Volkslieder and War-songs of the Fatherland.   Particularly the latter, all of them full of the true martial ring, the force and fire of the old Border ballads, including the translation of the 'Battle Prayer' of Korner 'Vater ich rufe dich'—the most beautiful of soldiers' prayers in the world's literature,

> 'Clouds from the thunder-voiced cannon envail me,
>   Lightnings are flashing, death's thick darts assail me ;
>   Ruler of battles, I call on thee,
>   Father, O lead me !'

Of 'The Wise Men of Greece,' I need only say that Professor Blackie considered this to be his most important contribution to literature.   And when we come to examine the volume, we see in what a masterly and scholarly fashion he has portrayed 'the philosophical significance, the intellectual dignity and moral power,' of such men as Socrates, Pythagoras, Xenophanes and Empedocles.   To quote his own words to Tom Taylor, 'I can only tell you that scholars and thinkers will get here no mere soap-bubbles lightly blown for a summer's recreation, but the produce of hard work and years of study.   I had no ambition, even if I had had the ability, to make a Pythagoras or an Empedocles, a mere mouthpiece

to spout my sentiments. I strove everywhere to give
a true picture of what was actually thought and said
by these old worthies, or at least of what lay in their
most distinctive maxims by plain implication; and if
the lines of the portraiture shall seem to agree in a
very striking way, sometimes, with certain recent
phases of modern thought, or the obvious opposite of
these phases, this is not that I have interpolated anything which, to the best of my judgment, did not lie
in the original, but because the fundamental principles
of all wisdom have always been present in the spiritual
world wherever human beings in a normal state of
culture have lived and thought. Reason is the light
of the soul; and though, like the sun in the heavens,
it may be largely overclouded, and shine only by
glimpses for a space, yet it is always there; and the
glimpse, whenever it appears, is a sure prophecy of
the full radiance, which under favourable circum-
stances will surely be revealed.'

The whole is comprised in a series of ten dramatic
dialogues, which are as rich in language as they are
in wisdom.

Of his prose works, besides those I have mentioned,
three stand out,—'The Four Phases of Morals,' the
essay 'On Beauty,' and 'Self-Culture.' In the first, to
use the words of the present Professor of Moral Philosophy in the University of Edinburgh, 'Professor
Blackie has given us a valuable addition to ethical
literature full of important exposition and criticism;' of
the second 'On Beauty;' Dr John Brown had written,
'If I am mistaken not, there is more in the honest
instincts, the broad sympathies, the genuine philosophy

and cordial love of all that is lovable, as expressed in these discourses, to take and to hold, and to impress the great mass of thinking men and women, than in all else that our century has yet seen, not excepting my own great Ruskin.' Of 'Self-Culture' I need not speak at length. It has been far and away the most widely circulated of all John Stuart Blackie's works, went through eleven editions in eight years, is now in its twenty-fifth, and has been translated into eleven different languages. As far north as the land of the Finns, south in the sunny lands of Italy and Spain, east of Suez amongst the many-tongued people of the Indian empire, this book has been read and re-read. Its simple, robust, straightforward common sense, has made it a power of its kind, and a power for good, difficult to estimate. 'It is many years ago since I read his "Self-Culture," wrote Professor Seth ; 'but it seemed to me then to be a masterpiece of its kind, full of the wisdom of life, ripe and true.' The germ of 'Self-Culture' is in these words quoted in 'The Wisdom of Goethe '—' Every man must think for himself, and he will always find upon his path some truth or, at least, a kind of truth, that will keep him through life. Yet he dare not allow himself to drift. He must be self-controlled. Mere naked instinct does not become a man.' 'How can a man learn to know himself?' asks Goethe, ' By reflection never, only by action. In the measure in which thou seekest to do thy duty shalt thou know what is in thee. But what is thy duty? The demand of the hour.'

In the region of poetry, from which I have selected for this volume many of the gems, besides his translations from the German, the Greek and the Latin, we must not omit reference to his translations from the Gaelic. These are in most cases extremely faithful, and convey the spirit of the original in a remarkable way. As an example, let me recommend the translation of Duncan Ban's 'Ben Dorain,' which will be found in this volume. As in an introduction I have spoken of his chief contributions to verse in other directions, it is not necessary for me to dwell further upon the subject.

It is not for me in this place to dwell on the many important affairs of a practical nature which engaged John Stuart Blackie throughout his life. These are all told in detail in Miss Stoddart's pages, and my reader will turn there for the history of the movement for university reform, the history of the foundation of the Celtic Chair, his endeavours in the question of reform in matters pertaining to education, his institution of travelling Greek fellowships, his work in the Greek and Latin classes, and last, but not least, the record of his persistent preaching in and out of season on the subject of the philological continuance of the Greek language and of the pronunciation of such. On this subject let me quote from a letter of M. Gennadius, ex-Envoy from the King of Greece.

'Greek newspapers received from Athens and other parts of Greece, contain obituary notices of the late Professor Blackie, all couched in terms of fond attachment and affectionate respect for the memory of one who was considered as much Greek in heart and mind as those in the Levant who now mourn his loss. He had made himself more known among the Greek-speaking populations in the East, and he had entered more thoroughly into their habits of thought and modes of speech than many scholars who visited Greece more often, or sojourned longer there than he had done. It may even be said that he was more full of a vivid conception of the language and life of ancient and modern Greece than they. To what was this attributable? He learned, considered and taught Greek as a living, not as a dead language. He did not confine its ranges within the narrow and artificial limits of Atticism, or even of Classicism; but recognised that Greek, as a tongue actually in use, has an unbroken record of 3000 years; that contemporary Greek presents one of the most interesting and most remarkable periods of an existence ever changing because ever alive. Finally, to quote from one of his letters to the *Times*, 'He did not perpetrate the English absurdity of pronouncing the language of Pericles and Plato with the vocalism of John Bull, and the accentuation of Old Cato, the Censor.'

And before he died it was one of his greatest joys to learn that the seed he had sown was bearing fruit, and letters from M. Drakoules and others from Oxford and elsewhere, cheered him with the news that emancipation had begun.

However many may differ as to the comparative merits and demerits of John Stuart Blackie's literary, academic and public works, no two opinions can be held with regard to the absolute sincerity and unassailable honesty of the man. Never have I met or heard of a man who was so absolutely truthful—truthful in word, truthful in deed—never did I know one who so absolutely refused to sacrifice one iota that a lie might be uttered or perpetuated.

> 'No dread of censure, and no lack of praise,
> Turned thee to right or left.'

If at times he seemed unreasonable in his persistency, it was because he was thoroughly convinced of the rectitude of his action. And this absolute honesty he carried into all his work. Here there was no trimming, no manufacture of facts to suit theories, his methods were absolutely scientific; many may have disputed his opinions, none ever disputed his facts. He tells us, as Mr Morley says of Goethe, 'the whole truth.' Over and over again have I seen him spend what appeared a superfluous amount of time, to find out the accuracy of a statement or fact, and so careful was he to keep in control the knowledge which he possessed, so careful so as to have it stored away in his brain that it might be reproduced with accuracy, that he often used to say to me,— 'Don't tell me what you think, tell me what you know!'

A good deal has been said with regard to Professor Blackie's supposed vanity. To me, who knew him in many phases of his mental and moral attitude, this charge of vanity is simply inexplicable. I never knew anybody so humble, so reverential, so careless of opinion. No vain man is humble, no vain man is truly reverential, every vain man is sensitive to a degree to opinion. Of course, he had tinges occasionally of what he called 'Oldie' (Old Adam), but so strong was his power of inhibition that these were quickly trodden down. A vain man is never charitable to those who attack him—Professor Blackie never spoke a harsh word against any man in his life. Some have even mentioned his dress as an evidence of his vanity, but would it be news for the public to learn that he never knew when he had adorned himself with new clothes. At night-time the old clothes were removed and new ones were substituted, and he lived in ignorance of the fact. He was so much above the consideration of his sartorial environment, that had it not been for the kindly and studied care of his devoted wife, we are afraid he would have cut a very sorry figure indeed. That he was one of the most picturesque figures of the day was hardly his fault, and only arose from the fact that Mrs Blackie thought it no crime to dress a naturally handsome and picturesque man in a picturesque manner.

Of his charity, I cannot speak too highly. To an opponent he behaved in a manner that was often quixotic. He never judged harshly ; he never attributed motives. When spiteful, sometimes cruel letters came to him, and we around his fireside gave vent to our honest indignation, in that sweet, fascinating way of his, he would bid us be charitable and would in many ways try to find a justification for the offender. Not that this ever detracted from his stern sense of duty which sometimes made him give vent to the expression, — 'Bad boys should be thrashed.' As for what he gave away to the poor, only a very few knew his great, unostentatious liberality. This was one of the most beautiful traits of his character, and if he erred at all, it was that sometimes an unworthy person gained by the largeness of his heart. Many a poor, struggling literary man ; many a poor, weak, broken-down schoolmaster, or impoverished student has had cause to thank God that John Stuart Blackie was alive. 'Many a poor man and woman will miss the half-crown and the jest—that made the pocket a little heavier, and the heart a little lighter.'

Of other marked characteristics may be mentioned his reverence and his patriotism. His reverence I have hinted at, and this virtue weighed so much with him, that it may with safety be said that it was the genesis of all his aspect to the Creator, and to the moral systems of the world. 'Think upon your knees,' was his metaphorical way of picturing the attitude of reverence which he deemed right in our intellectual life, and it was in this attitude that he himself went through life.

Reverence for, not fear of, the great all-ruling '*logos*' of the Universe, the 'all-father,' the dispenser and reasoning ruler of all the wonders of nature.

> 'Write them Jove, Buddha, Allah, Elohim,
> Apollo, Krishna, Vishna, Great All-father
> Or great All-mother, if it please you rather,
> They are but names that sound one self-same theme,
> Soul of all souls, and of all causes cause.'

And this reverence for the fatherhood was carried into the practical affairs of his life. It tempered his judgment, it made richer his charity, it broadened his conception of the variety of life. 'Keep yourself,' he wrote, 'always in an attitude of reverential dependence on the supreme source of all good. It is the most natural and speediest and surest antidote against that spirit of shallow self-confidence and brisk impertinence so apt to spring up with the knowledge without charity, which puffeth up and edifieth not.'

One of his favourite, perhaps the favourite, of his illustrations bearing on this aspect of reverence was taken from Goethe, and may be quoted in his own translation of Goethe's words. ' There is one thing by means of which every man that is born into the world becomes truly manly. This thing is reverence, of which there are three kinds, or, if you will, three stages. These we endeavour to implant in the minds of our pupils with the symbolical accompaniment of three attitudes or postures. The first kind is reverence for that which is above us, and the attitude connected with this is that in which, with the arms crossed over the breast, our pupils are taught to look joyfully towards the heavens. By this we ask from them an acknowledgment that there is a God on high, who reflects and reveals Himself in the person of parents, teachers and superiors. The second type is reverence for that which is beneath us. The hands clasped as though bound behind the back, the downward, smiling look, in the attitude belonging to the type indicate that we should look upon the earth graciously and cheerfully, for it is the earth that affords us means of subsistence and the source of innumerable joys. But from this attitude we set our pupil free as soon as possible, the moment we are assured the lesson it is intended to convey has had its proper effect, then we call on him to brace himself like a man, and turning to his comrades to pit himself against them. Now he stands firm and bold, but not selfishly isolated. Only in conflict with his fellows can the young man learn to face the world. Our third attitude indicates this; standing upright and with forward look, they take their stations no longer singly, but linked together in a row.'

Then again. 'The religion which is founded on reverence for what is above us we call *ethnic*, or as it is in vulgar English, *heathen*. It is the religion of the nations, and the first happy deliverance from abject fear. To this class belong all pagan religions, whatever names they may bear. The second type of religion founded upon the reverence we cherish for what is on a par with ourselves, we call philosophical; for the philosopher, who takes a central position, must draw down to his level what is above, while he seeks to elevate what is below; and only when in this middle state does he deserve the name of a sage. The third type is that founded on reverence for what is beneath us—this is Christanity, for in it chiefly is this sentiment dormant. It is the highest step in the ladder of reverence to which humanity can obtain. . . . From these three embodied types spring the consummation of all reverences, the reverence for our self, out of which the other three again develop themselves.'

And it is as well to note that he did not confuse the reverence for those great physical, intellectual, social and moral factors which in the ages have held the balance level for humanity, with that blind respect and worship of things born in prejudice, bred in ignorance, and perpetuated in mysticism. He was

always of the north and western world, though in-
fluenced by the wisdom which came from the east
and south, and he had no respect for what would clog
the higher developments of his human brothers.

When we come to analyse the Professor's religious
belief, we find, as I have said, this reverence at the root
of it all, and in the aspect of worship we find how wide,
almost pantheistic, was his conception of the worship
of the Creator.   It was really, when we look at it, the
first verse of the 19th psalm, and no choir, no chorus
of human voices in any temple made by hands was half
as expressive to him as the choir, whose units were
the rippling brook, the roaring cataract, the heaven-
pointing hills, and the changing clouds.

> ' Go not where sculptured tower or pictured dome
>   Invites the reeking city's jaded throngs,
> Some hoar old shrine of Rhine-land or of Rome
>   Where the dim aisle the languid hymn prolongs,
> Here rather follow me and take thy stand
>   By the grey cairn that crowns the lone Dunee,
> And let thy breezy worship be the grand
>   Old Bens, and the old grey knolls that compass thee ;
> The sky-blue waters and the snow white sand,
>   And the quaint isles far sown upon the sea.'

And again, at Ardlui,—

> ' In sooth a goodly temple, walled behind
>   With crag precipitous of granite grey,
> And by green birches corniced, which the wind
>   Sowed o'er the rim in random rich display,
> And for a roof the azure-curtained hall,
>   Light-floating cloud and broad benignant ray,
> And organed by the hum of waterfall
>   And plash of bright waves in the gleaming bay.
> And here's the pulpit, the huge granite mass
>   Erect, frost-sundered from the mossy crown

> And there the people sit on turfy grass,
> And here the fervid preacher thunders down ;
> Go kneel beneath Saint Paul's proud dome and say,
> If God be nearer there, or here to-day.'

And again, in Arran, in that most eloquent pantheistic poem, 'A Sabbath Meditation '—

> ' In the high-domed fane,
> Glorious with all the legendary pomp
> Of pictured saints, where skilful singers swell
> The curious chant, or on the lonely hill
> Where, on grey cliff and purple heather shines
> The shadowless sun at noon.   Thou hears't alike.
> Vainly the narrow wit of narrow men
> Within the walls which priestly lips have blest,
> In the fixed phases of a formal creed
> Would crib Thy presence ; Thou art more than all
> The shrines that hold Thee ; and our wisest creeds
> Are but the lispings of a forward child
> To spell the Infinite.'

And finally, in his eloquent apology for the poor Hindoos in his ' Trimurti.'

> ' Farewell ! your creed may nevermore be mine,
> I hold one God, but many forms Divine ;
> Your's best—so be it ! but I may not bind
> My heart to worship only in one kind ;
> Nor where flowers prink the mead with diverse hue
> Let one bright bloom usurp my wondering view ;
> And they are wise who love with like regard
> Both rose and lily, where to choose is hard.
> Leave me, my friend, the luxury of my error,
> To think that creeds are but a broken mirror
> With thousand suns for one that lights the skies,
> And one truth imaged in a thousand lies ! '

God, to him, was soul of all soul and substance of all creeds, and his interpretation of the meaning of the Trinity, was Thought, Word and Deed. Thought, the Father, Deed, the Son, and Word the Holy Spirit. His religion 'was one glowing furnace hot with moral emotion rather than the outcome of a theology bristling with stereotyped dogma and scholastic formulas.' It was a religion of action, of morals, of personal inhibition. In a sonnet to Mr Findlay of Aberlour, a wise and good landlord, he said :—

'Not all who catch the breeze can guide the ship,
Not all who mount the car can rein the steed,
Not all can quaff good wine with sober lip,
Some make their lives a slander on their creed.'

His ship was ever off the rock, not always riding smoothly, for—

'Far better to be tempest driven
Than rot upon the harbour mud,'

but never stranded.

With a steady hand he reined the steed, and his temperate, guileless and noble life was a better demonstration of his religious belief than all the creeds his lips could utter.

It was the love of the natural in religion that made him such an admirer of the æsthetic in places of worship which, indeed, inspired him in a sonnet to his old friend Dr M'Gregor of St Cuthbert's to write :—

'Thou are wise to feel
The pulse of the time and from high mitred station
Bring chant and hymn with soul compelling power
To fling a grace in worship's praiseful hour
O'er the grave-visaged Presbyterian nation.'

No doubt, much of the reverence in his nature helped to keep alive that intense passion for Fatherland which coloured most of his utterances on educational and social questions. Reverence for those who had secured for Scotland their civil liberty at Bannock-burn and their religious liberty at Drumclog.   To use the words of his friend, 'the wise young laird of Dalmeny,' as he was fond of calling Lord Rosebery, 'When we forget our individual national life as Scotsmen, you may be sure the history of Scotland has come to an end.   The principle of nationality, I take to be this, that we should cling to everything essential to us as a historical nation, and because we are a historical nation we should remember with all the more pride that we are one of many nations that go to make up the greatest empire the world has ever seen.'   Patriotism in the abstract to him was one of the greatest virtues of citizenship, and it hurt his right feelings of pride for the great historical traditions of his country, to see his countrymen forgetting that these traditions ever existed, that we never had a distinct national character, that we never inherited a distinc-tive type of manhood from the past, forgetting that Scotland was something more than a northern pro-vince of England.   He himself rejoiced every day in the traditions and heritages of his beloved country —the traditions of civil and religious strifes and conquest, the heritages of poetry and of song.   As I have said, patriotism in the abstract he counted among the higher virtues, and it is with this view that we hear him speak in such high terms of the three greatest national demonstrations he had witnessed— the first, when the German troops entered Berlin after the Franco-German war; the second, the Jubilee pro-cession in London in 1887; and the third, when he himself at Bannockburn, in the presence of thousands

c

of the Scottish people, unfurled the banner on the Borestone.

This was not the only occasion on which he took the principal part in a demonstration markedly Scottish in character. Some years ago he inaugurated a monument to Peden at Cumnock, in the presence of four thousand people; and in 1864, he made one of his most eloquent public appearances, when at Sanquhar he was present at the inauguration of an obelisk at the market cross, the place where Richard Cameron and his compatriots published their famous 'Declaration,' and which, eight years after, shook the Stuarts from the throne. 'There, then and afterwards,' in the words of Mr Tod, 'at the Old Castle, Blackie delivered great and glowing speeches; and in reference to the persecuted Covenanters, thundered out the lines carved upon the tall column :—

> ' If you would know the nature of their crime,
> Then read the story of that killing time.'

He loved to the end his 'ain Doric,' the sibilants of his 'ain braid Scots,' that language which Ruskin, in a letter to me, spoke of as 'the sweetest, subtlest, richest, most musical of all the living dialects of Europe,' he loved his Scottish songs, he loved the Scottish people, he loved his Scottish land.

> ' I've fed my eyes by land and sea,
> With sights of grandeur streaming o'er me,
> But still my heart remains with thee,
> Dear Scottish land, that stoutly bore me.
> O, for the land that bore me !
> O, for the stout old land !
> With mighty ben, and winding glen,
> Stout Scottish land—my own, dear land.'

In conclusion, perhaps it is not necessary for me to state that John Stuart Blackie was essentially, in all the elements that made up his personality, a man of affirmation, a man of action. The mere apostle of negation, the mere cynic, the mere looker-on, the mocker, may interest or startle for the moment, only to perish like a flash of lightning. Blackie often startled, but the intellectual or moral agitation aroused in his hearers or readers rose not from the dreary still-birth of negations, or the dead bones of pessimistic diatribes, but rather from a too glowing assertion, perhaps, of some living potent maxim or problem touching something that had a living bearing on human hopes and human aspirations. Many of us may have been annoyed at his persistency, but he believed with Herbert Spencer, that 'only by varied iteration can alien conceptions be forced on reluctant minds.'

Whether the high priests of the higher criticism, the door-keeper of the dovecots of the purists in style, will admit him into their sanctum is a different question. Like a very opposite man, Voltaire, he rated literature much lower than truth and action. He never was a mere literary man, he had too strong a personality for that, and in all he wrote that personality was not lost sight of.

It is not a matter, then, for much surprise that this Happy Warrior, fighting to the end with his sword in hand for what he thought to be right, absolutely sincere, generous-hearted, 'a man without guile,' patriotic, reverential, should become beloved at home, revered abroad. Loved by his peers, loved by the high, loved by the low;—his bright, rich, overflowing presentation, a lovable sight surely for gods and men. We will forgive him slapping the episcopal knee of Thirlwall, and for shaking Carlyle when he would not let his wife speak, because we knew how much of it was the result of his abnormal physical and mental vigour.

No one could come near him without being impressed with the greatness of his personality; and no young man certainly could fail to be impressed with the spirit of a joy in all things of good report, could not avoid being impressed by him by his creed, that 'this is a world of stern realities.' All his influence was for good, 'in an age of pessimism he held high the banner of human hope and human aims.' 'Speaking the truth in love,' and 'All noble things are difficult,' were his favourite mottoes; mottoes which helped him over many a hard stile in this, as he called it, 'pleasant pilgrimage.' He went through life working and singing. 'If you wish to be happy in this world, there are only three things that can secure you of your aim—the love of God, the love of truth, and the love of your fellowmen; and of this divine triad, the best and most natural exponent in my estimate is, neither a sermon, nor a lecture, nor even a grand article in a quarterly review, but just simply a good song.'

> ' Rocking on a lazy billow
>   With roaming eyes,
> Cushioned on a dreamy pillow
> Thou art not wise.
> Wake the power within thee sleeping,
>   Trim the plots that's in thy keeping,
> Thou wilt bless the task when reaping
>   Sweet labour's prize.

Work and wait, a sturdy liver
  (Life fleetly flies),
Work and pray, and sing, and ever
  Lift hopeful eyes.
Let no flaring folly din thee,
Wisdom when her charm may win thee,
Flows a well of life within thee,   .   .
  Young man, be wise.'

Born on 25th July 1809, John Stuart Blackie passed
on the 2nd of March 1895 into the valley of the dark
shadow, within the 'door which, opening, letting in,
lets out no more,' and was buried with all the honours
which a city and nation could command, on March 6th.
As Mr George Stronach says, 'everybody he loved,
but not a tithe of those who loved him, was there to
pay him a last homage ; Edinburgh, particularly the
High Street, presenting a spectacle which has never
been seen since the execution of Montrose, and will
never again be seen in our days. 'I have seen,' he
says, 'many impressive sights in historic St Giles'
Cathedral, but nothing to equal the awful solemnity
and the last honour paid to the great Scotsman, of
whom we were all so justly proud. Rich and poor,
high and low, the learned and the unlearned were
gathered outside or inside the famous old shrine, and
there were few dry eyes in the great crowd when the
funeral car slowly made its way to the church.' But,
as Professor Geddes puts it, 'the broad Cathedral was
but the sounding chancel, the square and street, the
silent transept and nave. Psalm and prayer, chorus
and organ rolled their deepest, yet the service had
a climax beyond the hallelujah, the pipes, as they led
the procession slowly out, giving the " Land of the

Leal " a new pathos, and stirring the multitude with
a penetrating and vibrating intensity, which is surely
in no other music. The big man beside me broke
down and sobbed like a child; the lump comes back
to one's own throat, the eyes dim again as one re-
members it. It was a new and strange instrument;
strangest perhaps to those who knew well its musical
call to dance, its demoniac scream and thrill of war. . . .
In front went a long procession of societies headed by
kilt and plaid; behind came the mourning kinsmen,
with the advocates, the Senate, the students and the
Town Council in their varied robes; then the in-
terminable carriages of personal friends. But better
than all these, the town itself was out; the working
people in their thousands and tens of thousands lined
the way from St Giles' to the Dean; the very windows
and balconies were white with faces. Coming down
the Mound, in full amphitheatre of Edinburgh, filled
as perhaps never before, with hushed assemblage of
city and nation, the pipers suddenly changed their song.
. . . For those who were not there, the scene is well
nigh as easy to picture as us to recall; the wavy lane,
close-walled with drawn and deepened faces, the long
black procession marching slow, sprinkled with plaid
and plume, crowded with college cap and gown, with
civic scarlet and ermine, marshalled by black draped
maces. In the midst the Black Watch pipers, marching their slowest and stateliest—then the four tall black-
maned horses—the open bier, with plain, unpolished
oaken coffin high upon a myriad of flowers, a mound
of tossing lilies, with Henry Irving's lyre of violets,
" To the beloved Professor," its silence fragrant at its

foot. Upon the coffin lay the Skye women's plaid, above his brow the Prime Minister's wreath, but on his breast a little mound of heather, opening into bloom.'

When on that spring morning the Scottish people had laid him to rest in the Dean Cemetery, he went as one of the last of those who had stood together in the days when his arm was strongest. Baron Bunsen and Edward Gerhard, 'the friends of his youth, and the directors of his early studies,' had long departed. Leigh Hunt and Thomas Carlyle, attached friends and early stimulators, had long closed their records. Moncreiff, a friend of the 'Spec.' days, Brewster, Lord Brougham, John Carlyle, Lord Cockburn, Froude, Kelland, Lushington, Dean Stanley, Tyndall Huxley and Manning, had all paid their last debts to nature. 'Rab,' the beloved Physician; Norman M'Leod, his soul bubbling over with human love and joy; Alexander Smith, with his life's tragedy unwritten; the sunny-souled Dean Ramsay, that metaphysical giant Sir William Hamilton, Sydney Dobell ' my chaste-souled Sydney,' Schliemann, Samuel Brown, Hunter of Craigcrook, D. O. Hill, Guthrie, 'the generous evangelist,' Robertson Smith, Alexander Nicholson, 'the Shirra,' Sir George Harvey and Robert Horne, friends indeed, Lord Neaves, Aytoun, Robert Wyld, the Duke of Sutherland, had all been laid to rest, most of them 'in good Scots clods.' Browning having written that 'he counted life just a stuff to try the soul's strength on,' had found his soul strong, and had gone unto the poet spirits that he loved of English race; and Tennyson had a few years before

'put out to sea.' Left to mourn their old comrade
are Sir Theodore Martin, whom he loved well;
Gladstone, the lord of destinies, who in a letter to
Mr Kennedy had written that he 'looks back with
interest, respect, and warm regard upon his life and
acts; so genuine, so simple, so susceptible of a pure
enthusiasm, so detached from self, so attached to
things kindly, pure, and noble;' David Masson, *ultimus Scotorum* indeed, who said of his old friend as
of Chaucer's knight,—

> ' He never yet no vileyne ne said
> In all his life unto no maner wight.'

Walter Smith, his soul still unlifted on the wings
of song, Campbell Fraser, Sir Douglas Maclagan,
James M'Gregor, full of the fire of human sympathy;
General Forlong, James Donaldson, Sir W. Geddes,
John Forbes White, and others less known to the
world, but none the less beloved, while she, the
faithful and loving companion of fifty-three years,
in her heart said with Tennyson—

> ' And doubtless unto thee is given
> A life that bears immortal fruit,
> In such great offices as suit
> The full-grown energies of Heaven.'

believing with Keats, that

> ' There is budding morrow in midnight.'

ARCHIBALD STODART WALKER.

POEMS

LAYS AND LYRICS

BEAUTIFUL WORLD

BEAUTIFUL world !
  Though bigots condemn thee,
My tongue finds no words
  For the graces that gem thee !
Beaming with sunny light,
  Bountiful ever,
Streaming with gay delight,
  Full as a river !
      Bright world ! brave world !
        Let cavillers blame thee !
      I bless thee, and bend
        To the God who did frame thee !

Beautiful world !
  Bursting around me,
Manifold, million-hued
  Wonders confound me !
From earth, sea, and starry sky,
  Meadow and mountain,
Eagerly gushes
  Life's magical fountain.

Bright world ! brave world !
  Though witlings may blame thee,
Wonderful excellence
  Only could frame thee !

The bird in the greenwood
  His sweet hymn is trolling,
The fish in blue ocean
  Is spouting and rolling !
Light things on airy wing
  Wild dances weaving,
Clods with new life in spring
  Swelling and heaving !
    Thou quick-teeming world,
      Though scoffers may blame thee,
    I wonder, and worship
      The God who could frame thee !

Beautiful world !
  What poesy measures
Thy strong-flooding passions,
  Thy light-trooping pleasures ?
Mustering, marshalling,
  Striving and straining,
Conquering, triumphing,
  Ruling and reigning !
    Thou bright-armied world !
      So strong, who can tame thee ?
    Wonderful power of God
      Only could frame thee !

Beautiful world !
   While godlike I deem thee,
No cold wit shall move me
   With bile to blaspheme thee !
I have lived in thy light,
   And, when Fate ends my story,
May I leave on death's cloud
   The bright trail of life's glory !
     Wondrous old world !
       No ages shall shame thee !
     Ever bright with new light
    From the God who did frame thee

THE SONG OF THE HIGHLAND RIVER

   Dew-fed am I
   With drops from the sky,
Where the white cloud rests on the old grey hill ;
   Slowly I creep
   Down the precipice steep,
Where the snow through the summer lies freezingly
   still ;
   Where the wreck of the storm
   Lies shattered enorm,
I steal 'neath the stone with a tremulous rill ;
   My low-trickling flow
   You may hear, as I go
Down the sharp-furrowed brow of the old grey hill,
   Or drink from my well,
   Grass-grown where I dwell,
The clear granite cell of the old grey hill.

In the hollow of the hill
With my waters I fill
The little black tarn where the thin mist floats;
The deep old moss
Slow-oozing I cross,
When the lapwing cries with its long shrill
notes;
Then fiercely I rush to the sharp granite edge,
And leap with a bound o'er the old grey ledge;
Like snow in the gale,
I drive down the vale,
Lashing the rock with my foamy flail;
Where the black crags frown,
I pour sheer down,
Into the caldron boiling and brown;
Whirling and eddying there I lie,
Where the old hawk wheels, and the blast howls by.

From the treeless brae
All green and grey,
To the wooded ravine I wind my way,
Dashing, and foaming, and leaping with glee,
The child of the mountain wild and free.
Under the crag where the stone-crop grows,
Fringing with gold my shelvy bed,
Where over my head
Its fruitage of red,
The rock-rooted rowan tree blushfully shows,
I wind, till I find
A way to my mind,
While hazel, and oak, and the light ash tree,
Weave a green awning of leafage for me.

Fitfully, fitfully, on I go,
Leaping, or running, or winding slow,
Till I come to the linn where my waters rush,
Eagerly down with a broad-face gush,
Foamingly, foamingly, white as the snow,
On to the soft green turf below ;
Where I sleep with the lake as it sleeps in the
glen,
Neath the far-stretching base of the high-peaked
Ben.

Slowly and smoothly my winding I make,
Round the dark-wooded islets that stud the clear
lake ;
The green hills sleep
With their beauty in me,
Their shadows the light clouds
Fling as they flee,
While in my pure waters pictured I glass
The light-plumed birches that nod as I pass.
Slowly and silently on I wend,
With many a bay and many a bend,
Luminous seen like a silvery line,
Shimmering bright in the fair sunshine,
Till I come to the pass, where the steep red scaur
Gleams like a watch-fire seen from afar,
Then out I ride,
With a full-rolling pride,
While my floods like the amber shine ;
Where the salmon rejoice
To hear my voice,
And the angler trims his line.

Gentlier now, with a kindly slope,
The green hills lie to the bright blue cope,
And wider the patches of green are spread,
Which Time hath won from my shifting bed.
    And many a broad and sunny spot,
        Where my waters wend,
        With a larger bend,
Shows the white-fronted brown-thatched cot,
Where the labouring man with sweatful care,
Hath trimmed him a garden green and fair,
        From the wreck of the granite bare.

And many a hamlet, peopled well
With hard-faced workmen, smokes from the dell;
        Cunning to work with axe and hammer,
        Cunning to sheer the fleecy flock,
        Cunning, with blast and nitrous clamour,
          To split the useful rock.
And many a rural church far-seen
Stands on the knolls of grassy green,
        Where my swirling current flows;
And, with its spire high-pointed, shows
How man, that treads the earthly sod,
        Claims fatherhood from God.

Now broader and broader my rich bed grows,
And deeper and deeper my full tide flows;
        And, while onward I sail,
        Like a ship to the gale,
With my big flood rolling amain,
The glen spreads out to a leafy vale,
        And the vale spreads out to a plain.

And many a princely mansion good
Looks from the old thick-tufted wood,
    On my clear far-winding line.
And many a farm, with acres spread,
Slopes gently to my fattening bed,
The farm, whose broad and portly lord
Loads with rich fare the liberal board,
    And quaffs the ruby wine.
And richly, richly, round and round,
With green and golden pride, the ground
Swells undulant, gardened o'er and o'er
With beauty's bloom, and plenty's store ;
    And many a sheaf of yellow corn,
      The farmer's healthful gain.
    Up my soft-shaded banks is borne,
      On the huge slow-labouring wain.
And many a yard well stacked with hay,
And many a dairy's trim array,
And many a high-piled barn I see,
And many a dance of rustic glee,
    Where sweats the jocund swain.
And many a town thick-sown with steeples,
With various wealth my border peoples,
    And studs my sweeping line ;
While frequent the bridge of well-hewn stone,
Arch after arch, is proudly thrown,
    My busy banks to join ;
Thus through the plain I wend my fruitful way,
To meet the sounding sea, and swell the briny
    bay.
    The briny bay ! how fair it lies
    Beneath the azure skies !

D

With its wide sweep of pebbly shore,
And the low far-murmuring roar
Of wave and wavelet sparkling bright
With a thousand points in the dancing light.
  There round the promontory's base,
  Bluff bulwark of the bay,
Free ranging with a lordly grace,
  I wind my surging way,
To mingle with the main.   Where wide
This way and that my turbid tide
Is spread, behold in pennoned pride
Strong Neptune's white-winged couriers ride !
  From east to west,
  Upon my breast,
Rich bales they bear, to swell the stores
Of merchant kings, who on my shores
Pile their proud palaces.   Busily plying,
And with fleet wings in fleetness vying,
The fire-fed steam-consuming boat
Casts from its high-reared iron throat,
The many-volumed smoke, while heaves
Beneath the boiling track it leaves
My furrowed flood.   Line upon line,
The ships that crossed the fretful brine,
Far-stretching o'er my spacious strand,
A myriad-masted army stand ;
While many a pier, and many a mole,
Breaks my strong current as I roll ;
And block and bolt, and bar and chain,
With giant-gates my flood detain,
To serve the seaman's need.   Around,
Thick as a forest, from the ground,

Street upon street, the city rears
Its pride, in strangely-clambering tiers
Of various-fashioned stone, while domes,
And spires, and pinnacles, and towers,
And wealthy tradesmen's terraced bowers
    Nod o'er my troubled bed,
And Labour's many-chambered homes,
    In straggling vastness, spread
There smoking lines. Thus, where I flow,
The stream of being, growing as I grow,
Floods to a tumult, and much-labouring man,
Who, with my small beginnings, small began,
Ends where I end, and crowns his swelling plan.

THE RIVER: AN ALLEGORY OF LIFE

I

Son of the mountain am I,
Born 'twixt the Earth and the Sky,
Where kindly cherished I lay
In my cradle of soft mossy green,
Looking with clear bright eye
On the clouds that curtained the day,
Floating in freakish display
With cerulean glimpses between.
Son of the mountain am I,
Born 'twixt the Earth and the Sky,

Where the old grey rocks stand out
'Mid the tempest's revel and rout,
Snorting with jagged old snout
    At the keen winds whistling by ;
Where the eagle spreads his van,
And the white-winged ptarmigan—
    Fed by rich dews from the sky
    There an infant of might I did lie.

II

Young was I, and lusty-hearted,
When first from the mountain I started,
    Down from the Ben's grey shoulders
    Over the old granite boulders,
    Scornful of rest and of ease,
Eagerly running and leaping,
Scooping the rocks with my sweeping,
    Tearing the roots of the trees ;
Swelling with torrent big-breasted,
Dashing with stream foamy-crested
Mighty and masterful then :
        Heaving and hurling,
        Whirling and swirling
O'er the harsh roots of the Ben ;
        Foaming and bubbling,
        Winding and doubling
Through the long stretch of the glen,
        So lusty was I,
        Son of Earth and of Sky,
So proud of my potency then !

III

Now I am grown to a River,
  With measured and equable strain
Rolling my waters, and never
  To toss and to tumble again ;
I am grown to a smooth-flooded River,
The mighty and merciful Giver
  Of wealth to the sons of the plain.
Through meadows and terraces pleasant
  In triumph of culture I ride,
With the home of the peer and the peasant
  To bless the rich roll of my tide ;
The firm-poised bridge I flow under,
  The fair-builded city I know,
And spires, domes, and turrets, a wonder,
  Nod their pride in my glass as I go ;
And high-tunnelled vessels are steaming
  And churning the foam of my tide,
And trafficking thousands are streaming
  With quick-eyed despatch at my side.
And millions are praising the River
  As he regally rolls to the main,
The mighty and merciful Giver
  Of wealth to the sons of the plain.

SPUT DUBH

(A Cascade near Pitlochrie.)

Son of the mountain,
Beautiful and strong,
Roaring and pouring
And sweeping along ;
Mighty art thou,
As I see thee now
Flinging the gathered floods of the Ben
Into the leafy shade of the glen ;
Like to a steed,
With galloping speed,
Tossing his mane,
And whisking his tail,
Art thou, when the pride
Of thy foaming tide
Leaps to the vale,
    Son of the mountain !
Most like a god,
Of things that I know,
On the earth below,
Art thou, in the pride
Of thy foaming tide,
    Son of the mountain !
Summers and winters,
Inconstant ever,
Roll their changes
Over thy head ;
Rocks tumble down
From the mountain's crown,

And stout old trees,
Root-wrenched by the breeze,
Fall with a crash
Into the dash
Of thy billowy bed ;
But thou dost abide
Unchanged in the swell
Of thy sky-fed well,
Most like in thy pride
To a deathless god,
    Son of the mountain !
Wise was the old Greek man who sang,
    ' Water is best.'
As from the breast
Of mighty Cybele,
Nurturing mother,
To every form
Of the breathing nation,
From eagle on wing
To creeping worm,
And man, the king
Of the vasty creation,
Flowed the redundant,
Life-sustaining,
Milky fountain ;
So, when thou pourest
Richly thy waters,
Budding and blowing
Follows thy flowing ;
Earth's sons and daughters
Rejoice in thy going.
Corn fields are waving

Near to thy laving,
Gardens are growing
With flower and with tree,
And proud cities rise
With towers to the skies,
Watered by thee,
   Son of the mountain !

Son of the mountain,
Lovely art thou,
Where thou leapest as now,
Silvery bright,
From the mountain's brow,
With the unspotted breadth of the blue above thee,
And the circling grace of the trees that love thee,
   Spiring larch, and the tresses fine
   Of waving birch,
And the red boled strength of the dark green
   pine,
Rejoicing with thee in the fair sunshine,
   Son of the mountain.
No fools were they who worshipped thee
So fair and bright, and wild and free,
   So beautiful, so strong.
They sought a god that they could see,
River god or nymph of fountain,
And poured their untaught litany
Responsive to thy bickering glee,
   Son of the mountain !

Son of the mountain,
Most like to a god

Art thou in the freedom and force of thy flow ;
A God must be in thee, or near thee, I know ;
      And Him I adore
      In this shrine of the glen,
      Mid the rush and the roar
      Where thy bright floods leap
      With silvery sweep,
Down from the crown of the old granite Ben,
      Strong son of the mountain !

WAIL OF AN IDOL

Μὴ δή μοι θάνατόν γε παραύδα, φαίδιμ' 'Οδυσσεῦ'
Βουλοίμην κ' ἐπάρουρος ἐὼν θητευέμεν ἄλλῳ,
'Ανδρὶ παρ' ἀκλήρῳ, ᾧ μὴ βίοτος πολὺς εἴη,
'Η πᾶσιν νεκύεσσι καταφθιμένοισιν ἀνάσσειν.—HOMER.

    O DREARY, dreary shades !
    O sad and sunless glades !
    O yellow, yellow meads
      Of asphodel !
    Where the dream-like idol strays,
    On lone and lifeless ways,
    Through Hades' weary maze,
      And sings his own sad knell.

    O sullen, solemn, silent clime !
    O lazy pace of noiseless time !
O where is the blythe and gamesome change
    Of the many-nurturing earth ?
    The dance of joy, the flush of mirth,
Life's vast and varied range ?

O dreary, dreary vales !
O heavy, heavy gales !
Fraught with the dreamy dew of sleep,
Over the joyless fields ye sweep ;
O sullen, sullen, streaky sky,
Where the changeless moon, with a leaden eye,
   Aloft hangs languidly,
And yellow vapours mount up high,
And flickering lights in a wild dance fly,
Like the last fleet flash when the strangled die,
Shooting across the darkling eye.

   O sullen, sullen sky !
Where the brown bat wings,
And the lone bird sings
A chant like the chant of death ;
   While sad souls wake
   The stagnant lake
With a sobbing, struggling breath.
O sad, O sad is the wail of the stream,
Mingling its sighs with the dead man's dream ;
   Winding, winding nine times round,
   Weary, wandering, 'scapeless bound !
     And the black, black kine,
      In lazy ranks,
Are cropping the sickly herb
   From the reedy Stygian banks ;
   And hissing things,
With poisoned blood,
Are crawling through the bubbling mud.
O sad, O sad is the endless row

Of poplars black; oh, sad and slow
Is the long-drawn train of the sons of woe,
    The silent-marching ghosts!
And they share no more in the feast of glee,
And the dance, and the song, and the wine-cup
    free;
Where the bard divine, with mellow lays,
Is singing the gods' and the heroes' praise;
      And they share no more
      Loud laughter's roar,
    The silent-marching ghosts!
      I hear their cry,
      As they flit swift by
        On noiseless wing,
Hurrying through the wide outspread
Gates that gape for the countless dead:
      I hear the cry
    Of the wailing ghosts;
      Their voices small,
      Like a drowning thing,
Drawn echoless along the long dim hall;
      And some are whirled,
    In the mighty void,
    Like a leaf in the gurgling tide
      And some are hurled,
      With a gusty fit,
    Into the deep Tartarean pit;
      And some do sway,
      Like a blind thing stray,
    To and fro in the pathless air;
And some, whom chance less stormy rules,
Sit sipping the blood from crimson pools.

O sad is the throne,
Dark, drear, alone,
Of the stern, relentless pair !
With gloom enveiled,
In judgment mailed,
A joyless sway they bear.
No circling years,
No sounding spheres,
No hopes and fears,
Are there ;
They sit on the throne,
Dark, drear, alone,
A stern relentless pair.
And beside them sits
A monster dire,
Watching the darkness with eyes of
fire,
The dog of the triform head ;
And his harsh bark splits,
Like thunder fits,
The realm of the silent dead.
Oh, sad is the throne,
Dark, drear, alone,
Of the stern, relentless pair !
O dreary, dreary shades !
O sad and sunless glades !
O yellow, yellow meads
Of asphodel !
O loveless, joyless homes !
O weary, starless domes !
Where the wind-swept idol roams,
And sighs his own sad knell.

O sullen, solemn, silent clime !
O lazy pace of noiseless time !
O where are the many-coloured joys of earth ?
O where is the loud strong voice of mirth ?
      The jubilant shout,
      Of the light-heeled rout,
Where the dance is whirling about and about ;
      The roving joy
      Of the bright-faced boy,
When he plays with life as he plays with a toy.
      O where is the change
      Of joy and woe ?
      The love of friend,
      The hate of foe ?
O where is the bustle of many-winged life,
And of man with man the many-mingling strife ?
      Where to live was to fight,
      And to fight was delight,
Where the fair face smiled on the strong-armed knight.
      O Hermes ! leader of the dead,
      Thou wingèd god
      Of the golden rod,
      O lead me, lead me further still !
Lead me to Lethe's silent stream,
   That I may drink, deep drink my fill,
And wash from my soul this long life-dream !
      O lead me, lead me to Lethe's shore,
      Where Memory lives no more !

SONG OF BEN CRUACHAN

(Argyleshire)

BEN CRUACHAN is king of the mountains,
　　That gird in the lovely Loch Awe,
Loch Etive is fed from his fountains,
　　By the stream of the dark-rushing Awe.
　　　　With his peak so high,
　　　　He cleaves the sky,
　　That smiles on his old grey crown,
　　　　While the mantle green,
　　　　On his shoulders seen,
　　In many a fold flows down.

He looks to the North, and he renders
　　A greeting to Nevis Ben,
And Nevis, in white snowy splendours,
　　Gives Cruachan greeting again.
　　　　O'er dread Glencoe
　　　　The greeting doth go,
　　And where Etive winds fair in the glen ;
　　　　And he hears the call,
　　　　In his steep North wall,
　　'God bless thee, old Cruachan Ben !'

When the North winds their forces muster,
　　And Ruin rides high on the storm,
All calm, in the midst of their bluster,
　　He stands, with his forehead enorm.
　　　　When block on block,
　　　　With thundering shock,
　　Comes hurtled confusedly down,

No whit recks he,
But laughs to shake free
The dust, from his old grey crown.

And while torrents on torrents are pouring
In a tempest of truculent glee,
When louder the loud Awe is roaring,
And the soft lake rides like a sea ;
He smiles through the storm,
And his heart grows warm,
As he thinks how his streams feed the plains ;
And the brave old Ben
Grows young again,
And swells with enforcèd veins.

For Cruachan is king of the mountains,
That gird in the lovely Loch Awe,
Loch Etive is fed from his fountains,
By the stream of the dark-rushing Awe.
Ere Adam was made,
He reared his head
Sublime o'er the green-winding glen ;
And, when flame wraps the sphere,
O'er Earth's ashes shall peer
The peak of the old Granite Ben !

———

THE OLD MAN OF HOY

(Orkney)

THE old man of Hoy
Looks out on the sea,
Where the tide runs strong, and the wave rides free :
He looks on the broad Atlantic sea,
And the old man of Hoy
Hath this great joy,
To hear the deep roar of the wide blue ocean,
And to stand unmoved 'mid the sleepless motion,
And to feel o'er his head
The white foam spread
From the wild wave proudly swelling,
And to care no whit
For the storm's rude fit
Where he stands on his old rock-dwelling,
This rare old man of Hoy.

The old man of Hoy
Looks out on the sea,
Where the tide runs strong and the wave rides free :
He looks on the broad Atlantic sea,
And the old man of Hoy
Hath this great joy,
To look on the flight of the wild sea-mew,
With their hoar nests hung o'er the waters blue ;
To see them swing
On plunging wing,
And to hear their shrill notes swelling,

And with them to reply
To the storm's war cry,
As he stands on his old rock-dwelling;
This rare old man of Hoy.

The old man of Hoy
Looks out on the sea,
Where the tide runs strong, and the wave rides free:
He looks on the broad Atlantic sea,
And the old man of Hoy
Hath this great joy,
When the sea is white and the sky is black,
And the helmless ship drives on like wrack,
To see it dash
At his feet with a crash,
And the sailors' death-note knelling,
And to hear their shrieks
With pitiless cheeks,
This stern old man of Hoy.

The old man of Hoy
Looks out on the sea,
Where the tide runs strong, and the wave rides free:
He looks on the broad Atlantic sea,
And the old man of Hoy
Hath this great joy,
To think on the pride of the sea-kings old,
Harolds, and Ronalds, and Sigurds bold,
Whose might was felt,
By the cowering Celt,
When he heard their war-cry yelling;

E

But the sea-kings are gone,
And he stands alone,
Firm on his old rock-dwelling,
This stout old man of Hoy.

The old man of Hoy
Looks out on the sea,
Where the tide runs strong, and the wave rides free:
He looks on the broad Atlantic sea,
And the old man of Hoy
Hath this great joy,
To think on the gods that were mighty of yore,
Braga, and Baldur, and Odin, and Thor,
And giants of power
In fateful hour,
'Gainst the great gods rebelling:
But the gods are all dead,
And he rears his head
Alone from his old rock-dwelling,
This stiff old man of Hoy.

But listen to me,
Old man of the sea,
List to the Skulda that speaketh by me;
The Nornies are weaving a web for thee,
Thou old man of Hoy,
To ruin thy joy,
And to make thee shrink from the lash of the ocean,
And teach thee to quake with a strange commotion,
When over thy head
And under thy bed
The rampant wave is swelling,

And thou shalt die
'Neath a pitiless sky,
And reel from thine old rock-dwelling,
Thou stout old man of Hoy !

A SONG OF BEN LEDI

(Perthshire)

Come, sit on Ledi's old grey peak,
   And sing a song with me,
Where the wild bird whirrs o'er the mosses bleak,
   And the wild wind whistles free !
'Tis sweet to lie on the tufted down,
   Low, low in the gowany glen ;
But proud is the foot that stands on the crown
   Of the glorious Ledi Ben.

Come hither, ye towsmen, soot-besoiled,
   Who cower in dingy nooks,
On whom no ray of the sun hath smiled,
   To shame your sombre looks.
Come, closely mewed in steaming lanes,
   Whom musty chambers pen,
And look abroad on the world of God
   From the top of this glorious Ben !

Come ye who sit with moody pains,
   And curious-peering looks,
Clogging the veins of your laden brains
   With the dust of your maundering books.

Not in your own dim groping souls,
  Nor in words of babbling men,
But here His wonders God unrolls—
  On the peak of the Ledi Ben.

Look forth on these far-stretching rows
  Of huge-ridged mountains high ;
There God His living Epos shows
  Of powers that never die.
Far north, far west, each glowing crest
  Thy sateless view may ken,
Where proudly they stand to rampart the land,
  With this glorious Ledi Ben.

And lo ! where eastward, far beneath,
  The broad and leafy plain
Spreads on the banks of silvery Teith
  ' Stout labour's fair domain ;
The smoke from the long white-glancing town,
  The loch that gleams in the glen,
All rush to thine eye when castled high
  On this glorious Ledi Ben.

Come, sit with me, ye sons of the free,
  Join hearty hand to hand,
And claim your part in the iron heart
  Of the Grampian-girded land ;
Soft lands of the South on rosy beds
  May cradle smoother men.
But the Northern knows his strength when he treads
  The heath of the old grey Ben.

Come, sit with me and praise with glee,
  On the peak of this granite Ben.
The brave old land, where the stream leaps free
  Down the rifts of the sounding glen.
Land of strong hands and glowing hearts,
  And mother of stalwart men,
Who nurse free thoughts where the wild breeze floats
  On the peak of the Ledi Ben.

TO THE DIVINE SPIRIT

SPIRIT that shaped the formless chaos,
  Breath that stirred the sluggish deep,
When the primal crude creation
  Started from its dateless sleep ;
Spirit that heaved the granite mountains
  From the central fiery wells,
Breath that drew the rolling rivers
  From the welkin's dewy cells,
      Spirit of motion,
      Earth and ocean
Moulding into various life,
      Within, without us,
      And round about us
Weaving all in friendly strife :
Come, O come, thou heavenly guest,
Shape a new world within my breast !

Spirit that taught the holy fathers
  Wandering through the desert drear,
To know and feel, through myriad marchings,
  One eternal presence near.

Breath that touched the Hebrew prophets'
  Lips with words of wingèd fire,
Through the dubious gloom of ages,
  Kindling hope and high desire ;
      Spirit revealing
      To pure feeling,
  In the inward parts of man,
      Fitful-shining
      Dim-divining
  Vast foreshadowings of Thy plan ;
Come, O come, thou prophet guest,
Watch and wait within my breast !

Spirit, that o'er Thine own Messiah
  Hovered like a brooding dove,
When Earth's haughty lords he conquered,
  By the peaceful march of love.
Breath that hushed loud-vaunting Cæsars,
  And in triumph yoked to Thee
Iron Rome, and savage Scythia,
  Bonded brethren and the free.
      Spirit of union,
      And communion
  Of devoted heart with heart,
      Pure and holy,
      Sure and slowly
  Working out thy boastless part :
Come, thou calmly-conquering guest,
Rule and reign within my breast !

Spirit that, when free-thoughted Europe
  With the triple-crowned despot strove,

In the gusty Saxon's spirit
  Thy soul-stirring music wove;
Then when pride's piled architecture
  At a poor monk's truthful word
Crashing fell, and thrones were shaken
  At the whisper of the Lord.
      Spirit deep-lurking,
      Secret-working
Weaver of strange circumstance,
      All whose doing
      Is rise or ruin
Named by shallow mortals chance;
Come, let fruitful deeds attest
Thy plastic virtue, in my breast!

Spirit, that sway'st the will of mortals,
  Every wish, and every hope,
Shaping to Thy forethought purpose
  All their striving, all their scope.
Central tide that heavest onward
  Wave and wavelet, surge and spray,
Making wrath of man to praise Thee,
  And his pride to pave Thy way:
      Spirit that workest,
      Where thou lurkest,
Death from life, and day from night,
      Peace from warring,
      And from jarring,
Songs of triumph and delight;
Come, O come, Thou heavenly guest,
Work all Thy will within my breast!

NIGHT

Ἱερὰ Νύξ.—HOMER

HOLY NIGHT! in silence
 From thy starry throne
Swaying, thee I worship,
 Silent and alone.

Holy Night! how calmly
 Sails the mellow moon
Through the deep blue welkin,
 Fairer than the noon.

Mellow Moon! how gently
 Through the voiceless night,
O'er the sleeping waters,
 Streams thy silver light.

Holy Night! how lovely
 Shoot, with sudden birth,
Hosts of shimmering arrows
 From the lambent north.

Holy Night! thou reignest
 Solemn, still, serene;
Hushed the tribes of mortals
 Bow before their queen.

Now the battling voices
 Of the babbling throng
Cease; and thou may'st listen,
 As it treads along,

To the steps of Godhead
    Beating march of Time,
Slowly, surely, wisely,
    Beautiful, sublime;

Beating thought and feeling,
    Beating vital power
In renewed creation's
    Pulse, from hour to hour.

Holy Night! devoutly
    While I worship thee,
Babbling Folly's echo
    Dies away from me.

A SABBATH MEDITATION

THE Sabbath bells are travelling o'er the hill;
The gentle breeze across the fresh-reaped fields
Blows fitful; scarcely, on the broad smooth bay,
With full white-gleaming sail, the slow ship moves;
Thin float the clouds; serene the mountain stands;
And all the plain in hallowed beauty lies.
God of the Sabbath, on Thy holy day
'Tis meet to praise Thee!   In the high-domed fane,
Glorious with all the legendary pomp
Of pictured saints, where skilful singers swell
The curious chant, or on the lonely hill,
Where, on great cliff and purple heather, shines
The shadowless sun at noon, Thou hear'st alike.
Vainly the narrow wit of narrow men

Within the walls which priestly lips have blest,
In the fixed phrases of a formal creed,
Would crib thy presence ; Thou art more than all
The shrines that hold Thee ; and our wisest creeds
Are but the lispings of a prattling child,
To spell the Infinite.   Kings have drawn the sword,
Lawyers have wrangled, to declare Thy being ;
And convocations of high-mitred men
The foaming vials of sacerdotal wrath
Outpoured, and, with tempestuous proud conceit,
Shook the vast world about a phrase to name Thee,
In vain.   Thou, like the thin impassive air,
Dost cheat the grasp of subtlest-thoughted sage ;
And half our high theology is but
The shadow, which man's poor and clouded ken
Hath cast across Thy brightness.   I would sing
Thy praise with humble heart, and, like the lyre
Wind-swept, the comings of thy breath would wait,
To wake my rapture.   Lift up your heads, ye hills,
And nod His praise, ye sharp far-stretching lines
Of crags storm-shattered, and ye jagged peaks
Sky-cleaving ! you His mighty power upshot
From the red ocean of His nethermost fire,
In primal ages : there inform ye lay,
In seething lakes, your molten masses huge,
In turbid waves, with inorganic roll,
Far-heaving through the dark abysmal space
Chaotic ; thence His word creative hove
Your marshalled ridges ; rank on rank ye rose,
Granite and gneiss, and every ordered kind
That careful science counts ; the giant frame
Of this fair world, of peace-enfolden vales

Storm-fronting fence, and bulwark ever sure.
Ye mountain torrents, with far-sweeping foam,
Ye leaping cataracts, and deep-swirling pools,
Ye streams with the full-gathered grandeur rolling
Of countless rills, from huge far-sundered Alps,
Ye waters, with your thousand voices, praise
The mighty Lord! He of your sleepless floods
Is the unsleeping soul. All motion comes
From Him. Thou Ocean, with thy living belt
Girdling the Earth, whether serene, as now,
Thou liest, licking with an innocent ripple
The feet o' the green-throned isles, or, like a spurred
And furious charger, wild from coast to coast
Drivest far-sounding—thou, in all thy changes,
Art full of God; yea, all thy works, O Lord,
Are full of Thee! and who is dull to these
Shall from the teaching of the schools come back
With beggarly blindness. He shall mount in vain
His telescope, to spy Thee in the clouds,
Who in green herb and starry flower, beneath
His vagrant foot, hath failed to see and love
Thy manifest beauty. O make clear my sense,
Thou great Revealer, to the grand array
Of open mysteries that encompass round
Our daily walk with Godhead, that no vain
And wordy fool may cheat my facile ear
With echoed volleys of man's crude conceit,
Misnamed God's thunder! From Thyself direct
Thy secret comes to all, whom Thou shalt deem
Worthy to find it. Councils, doctors, priests,
Are but the signs that point us to the spring
Whence flow thy living waters; and, alas!

Too oft with wavering, or with cowardly hand
Back-turned, they point.   Teach Thou my 'stablished
      soul
To seek Thy teaching, Lord, and trust in Thee.

The generations of uncounted men
Have hymned Thy praises, Lord.   Their stammering
      tongues
With strange crude doctrine magnify the power
Of Him, whose vastness they were fain to grasp,
But could not.   Even the folly of the fool
Shall praise Thee, Lord.   Thou hast a place for all.
The wicked and the weak are but the steps,
Whereon the wise shall mount, to see Thy face ;
And mighty churches, and high-vaunted faiths,
Are but the schools, wherein Thy centuries train
The infant peoples to the manly reach
Of pure devotion ; and most wise are they,
Who hear one hymn of varied truth through all
The harmonious discord of strange witnesses,
Prophets and martyrs, priests, and meek-eyed saints,
And rapt diviners, with imperfect tongue,
Babbling Thy praises.   Egypt's brutish gods,
Dog-faced, hawk-headed, crocodile, and cat,
Snake-eating ibis, and the spotted bull,
Not without apt significance did type
Thy severed functions to a sense-bound race.
In sea and sky, green tree, and flowing stream,
In flying bird, and creeping beast, they found
Pictorial speech, and speaking signs of what
They crudely guessed of Thee.   To clearer Greeks
Stout Briareus, celestial Titans strong,

And supreme Jove, with weight of thunderous locks,
Throned like a king, and sceptre in his hand,
And ministrant eagle, spake Thy mighty power
With awful grace. Each seized a part of Thee,
And, with a fond assurance, deemed to hold
Thy whole infinity in earthly bonds
For human needs. Nor less the Christian priest
Portentous erred, when with rash hand he clutched
The awful Triune symbol, and defined
The immeasurable Majesty Supreme
With curious phrase and scientific rule,
And with the thorns of wiry logic fenced
Thy bristling name, from touch of thought profane;
Then, from a throne high-seated, and girt round
With triple-tiered presumption, grasped Thy bolt,
Sported Thy thunder, and with Thy best friends
Filled a far-dreaded Hell, that he might seem
A god on earth, whom awe-struck, grovelling men
Might see, and feel, and handle. The pale monk,
Wasting his flesh within a cold damp cell,
And straining his dull vision, till he saw
God's features, in the dim putrescent light
Of his own sick imaginings—this man caught
A glimpse of Thee, and, with such fiery haste
Did hold Thee, and with prostrate worship hug,
That nevermore his head he dared to lift
Erect, and with proud-sweeping glance survey
The riches of Thy wide luxuriant world,
Man's privilege. On so nice a pivot turns
True wisdom; here an inch, or there, we swerve
From the just balance; by too much we sin,
And half our errors are but truths unpruned.

The errors of Thy creatures praise Thee, Lord.
Not they who err are damned; but who, being
    wrong,
In obdurate persistency to err
Refuse all bettering.   Hope for such is none.
Hope lives for all, who flounder boldly on
Through quaggy bogs, till firmer footing found
Gives glorious prospect.   One Deceiver haunts
The hearts of faithless men; his name is FEAR.
O Thou, who ridest glorious through the skies,
In thunder or in sunshine strong the same,
The Almighty builder of this fair machine,
Whose beauty blinds star-eyed philosophy,
Whose vastness makes our staggered thinking pant
For utterance vainly,—Father of all Power,
Eternal Fount of liberty and life,
Free, measureless, unspent—if e'er my voice
Rose to Thy throne, in reverent truthful prayer,
Slay me this demon, yellow Fear, that maims
The arm of enterprise, nips the bud of hope,
And freezes the great ocean of our life,
That should run riot in the praise of Thee,
With wave on wave of proud high-venturing deeds.
O may this Sabbath, with its gentle dews
Shed by Thy Spirit on my chastened soul,
Restore my blighted bud of thought, and lift
This low-crushed life into a mighty tree,
Branchy, and blooming with fair summer fruits
Exuberant-clustered!—May all Sabbaths be
A ripe and mellow season to my heart,
Lovely as golden autumn's purple eve,
Genial as sleep, whence the tired limb refreshed

Leaps to new action, and appointed toil,
With steady hope, sure faith, and sober joy.

THE SEA

WHAT dost thou say,
Thou old grey sea,
Thou broad briny water
   To me?
With thy ripple and thy plash,
And thy waves as they lash
The old grey rocks on the shore?
With thy tempests as they roar,
And thy crested billows hoar,
And thy tide evermore,
   Fresh and free;
With thy floods as they come,
And thy voice never dumb,
What thought art thou speaking to me?
What thing should I say
On this bright summer day,
Thou strange human dreamer, to thee?
One wonder the same
All things do proclaim
In the sky, and the land, and the sea;
'Tis the unsleeping force
Of a GOD in his course,
Whose life is the law of the whole,
As he breathes out his power
In the pulse of the hour,
And the march of the years as they roll;

You may measure his ways
In the weeks and the days,
And the stars as they wheel round the pole,
But no finger is thine
To touch the divine
All-plastic, all-permeant soul,
As it shapes and it moulds,
And its virtue unfolds,
In the garden of things as they grow,
And flings forth the tide
Of its strength far and wide,
In wonders above and below.

Thou huge-heaving sea
That art speaking to me
Of the power and the pride of a God,
I would travel like thee
With force fresh and free
Through the breadth of my human abode,
Never languid and low,
But with bountiful flow,
Of thoughts that are kindred to God;
Ever surging and streaming,
Ever beaming and gleaming,
Like the lights as they shift on thy glass,
Ever swelling and heaving,
And largely receiving
The beauty of things as they pass.

Thou broad-billowed sea
Never sundered from thee
May I wander the welkin below;

May the plash and the roar
Of thy waves on the shore
Beat the march to my feet as they go ;
Ever strong, ever free,
When the breath of the sea
Like the fan of an angel I know ;
Ever rising with power,
To the call of the hour,
Like the swell of thy tides as they flow.

THE BOULDER

Thou huge grey stone upon the heath,
With lichens crusted well,
I marvel much, if thou found breath,
What story thou would'st tell.
Oft wandering o'er the birch-grown hill,
To hear the wild winds moan,
I wonder still what chance or skill
Hath pitched thee here alone.

Where wert thou when Sire Adam first
Drew his mischanceful breath,
And in the bowers of bliss was cursed
With everlasting death,
Then when the damned fiend, who loves
The mask of snake and toad,
Crept into Paradisian groves,
And stole Eve's heart from God ?

F

Thee in some seaward glen, I ween,
   On sharp Loffodin's shore,
In frozen folds of gleaming green
   The giant glacier bore,
Then down the steep it harshly slid,
   Till, loosen'd from the high land,
With wrench enorm its compact form
   Was launch'd, a floating island,

Into the Artic deep.   And thou,
   In its stark bosom buried,
Through seas which huge Leviathians plough,
   To this South strand wert hurried.
Then, from its cold close gripe unbound
   By summer's permeant breath,
Thy wandering bulk à station found
   On this wide sandy heath.

And here thy watch hath been, God knows
   How long, and what a strange
Masque of Time's motley-shifting shows
   Hath known thee without change.
Seas thou hast seen to dry land turned,
   And dry land turned to seas,
And fiery cones that wildly burned,
   Where flocks now feed at ease.

By thee the huge-limbed breathing things,
   Crude Earth's portentous race,
Passed, and long lizard-shapes with wings
   Swept o'er thy weathered face.

To thee first came man's jaded limb
   From Eastern Babel far ;
Around thee rose the Druid's hymn,
   And the cry of Celtic war.

By thee the Roman soldier made
   The mountain-cleaving road,
The Saxon boor beside thee strayed,
   The lordly Norman strode.
The Papal monk thy measure took ;
   The proud priest triple-crowned
Mumbled a blessing from his book,
   And claimed the holy ground.

By thee the insolent Edward passed,
   When mad with eager greed,
A bridge of law-spun lies he cast
   Across the Scottish Tweed.
And thou that vengeful day didst know,
   When strong with righteous scorn
Young Freedom rose, and smote the foe,
   At glorious Bannockburn.

Thou saw'st when 'neath thy hoary shade
   Upon the old brown sod
The plaided preacher sate, and made
   His fervent prayer to God,
What time men tried by courtly art
   To trim, and craft of kings,
The faith that soars from a people's heart
   And flaps untutored wings.

Thou saw'st, from out old unkempt bowers,
　Huge peopled cities rise,
And merchant kings with stately towers
　Invade the troubled skies.
Thick rose the giant vents, that mar
　Heaven's lustrous blue domain,
And whirling wheel and hissing car
　Disturb thy silent reign.

And thou—but what thou yet may'st see
　The pious Muse witholds ;
The curious art be far from me,
　To unroll Time's fateful folds.
When Earth, that wheels on viewless wing,
　Is twenty centuries older,
Some bard, where Scotland was, shall sing
　The story of the Boulder.

MY SCOTCH LASSIE

If I had the brush of angel,
Dipt in colours rich and rare,
I would paint with choicest limning
My Scotch lassie fresh and fair.

Fresh is she as dewy morning,
Fair as blossom on the spray,
Fragrant as the birch tree waving
In the fresh breeze of the May.

O my bright and blooming lassie !
Maids more stately well may be ;
But no stateliest maiden ever
Breathed a smile so sweet as she.

O my bonnie blithe-faced lassie,
Mild as bloom on hawthorn tree,
Rich as June, and ripe as Autumn,
Flower and fruit in one is she.

Saw you ever cowslip warmer
When the zephyrs came to woo ?
Saw you bright-eyed speedwell peeping
'Neath the hedge with purer blue ?

Warmer than her keen pulse keeping
Time to all things true and good,
Bluer than her blue eye swelling
In young love's divinest mood ?

Softer floats no plumy sea-gull
Than her bosom's heaving charms,
Swan on lake not whiter swimmeth
Than the whiteness of her arms.

If I had the brush of angel,
Dipt in colours rich and rare—
No ! no trick of brush or pigment
Ever limned a form so fair.

Let them limn who live in dreamland,
Where the brain-born phantoms sway ;

I have feasted on the substance,
And the shadow pales away.

I will not make dainty mockery
With a painted thin display   .
Of a life that breathes and burgeons
With the fulness of the May.

I will see my dear Scotch lassie
In the ray that sweeps the hills,
In the bright far-shimmering ocean,
In the silver-flashing rills.

I will see her where the wandering
Bee sucks honey from the brae,
Where the mavis to the mavis
Pours his rich full-throated lay.

I will feed upon the sweetness
Of her presence near to me,
And her wealth of grace that hangeth
Like a peach upon a tree.

I will live on the dear memory
Of that hour of burning bliss,
When she lent her lips and thrilled me
With the rapture of her kiss !

———

STUDENTS' MAY-SONG

BLITHE birds are singing now,
   Light clouds are winging now,
Easter bells ringing now
   Anthems of glee !
Come from your dusty nooks,
   Fling away musty books,
Hear how the lusty rooks
   Caw merrily !
List to the happy note,
   Trolled from the mavis' throat,
Where breezy zephyrs float,
   Cradling the trees !
Broad seas are glancing,
   Bright waves are dancing,
Light skiffs advancing
   With undulant ease !
All things are buoyant and bright with the May,
All things rejoice in the fresh-streaming ray ;
   Come away ! Come away ! Come away !

Wilt thou be lagging now,
   Fretting and fagging now,
   Moping and groping,
     With down-drooping head ?
Over the yellow leaf,
Wasting thy summers brief,
   Building and gilding
     The bones of the dead !

Digging from mouldy graves,
Old Greek and Roman knaves,
　　Scratching and patching
　　　　Their mummies to life ;
Muddily diving,
Thornily striving,
Idly reviving
　　　　Some foolish old strife,
Deaf to the charm of the lusty-voiced May,
Deaf to the call of sweet birds from the spray ;
　　Come away ! Come away ! Come away !

Wilt thou be dreaming still,
Restlessly teeming still
　　With bubbles and troubles
　　　　That rise from the brain ?
Guessing and gaping,
Theories shaping,
　　Wondering, blundering,
　　　　Ever in vain ?
With thoughts never steady,
With words ever ready,
　　Spouting and routing,
　　　　And troubling the pool ;
Rushing in boldly,
Cutting up coldly,
　　Weighing, surveying,
　　　　All things by a rule !
Burrowing blindly far from the day,
Deaf to the sweet birds that call from the spray ;
　　Come away ! Come away ! Come away !

Come where the mountain high
Cleaveth the mottled sky,
Where white clouds lightly fly
        Dappling the noon !
Where the lone mountain tarn,
Fringed by the plumy fern,
    Shimmers and glimmers
        Beneath the pale moon ;
Where the green birchen spray
Waves o'er the cliffy way,
    Fragrantly, vagrantly,
        Skirting the Ben ;
And the flood roaring free,
Bubbling with foamy glee,
    Gushes and rushes
        And leaps to the glen !
Where winter's cold cerements are bursting away,
And Zephyrs are piping the birth hymn of May,
    Come away ! Come away ! Come away !

Where the wide leafy bower,
Sprouting with snowy flower,
Richly with drooping power,
        Nods o'er the lea ;
And the brook slowly wandering,
Broadly meandering,
    Lispingly, crispingly,
        Creeps to the sea !
Where crown, bell, and starlet,
White, purple, and scarlet,
    Loosely, profusely,
        Spread over the mead ;

Where the white lambs are playing
And reeling and swaying,
The bee goes a-Maying
     With light buzzing speed;
Where Nature is vested in light from the May,
And all things with vegetive splendour are gay,
     Come away! Come away! Come away!

Come where broad seas of light,
Flooding with noiseless might,
Sweep with new glory bright
     O'er earth and sky!
Wilt thou be lurking then,
Owlishly far from men,
Dark in this musty den,
     Blinding thine eye?
Not from dry learning's mine,
Not from dead printed line,
Gushes the lore divine
     Living to thee;
Shake rusty bonds away,
Leap into open day,
Wander in face of May,
     Bravely with me;
Things that were dead shall be quickened to-day,
Touched with new transport of life from the May,
     Come away! Come away! Come away!

ADVICE TO A FAVOURITE STUDENT
ON LEAVING COLLEGE

DEAR youth, grey books no blossoms bear ;
   Thou hast enough of learning ;
For life's green fields thy march prepare,
   And take my friendly warning.
I would not have thee longer stay,
   To read of other's striving ;
Wield thine own arm !—the only way
   To know life is by living.

The brain's a small part of a man ;
   Though thought has wide dominions,
Thou canst not lift the smallest stone
   By Speculation's pinions.
Who learns an art by lifeless rule,
   Through mists will still be blinking ;
The subtlest thinker is a fool,
   Who spins mere webs of thinking.

The times are feverish ; mark me well !
   Have faith and patience by thee ;
Unless thou curl into thy shell,
   Thou'lt find enough to try thee.
But that's a weak device.   I know
   Thou'lt face it free and fearless ;
But O ! beware the greater foe,
   A spirit proud and prayerless !

I love a bold and venturous boy,
  Who, full of fresh emotion,
Launches with large and liberal joy
  On life's wide-rolling ocean.
But there are rocks; and blind to steer
  Were thoughtless folly's merit:
Curb thou thy force with holy fear,
  And keep a watchful spirit.

Where eager crowds contend for pelf,
  The seller and the buyer,
Each one free range seeks for himself,
  And cares for nothing higher.
Make honey in an ordered hive,
  Nor join the lawless scramble
Of men, with whom in life to thrive
  Is with good luck to gamble.

We live in days when all would climb
  With hot, high-strung employment;
Some rage in prose, some writhe in rhyme,
  All hate a calm enjoyment.
Freedom's the watchword of the hour;
  But O! tis melancholy
When every bubbling brain has power
  To drown calm thought with folly!

The age is full of talkers.   Thou
  Be silent for a season,
Till slowly-ripening facts shall grow
  Into a stable reason.

Pert witlings fling crude fancies round,
　As wanton whim conceits them,
Pleased when from fools the echoed sound
　Of their own folly greets them.

Nurse thou, where eager babble spreads,
　A quiet brooding nature,
Nor strive, by lopping taller heads,
　To raise thy lesser stature.
Eschew the cavilling critic's art,
　The lust of loud reproving ;
The brain by knowledge grows, the heart
　Is larger made by loving.

All things we cannot know.　At sea
　As when a good ship saileth,
Our steps within the planks are free,
　Beyond all cunning faileth.
So man as by a living bond
　Of circling powers is bounded ;
Within the line is ours, beyond
　The sharpest wit's confounded.

What thing thou knowest, nicely know
　With curious fine dissection ;
The smallest mite can something show
　That chains thy rapt inspection.
Allwhere with holy caution move,
　In God thy life is moving ;
All things with reverent patience prove,
　'Tis God's will thou art proving.

What thing thou doest, bravely do ;
　　When Heaven's clear call hath found thee,
Follow !—with fervid wheels pursue,
　　Though thousands bray around thee !
Yet keep thy zeal in rein ; depise
　　No gentle preparation ;
Flash not God's truth on blinking eyes,
　　With reckless inspiration !

Farewell, my brave, my bright-eyed boy !
　　And from the halls of learning,
Thy face, my long familiar joy,
　　Take, with this friendly warning.
And when with weighty truth thou'rt fraught
　　From life, the earnest preacher,
Think sometimes with a kindly thought
　　On me, thy faithful teacher.

VACATION ODE

(Read at the end of the Winter Session of the
Greek Classes, Edinburgh.)

　　YE sons of learned toil,
　　Who with hard purpose moil
O'er grammar's thorny ways, and heaps of dusty
　　　tomes,
　　Your posts are run.　Be free,
　　And with unchartered glee
Sport where the springy foot o'er lush green meadow
　　　roams

Not from the gaunt array
Of mouldy parchments grey,
Drops the fine dew that slakes the knowledge-thirst-
    ing soul !
But where from blade and spray
Glances the fresh green May,
And rose-tipt flowerets blow, and lucid waters roll.

Rise, and no more be vext
From harsh disjointed text,
With learned strain to wrench the dubious-worded
    lore !
Up ! and redeem your sight
With Heaven's broad-streaming light,
And pictured skies, and plains with beauty dappled
    o'er !

And let the genial note
That through green woods doth float
From viewless cuckoo, win your rapt ear's wise regard,
More than the cunning chime
Of curious-builded rhyme
From craft of smooth-lipped Greek, or deep-mouthed
    Roman bard.

Let roar of foaming floods,
And breath of growing woods,
Wave round you with more joy than flags of conquer-
    ing kings !
Nor let your dull thought go
With painful pace and slow,
When every bursting grove with twittering gladness
    rings !

Not wise who stern refuse
With gracious hand to use
The chance-sown sport, stray whim, and random-
        started joy;
In many a shifting mood,
With gamesome lustihood,
Quaint Nature respite finds from life's severe employ.

You to familiar halls
A father's voice recalls,
And tells your virtues' roll with broad benignant pride;
While eager at the gate
A mother's love doth wait
To gain her laurelled boy back to her careful side.

And troops of sisters fair,
Whose smiles make blithe the air,
And rings of lusty boys, with merry sun-brown faces,
These wait your skill to guide
Their steps by mountain side,
To lone green glens remote, and strange old castled
        places!

Now home!   You need no goad
From me on such a road;
Your native steam will urge this taskless travel duly;
And may God love you so,
Your strength through weal and woe,
As I did love you well, and strove to serve you truly!

A SONG FOR THE ROAD, AND A RULE
FOR THE LIFE

A SONG for the road, and a rule for the life,
    Receive from a lusty old man, Tom ;
Fear God, and march on, and make war to the knife,
    When the enemy crosses your plan, Tom.
For Life's a campaign ; then foot it apace,
    There are dangers enough in your track, Tom ;
Still keep a sharp out-look, and show a bold face,
    Or the foe will be soon on your back, Tom !
        For this is true wisdom, I wish you to know,
        Sail close to the wind when you tack, Tom !
        We live, while we live, by the pluck that we show,
        And if we don't stand, we must flee from the foe
        And fall with a stab in the back, Tom !

You see yon huge Ben that runs up to the sky,
    So ruggedly grand and sublime, Tom ;
A staircase so steep, you think, would defy
    The cat o' the mountain to climb, Tom !
But, 'tis all a delusion—just wisely survey
    With your eye, and then take it aslant, Tom,
And you'll find what they say, that you can't find a way,
    Is a tissue of cowardly cant, Tom.
        For this, etc.

The worst of all words in the language is—*But*,
    For whatever you purpose or plan, Tom,
This weak monosyllable comes in to cut
    The sinews that make you a man, Tom.

G

'Tis noble to dare, *but* not pleasant at all
   A lion to meet, where you fare, Tom ;
It may suit you to ride, *but* a rider may fall,
   So you sit and you rot in your chair, Tom
     For this, etc.

Some people's devotion delights in this notion
   Of heaven, that when we get there, Tom,
We'll have nothing to do but to float in the blue,
   And pipe a psalm tune in the air, Tom !
If 'tis so in the sky, we shall know by-and-by,
   But on earth 'tis much otherwise now, Tom,
Where the battle we fight brings a keener delight
   Than the laurels we wear on the brow, Tom.
     For this, etc.

The end of all living is simply to live,
   Is what Aristotle would say, Tom ;
And form to the formless by labour to give
   Is to live the most excellent way, Tom !
A moth in the sunbeam may flutter an hour,
   To flutter is all that it can, Tom ;
But to fashion great thoughts into deeds is the dower
   God gave to high-reasoning man, Tom !
     For this, etc.

If you shrink from no danger where valour avails,
   There's nothing can stand in your way, Tom ;
You may start, like stout Lincoln, a splitter of rails,
   And be king of the people some day, Tom.
The Romans were lords of the sea and the land,
   And what was the reason of that, Tom ?

At the word of command, they marched on sword in
      hand,
  And they laid all their enemies flat, Tom.
    For this, etc.

My sermon is done—still rejoice in the toils
  That the travel of life may attend, Tom.
Put foot after foot; never number the miles;
  You will know when you come to the end, Tom!
Fear God; every atom takes rank at His call;
  For the world is no rope of sand, Tom;
Link hangs upon link; and 'tis profit to all
  That each march at the word of command, Tom.
    For this is true wisdom, I wish you to know,
    Sail close to the wind when you tack, Tom!
    We live, while we live, by the pluck that we show,
    And if we don't stand, we must flee from the foe,
    And fall with a stab in the back, Tom!

A SONG OF SUMMER

'Always in your darkest hours strive to remember your brightest.'
              J. P. RICHTER

  SING me a song of Summer,
    For my heart is wintry sad,
  That glorious bright new-comer,
    Who makes all Nature glad!
  Sing me a song of Summer,
    That the dark from the bright may borrow,
  And the part in the radiant whole of things
    May drown its little sorrow!

Sing me a song of Summer,
　When God walks forth in light,
And spreads his glowing mantle
　O'er the blank and the grey of the night;
And where he comes, his quickening touch
　Revives the insensate dead,
And the numbed and frozen pulse of things
　Beats music to his tread.

Sing me a song of Summer,
　With his banners of golden bloom,
That glorious bright new-comer,
　Who bears bleak winter's doom,
With banners of gold and of silver,
　And wings of rosy display,
And verdurous power in his path,
　When he comes in the pride of the May;

When he comes with his genial sweep
　O'er the barren and bare of the scene,
And makes the stiff earth to wave
　With an ocean of undulant green;
With flourish of leafy expansion,
　And boast of luxuriant bloom,
And the revel of life as it triumphs
　O'er the dust and decay of the tomb

Sing me a song of Summer;
　O God! what a glorious thing
Is the march of this mighty new-comer
　With splenpour of life on his wing!

When he quickens the pulse of creation,
  And maketh all feebleness strong,
Till it spreads into blossoms of beauty,
  And burst into pæans of song!

Sing me a song of Summer!
  Though my heart be wintry and sad,
The thought of this blessed new-comer
  Shall foster the germ of the glad.
'Neath the veil of my grief let me cherish
  The joy that shall rush into day,
When the bane of the winter shall perish
  In the pride and the power of the May.

FAREWELL TO SUMMER

(Written at Oban)

I HEARD the whistling North wind say
  When it came down with power,
Athwart the russet ferny brae,
  And by the old grey tower:
I heard the whistling North wind say,
  Bright Summer suns no more
Shall shine on Oban's dimpled bay,
  And green Dunolly's shore.

I saw a fox-glove in the dell
  Beneath the crag so grey,
One lonely, lean, belated bell,
  And thus it seemed to say:

The glory of the June is past,
  My purple kin are gone,
And I am left a poor outcast
  To die in the cold alone!

I saw the long black ragged cloud
  O'ercap the frowning Bens,
And trails of thick blue mist enshroud
  The green far-gleaming glens;
And thus the black cloud seemed to say,
  Now Summer suns are dim,
The stout old Winter holds his sway,
  And I will reign with him.

And is it so?—brightest of things,
  God's beauty-vested Summer,
Shall it depart on hasty wings
  That was so late a comer,
And I who lived with fragrant breeze,
  Blue skies, and purple braes,
On hueless flowers and leafless trees
  Must feed my widowed gaze?

It may not be: up! let us go!
  I will not stay and look
Where gorgeous Nature's pictured show
  Is now a blotted book.
Let Nature die! She'll live again
  When six dull months expire;
Meanwhile against both wind and rain
  Heap we the blazing fire,

Snug in the chambered town ! and call
  My troup of friends together,
And for six months let no word fall
  Of Nature, wind, or weather ;
And ply the work of thought or art
  That helps both self and neighbour,
And sing with glad and guileless heart
  The song that seasons labour.

And bring the grey tomes from the shelves
  And learn strong will from Cato.
And take high value of ourselves
  From lofty-thoughted Plato :
And, while with friendly cheer we pass
  The rare, rich-blooded bottle,
Give learnèd flavour to the glass
  By saws from Aristotle !

 And then we'll talk of Church and State,
  And wish the hangman's rope
To wed their necks to righteous Fate
  Who love the Roman Pope !
And blame the loons who gave the sway
  To the mere polled majority,
With clamorous yells to overbray
  The voice of grave authority.

And then,—why then, we'll go to bed,
  And wake, above all sorrow
Of factious brawls to lift our head,
  By faithful work to-morrow,—

Work through long weeks of blustering storm,
  And winter's gloomy reign,
'Till the great pulse of things grow warm,
  And Nature lives again.

And suns shall shine, and birds shall sing,
  And odorous breezes blow,
And ferns uncurl their folded wing
  Where star-eyed flowerets grow ;
And surly blasts shall cease to bray,
  And stormy seas to roar
On Oban's warm sun-fronting bay,
  And green Dunolly's shore.

A SONG OF THE COUNTRY

(Written near Witley, in Surrey)

AWAY from the roar and the rattle,
  The dust and the din of the town,
Where to live is to brawl and to battle,
  · Till the strong treads the weak man down !
Away to the bonnie green hills
  Where the sunshine sleeps on the brae,
And the heart of the greenwood thrills
  To the hymn of the bird on the spray.

Away from the smoke and the smother,
  The veil of the dun and the brown,
The push and the plash and the pother,
  The wear and the waste of the town !

Away where the sky shines clear,
   And the light breeze wanders at will,
And the dark pine-wood nods near
   To the light-plumed birch on the hill.

Away from the whirling and wheeling,
   And steaming above and below,
Where the heart has no leisure for feeling,
   And the thought has no quiet to grow.
Away where the clear brook purls,
   And the hyacinth droops in the shade,
And the wing of the fern uncoils
   Its grace in the depth of the glade.

Away to the cottage so sweetly
   Embowered 'neath the fringe of the wood,
Where the wife of my bosom shall meet me
   With thoughts ever kindly and good.
More dear than the wealth of the world,
   Fond mother with bairnies three,
And the plump-armed babe that has curled
   Its lips sweetly pouting for me.

Then away from the war and the rattle
   The dust and the din of the town,
Where to live is to brawl and to battle
   Till the strong treads the weak man down.
Away where the green twigs nod
   In the fragrant breath of the May,
And the sweet growth spreads on the sod,
   And the blithe birds sing on the spray.

THE MUSICAL FROGS *

BREKEKEKEX! coax! coax! O happy happy frogs!
   How sweet ye sing!   Would God that I
   Upon the bubbling pool might lie,
      And sun myself to-day
   With you!   No curtained bride, I ween,
   Nor pillowed babe, nor cushioned queen,
   Nor tiny fay on emerald green,
      Nor silken lady gay,
   Lies on a softer couch.   O Heaven!
   How many a lofty mortal, riven
      By keen-fanged inflammation,
   Might change his lot with yours, to float
   On sunny pond with bright green coat,
   And sing with gently throbbing throat
      Amid the croaking nation,
Brekekekex! coax! coax! O happy happy frogs!

Brekekekex! coax! coax! O happy happy frogs!
   Happy the bard who weaves his rhyme
   Recumbent on the purple thyme,
      In the fragrant month of June;

* Some dozen or more years ago, while living at Liebenstein, a German hydropathic establishment in Sachse-Meiningen, I took a stroll across the country on a hot summer's day; when coming near some low marshy ground I became aware of a concert of soft musical notes, floating up gently from the pools of water among the reeds.   Never having heard anything of the kind before, I went close up to the brink of the water, and soon found that this most sweet discourse came from a colony of green frogs.   Their music made such an impression on me, that on the way back to my water-quarters I wrote some lines as a memorandum of the event, and as a sample of the philosophy of enjoyment. in which frogs belike are sometimes wiser than men.—J.S.B.

Happy the sage, whose lofty mood
Doth with far-searching ken intrude
Into the vast infinitude
  Of things beyond the moon ;
But happier not the wisest man
Whose daring thought leads on the van
  Of star-eyed speculation,
Than thou, quick-legged, light-bellied thing,
Within the green pond's reedy ring,
That with a murmurous joy dost sing
  Among the croaking nation,
Brekekekex ! coax ! coax ! O happy happy frogs !

Brekekekex ! coax ! coax ! O happy happy frogs !
  Great Jove with dark clouds sweeps the
   sky,
Where thunders roll and lightnings fly,
  And gusty winds are roaring ;
Fierce Mars his stormy steed bestrides,
And, lashing wild its bleeding sides,
O'er dead and dying madly rides,
  Where the iron hail is pouring.
'Tis well ; such crash of mighty Powers
Must be : the spell may not be ours
  To tame the hot creation.
But little frogs with paddling foot
Can sing when gods and kings dispute,
And little bards can strum the lute
  Amid the croaking nation,
With Brekekekex ! coax ! coax ! O happy happy
  frogs !

Brekekekex! coax! coax! O happy happy frogs!
   Farewell! not always I may sing
   Around the green pond's reedy ring
      With you, ye boggy Muses!
   But 1 must go and do stern battle
   With herds of stiff-necked human cattle,
   Whose eager lust of windy prattle
      The gentle rein refuses.
   O if!—but all such *ifs* are vain;
   I'll go and blow my trump again,
      With brazen iteration:
   And when, by Logic's iron rule,
   I've quashed each briskly babbling fool,
   I'll seek again your gentle school,
   And hum beside the tuneful pool
      Amid the croaking nation,
Brekekekex! coax! coax! O happy happy frogs!

THE SONG OF MRS JENNY GEDDES

Air—'British Grenadiers'

SOME praise the fair Queen Mary, and some the good
   Queen Bess,
And some the wise Aspasia, beloved by Pericles;
But o'er all the world's brave women there's one that
   bears the rule,
The valiant Jenny Geddes, that flung the four-legged
   stool.
With a row-dow—at them now!—Jenny fling the stool!

'Twas the twenty-third of July, in the sixteen thirty-
    seven,
On Sabbath morn from high St Giles', the solemn
    peal was given :
King Charles had sworn that Scottish men should
    pray by printed rule ;
He sent a book, but never dreamt of danger from a
    stool.
With a row-dow—yes, I trow !—there's danger in a
    stool !

The Council and the Judges, with ermined pomp elate,
The Provost and the Bailies in gold and crimson state,
Fair silken-vested ladies, grave Doctors of the school,
Were there to please the King, and learn the virtue of
    a stool.
With a row-dow—yes, I trow !—there's virtue in a
    stool !

The Bishop and the Dean came wi' mickle gravity,
Right smooth and sleek, but lordly pride was lurking
    in their e'e ;
Their full lawn sleeves were blown and big, like seals
    in briny pool ;
They bore a book, but little thought they soon should
    feel a stool.
With a row-dow—yes, I trow !—they'll feel a four-legged
    stool !

The Dean he to the altar went, and, wi' a solemn look,
He cast his eyes to heaven, then read the curious-
    printed book ;

In Jenny's heart the blood upwelled with bitter anguish
    full ;
Sudden she started to her legs, and stoutly grasped
    the stool !
With a row-dow—at them now !—firmly grasp the stool !

As when a mountain cat springs upon a rabbit small.
So Jenny on the Dean springs, with gush of holy gall ;
Wilt thou say the mass at my lug, thou Popish-puling
    fool ?
No ! no ! she said, and at his head she flung the four-
    legged stool.
With a row-dow—at them now !—Jenny fling the stool !

A bump, a thump ! a smash, a crash ! now gentle folks
    beware !
Stool after stool, like rattling hail, came tirling through
    the air,
With, Well done, Jenny ! bravo, Jenny ! that's the
    proper tool !
When the Deil will out, and shows his snout, just
    meet him with a stool.
With a row-dow—at them now !—there's nothing like
    a stool !

The Council and the Judges were smitten with strange
    fear,
The ladies and the Bailies their seats did deftly clear,
The Bishop and the Dean went, in sorrow and in dool,
And all the Popish flummery fled, when Jenny showed
    the stool !
With a row-dow—at them now !—Jenny show the
    stool !

And thus a mighty deed was done by Jenny's valiant
   hand,
Black Prelacy and Popery she drave from Scottish
   land;
King Charles he was a shuffling knave, priest Laud a
   pedant-fool,
But Jenny was a woman wise, who beat them with a
   stool !
With a row-dow—yes, I trow !—she conquered by the
   stool !

MOMENTS

IN the beauty of life's budding,
   When young pulses beat with hope,
And a purple light is flooding
   Round thought's blossoms as they ope;
When the poet's song is dearest,
   And, where sacred anthems swell,
Every word of power thou hearest
   Holds thy spirit like a spell;
      O these are moments, fateful moments,
      Big with issue—use them well !

When a sudden gust hath tumbled
   Hope's bright architecture down ;
When some prouder fair hath humbled
   Thy proud passion with a frown ;
When thy dearest friends deceive thee,
   And cold looks thy love repel,

And the bitter humours grieve thee,
  That make God's fair earth a hell;
    O these are moments, trying moments,
    Meant to try thee—use them well!

When a flash of truth hath found thee,
  Where thy foot in darkness trod,
When thick clouds dispart around thee,
  And thou standest nigh to God.
When a noble soul comes near thee,
  In whom kindred virtues dwell,
That from faithless doubts can clear thee,
  And with strengthening love compel;
    O these are moments, rare fair moments;
    Sing and shout, and use them well!

When a haughty threat hath cowed thee,
  And with weak, unmanly shame,
Ignoble thou hast bowed thee
  To the terror of a name;
And then God holds the mirror
  Where thy better self doth dwell,
And thou dost start with terror,
  And thy tears gush like a well;
    O these are moments, blessèd moments;
    Weep and pray, and use them well!

In the pride of thy succeeding,
  When, beneath thy high command,
Every soul must own the leading
  Of thy strong controlling hand;
When wide cheers of acclamation
  Round thy march of triumph swell,

And the plaudits of a nation
  Every thought of fear expel ;
      O these are moments, slippery moments ;
      Watch and pray, and use them well !

When the term of life hath found thee,
  And thou smilest upon Fate,
And the golden sheaves around thee
  For the angels' sickle wait ;
When the pure love thou achievest
  Doth the mortal pang expel,
And a shining track thou leavest
  To dear friends that love thee well ;
      O these are moments, happy moments ;
      Bless God, with whom all issues dwell !

SABBATH HYMN ON THE MOUNTAINS

      PRAISE ye the Lord !
Not in the temple of shapeliest mould,
Polished with marble and gleaming with gold,
Piled upon pillars of slenderest grace,
But here in the blue sky's luminous face
      Praise ye the Lord !

      Praise ye the Lord !
Not where the organ's melodious wave
Dies 'neath the rafters that narrow the nave,
But here with the free wind's wandering sweep,
Here with the billow that booms from the deep,
      Praise ye the Lord !

H

Praise ye the Lord !
Not where the pale-faced multitudes meet
In the sweltering lane and the dun-visaged street,
But here where bright ocean, thick sown with green
    isles,
Feeds the glad eye with a harvest of smiles,
Praise ye the Lord !

Praise ye the Lord !
Here where the strength of the old granite Ben
Towers o'er the greenswarded grace of the glen,
Where the birch flings its fragrance abroad on the
    hill,
And the bee o'er the heather-bloom wanders at will,
Praise ye the Lord !

Praise ye the Lord !
Here where the loch, the dark mountain's fair daughter,
Down the red scaur flings the white-streaming water,
Leaping and tossing and swirling for ever
Down to the bed of the smooth-rolling river,
Praise ye the Lord !

Praise ye the Lord !
Not where the voice of a preacher instructs you,
Not where the hand of a mortal conducts you,
But where the bright welkin in scripture of glory
Blazons Creation's miraculous story,
Praise ye the Lord !

Praise ye the Lord!
The wind and the welkin, the sun and the river,
Weaving a tissue of wonders for ever;
The mead and the mountain, the flower and the
    tree,
What is their pomp but a vision of Thee,
    Wonderful Lord?

Praise ye the Lord!
Not in the square-hewn, many-tiered pile,
Not in the long-drawn, dim-shadowed aisle,
But where the vast world, with age never hoary,
Flashes His brightness and thunders His glory,
    Praise ye the Lord!

LAWS OF NATURE

THE fool hath in his heart declared,—by laws
    Since time began,
Blind and without intelligential cause,
    Or reasoned plan,
All things are ruled.   I from this lore dissent,
    With sorrowful shame
That reasoning men such witless wit should vent
    In reason's name.
O Thou that o'er this lovely world hast spread
    Thy jocund light,
Weaving with flowers beneath, and stars o'erhead
    This tissue bright

Of living powers, clear Thou my sense, that I
    May ever find
In all the marshalled pomp of earth and sky
    The marshalling mind !
Laws are not powers ; nor can the well-timed courses
    Of earths and moons
Ring to the stroke of blind unthinking forces
    Their jarless tunes.
Wiser were they who in the flaming vault
    The circling sun
Beheld, and in his ray, with splendid fault,
    Worshipped the one
Eye of the universe that seeth all,
    And shapeth sight
In man and moth through curious visual ball
    With fine delight.
A blessed beam, on whose refreshful might,
    Profusely shed
Eight times ten years, with ever young delight
    Mine eye hath fed,
Still let me love thee, and with wonder new,
    By flood and field,
Worship the fair, and consecrate the true
    By thee revealed !
And loving thee, beyond thee love that first
    Father of Lights
From whom the ray vivific marvellous burst,
    Might of all mights,
Whose thought is order, and whose will is law.
    That man is wise
Who worships God wide-eyed, with cheerful awe
    And chaste surprise.

BENEDICITE

ANGELS holy,
High and lowly,
Sing the praises of the Lord!
Earth and sky, all living nature,
Man, the stamp of thy Creator,
Praise ye, praise ye, God the Lord!

Sun and moon bright,
Night and noonlight,
Starry temples azure-floored,
Cloud and rain, and wild winds' madness,
Breeze that floats with genial gladness,
Praise ye, praise ye, God the Lord!

Ocean hoary,
Tell His glory,
Cliffs, where tumbling seas have roared!
Pulse of waters blithely beating,
Wave advancing, wave retreating,
Praise ye, praise ye, God the Lord!

Rock and high land,
Wood and island,
Crag where eagle's pride hath soared,
Mighty mountains purple-breasted,
Peaks cloud-heaving, snowy-crested,
Praise ye, praise ye, God the Lord!

Rolling river,
Praise Him ever,
From the mountain's deep-vein poured ;
Silver fountain clearly gushing,
Troubled torrent madly rushing,
Praise ye, praise ye, God the Lord !

Bond and free man,
Land and sea man,
Earth with' peoples widely stored,
Wanderer lone o'er prairies ample,
Full-voiced choir in costly temple,
Praise ye, praise ye, God the Lord !

Praise Him ever,
Bounteous Giver !
Praise Him, Father, Friend, and Lord !
Each glad soul its free course winging,
Each blithe voice its free song singing,
Praise the great and mighty Lord ! *

CREEDS AND CANARIES

I HAD a sweet canary bird,
Whose little wing was never stirred
    Beyond the wires around it ;
I looked upon my dainty bird,
And, while I looked, my heart was stirred
To think that pretty prisoned thing
May never flap its native wing
    Beyond the bars that bound it !

* (Set to the air *Alles Schweige*, also set to music by Mr W.
H. Jude and by A. S. W.).

I went and ope'd the little door,
And looked; but, sooth, I wondered sore
   To see my small canary:
With jerking head and pecking bill,
Within the wires it tarried still,
And had no lust abroad to spring,
And flit about with ransomed wing
   In ample range and airy!

Well, well! quoth I, 'tis plain to see
You have no notion to be free,
   So stay within your cage now!
And yet, methinks you are no fool,
And, safely bound by customed rule,
You wisely shun a larger home,
Where cats and deathful dogs may roam,
   If you should leave your cage now!

If birds are wise, men are not fools,
For they too have their customed rules
   And pretty gilded cages;
And, should you wish to make them free,
Just ope the door, and you will see
No folded wing they 'gin to stir,
But much the prudent ease prefer
   Of their own gilded cages.

The lawyer and the grave D.D.,
Who find strong bond of unity
   In old time-hallowed pages,

With sanctioned text and hoary creed
And fond tradition serve their need,
And live as safe and shielded well
As lobsters in close mailèd shell,
    Or birds in gilded cages.

And, though you make a dusty din,
They wrap them closer in their skin,
    And con their ancient lessons ;
And they are wise ; for who can tell
What risks may lurk and dangers fell
To helmless souls all tossed about
In seas of drivel and of doubt,
    Unmoored from old Confessions ?

HYMN

Air—' Belmont '

O FOR a heart from self set free,
    And doubt and fret, and care,
Light as a bird, instinct with glee,
    That fans the breezy air !

O for a mind whose virtue moulds
    All sensuous fair display,
And, like a strong commander, holds
    A world of thoughts in sway !

O for an eye that's clear to see,
    A hand that waits on Fate,
To pluck the ripe fruit from the tree,
    And never comes too late !

O for a life with firm-set root,
  And breadth of leafy green,
And flush of blooming wealth, and fruit
  That glows with mellow sheen !

O for a death from sharp alarms
  And bitter memories free :
A gentle death in God's own arms,
  Whose dear Son died for me !

A SONG OF FATHERLAND BY A TRAVELLER

Air—' Ho ! are ye sleeping, Maggie ? '

I'VE wandered east, I've wandered west,
  In gipsy-wise a random roamer ;
Of men and minds I've known the best,
  Like that far-travelled king in Homer.
      But O ! for the land that bore me,
      O ! for the stout old land,
      Of breezy Ben and winding glen,
      And roaring flood and sounding strand !

I've seen the domes of Moscow far,
  In green and golden glory gleaming ;
And stood where sleeps the mighty Czar,
  By Neva's flood so grandly streaming.
      But O ! etc.

I've stood on many a storied spot,
  Where blood of heroes flowed like rivers,
Where Deutschland rose at Gravelotte,
  And dashed the strength of Gaul to shivers.
    But O ! etc.

I've stood where stands in pillared pride,
  The shrine of Jove's spear-shaking daughter,
And humbled Persia stained the tide
  Of free Greek seas with heaps of slaughter.
    But O ! etc.

I've stood upon the rocky crest,
  Where Jove's proud eagle spreads his pinion,
Where looked the God far east, far west,
  And all he saw was Rome's dominion.
    But O ! etc.

I've fed my eyes by land and sea,
  With sights of grandeur streaming o'er me,
But still my heart remains with thee,
  Dear Scottish land, that stoutly bore me.
      O ! for the land that bore me,
      O ! for the stout old land,
      With mighty Ben, and winding glen,
      Stout Scottish land, my own dear land !

HAIL, LAND OF MY FATHERS!

Hail, land of my fathers! I stand on thy shore,
'Neath the broad-fronted bluffs of thy granite once
    more;
Old Scotland, my mother, the rugged, the bare,
That reared me with breath of the strong mountain
    air.
No more shall I roam where soft indolence lies
'Neath the cloudless repose of the featureless skies,
But where the white mist sweeps the red-furrowed
    scaur,
I will fight with the storm and grow strong by the
    war!

What boots all the blaze of the sky and the billow,
Where manhood must rot on inglorious pillow?
'Tis the blossom that blooms from the taint of the
    grave,
'Tis the glitter that gildeth the bonds of the slave.
But, Scotland, stern mother, for struggle and toil
Thou trainest thy children on hard, rocky soil;
And thy stiff-purposed heroes go conquering forth,
With the strength that is bred by the blasts of the
    north.

Hail, Scotland, my mother! and welcome the day
When again I shall brush the bright dew from the
    brae,
And, light as a bird, give my foot to the heather,
My hand to my staff, and my face to the weather:

Then climb to the peak where the ptarmigan flies,
Or stand by the linn where the salmon will rise,
And vow never more with blind venture to roam
From the strong land that bore me—my own Scottish
home.

CAPPED AND DOCTORED AND A'

A SONG OF DEGREES

FOR THE UNIVERSITY OF EDINBURGH

Air—'Woo'd and Married and a' '

I YINCE was a light-headed laddie,
    A dreaming and daundering loon,
Just escaped from the rod o' my daddie,
    And the skirts o' my mither's broun goun.
But now I cut loftier capers,
    And the beer that I drink is nae sma',
When I see my ane name in the papers,
    Capped and Doctored and a'.
        Capped and Doctored and a',
        Doctored and Capped and a'!
        Right sure 'tis a beautiful thing
        To be Capped and Doctored and a'!

My parish I wadna besmutch
    Wi' words that look heartless and hard ;
But I knew there of life just as much,
    As a hen in the farmer's kail yard.
I got a good tailor to suit me,
    My feet were richt decently shod ;

But the smell o' the peat was about me,
  And my manners were awkward and odd !
     Capped and Doctored and a',
     Doctored and Capped and a',
     I'm as proud as a Pope or a King,
     To be Capped and Doctored and a' !

Frae the school I came up to the College,
  As a calf comes up to a cow ;
Wi' a wonderful thirst for all knowledge,
  And scraps of learning a few !
Through Virgil I stoutly could hammer,
  A book, or it may be twa ;
And Greek, just a taste o' the grammar,
  To look better than naething ava !
     Capped and Doctored and a',
     Doctored and Capped and a' !
     I'm as proud as a Pope or a King,
     To be Capped and Doctored and a' !

A wonderful place is the College ;
  I felt like a worm getting wings,
When I heard the great mill-wheel of knowledge
  Turn round with all possible things !
A marvellous place is the College ;
  Professor's a marvellous man,
To find for such mountains of knowledge
  Such room in a single brain-pan !
     Capped and Doctored and a',
     Doctored and Capped and a' !
     I feel like a bird on the wing,
     When I'm Capped and Doctored and a' !

All races and peoples and nations
    Were lodged in that wonderful brain;
Proud systems and big speculations,
    All possible things to explain.
All creatures at various stages,
    From mollusc and monkey to man,
Through millions of billions of ages.
    That make up life's wonderful plan !
            Capped and Doctored and a',
            Doctored and Capped and a' !
            It gives one a wonderful swing
            To be Capped and Doctored and a' !

I confess I was glamoured at first—
    Looked round wi' a stupid surprise;
But from session to session their burst
    New light on my widening eyes :
I could talk of attraction and force,
    Of motion and mind and matter ;
And thought it a thing quite of course,
    When phosphorus burnt in the water.
            Capped and Doctored and a',
            Doctored and Capped and a' !
            The lad has the genuine ring
            Who is Capped and Doctored and a'.

My logic is lithe as an eel,
    My philosophy deep as a well ;
My rhetoric spins like a wheel,
    My Greek for a Scot pretty well.
Of my Bible I know quite enough,
    Not, like Chalmers, to preach and to pray,

But to give a glib fool a rebuff,
   And to keep the black devil at bay!
      Capped and Doctored and a',
      Doctored and Capped and a'!
      I leap and I dance and I sing,
      Now Capped and Doctored and a'!

You may ca' me a lean, lanky student,
   A chicken new out o' the shell;
But with time, if I'm patient and prudent,
   I may be Professor mysel'.
My head with citations well stocket,
   I may sit in the chair at my ease,
With a thousand a year in my pocket,
   And six months to do what I please.
      I'll know how to find my own place
      In the world, with great and with sma';
      And I'll no be the last in the race,
      Being Capped and Doctored and a'!

Then fill your glasses, my boys,
   Let mirth and jollity sway!
'Tis fit with my friends to rejoice,
   When I'm Capped and Doctored to-day!
This night may not stupidly pass
   With beer, or coffee, or tea;
But of champagne a bright sparkling glass
   Shall foam to my noble degree!
      Brim your glasses, my boys!
      In the Church, or it may be the law,
      Tom Tidy will yet make a noise,
      Being Capped and Doctored an a'!

A SONG OF GOOD GREEKS

Air—'Seit Vater Noah in Becher goss'

SINCE Martin Luther the ink-horn threw,
   Which worked the Devil much woe,
The power of Greek in Europe grew,
   And groweth and ever shall grow ;
     For never was language at all,
       So magical-swelling,
       So spirit-compelling,
       As Homer rolled,
       In billows of gold,
     And Plato, and Peter, and Paul.

Etruscan, Hebrew, and Sanscrit are dead,
   And Latin will die with the Pope,
But Greek still blooms like a thymy bed,
   On brown Hymettus' slope ;
     For never was language at all,
       That billowed so grandly,
       And flowed out so blandly,
       And never will die
       Till men deny
     The faith both of Plato and Paul.

Who'll buy my wares, my old Greek wares ?
   Here's Homer, who sang of old Troy,
A sunny sprite all robed in light,
   And crowned with beauty and joy ;

For surely no minstrel at all
    E'er poured such a river,
    Of verses that never
    Will cease to flow,
    While men shall know
The Gospel of Peter and Paul.

Who'll buy my wares, my old Greek wares?
  Here's Pindar, the eagle sublime,
Who soars where Jove's red lightning flares,
  And his awful thunders chime;
    For never was poet at all,
    In boxing and racing,
    And pedigree-tracing,
    So learned as he,
    And worthy to be
Canonised both with Peter and Paul.

Who'll buy my wares? here's Socrates,
  Who first by logical spell
From Olympus' crown brought wisdom down,
  With mortal men to dwell;
    And sure never sage was at all,
    Who mingled sound reason
    With such pleasant season
    Of mirth and fun,
    And died like one
Well gospelled by Peter and Paul.

Who'll buy my wares, my old Greek wares?
  Here's Plato will pass for a god,

I

Who for new worlds new men prepares,
On a plan both pleasant and odd ;
For sure never sage was at all
So loftily soaring,
So lavishly pouring
Of nectar fine,
The draught divine,
Only second to Peter and Paul.

Who'll buy my wares, my old Greek wares ?
Here's Aristotle, the wise,
Who sniffs about with learnèd snout,
And scans with critical eyes ;
And sure never sage was at all
So crammed with all knowledge,
A walking college,
Who many things knew,
I tell you true,
Unknown both to Peter and Paul !

Who'll buy my wares, my old Greek wares ?
Here's mighty Demosthenes, who,
When traitors sold fair Greece for gold,
Alone stood faithful and true ;
For sure never man was at all
Who flung his oration
With such fulmination
Of scorching power
'Gainst the sins of the hour,
Like epistles of Peter and Paul.

Who'll buy my wares, my old Greek wares?
  Here's Zeno, Cleanthes, and all,
Who set their face, with a manly grace,
  To follow where duty might call;
    For sure never men were at all
        So steeled in all virtue
        That flesh may be heir to,
        And ready to die,
        With never a sigh,
    For the truth, just like Peter and Paul.

Who'll buy my wares, my old Greek wares?
  Here's Proclus, Plotinus, and all,
Who clomb on Plato's golden stairs
  To the super-celestial hall;
    And sure never men were at all
        Who lived so devoutly,
        And grappled so stoutly
        With flesh and blood,
        And tramped in the mud
    The Devil, like Peter and Paul.

Come, buy my wares, each learned elf.
  Who culls Parnassian herbs,
And swears by Liddell and Scott, and Jelf,
  And Veitch's irregular verbs!
    For this I declare to you all,
        Greek gives you a station
        Sublime with the nation
        Of gods above,
        All hand and glove
    With Plato, and Peter, and Paul.

Of all the thoughtful sons of Time,
  The Greeks were wisest, that's clear ;
The Germans preach a lore sublime,
  But it smells of tobacco and beer ;
    And this I declare to you all,
        Though Kant, and such fellows
        Know something, they tell us,
        They never will do
        To tie the shoe
    To Plato, or Peter, or Paul.

Some think that man from a monkey grew
  By steps of long generation,
When, after many blunders, a few
  Good hits were made in creation ;
    But I can't comprehend this at all ;
        Of blind-groping forces
        Though Darwin discourses,
        I rather incline
        To believe in design,
    With Plato, and Peter, and Paul.

There's one Thomas Buckle, a London youth,
  Who taught that the world was blind
Till he was born to proclaim the truth,
  That matter is moulder of mind ;
    But I really can't fancy at all
        How wheat, rice, and barley,
        Made Dick, Tom, and Charlie
        So tidy and trim,
        Without help from Him
    Who was preached both by Plato and Paul.

There's one John Bright, a Manchester man,
  Who taught the Tories to rule
By setting their stamp on his patent plan
  For renewing the youth of John Bull ;
    But I say that it won't do at all.
      To seek for salvation
      By mere numeration
      Of polls would surprise,
      If they were to rise,
    Not a little both Plato and Paul.

Then praise with me the old Greek times,
  When men were lusty and strong,
And gods laughed merry in sunny climes,
  And wisdom was wedded to song ;
    For this I declare to you all,
      Bright may tickle your palate
      With suffrage and ballot,
      But you'll die a fool
      If you don't go to school
    With Plato, and Peter, and Paul.

A SONG OF GEOLOGY

I'LL sing you a ditty that needs no apology—
  Attend, and keep watch in the gates of your
    ears !—
Of the famous new science which men call Geology,
  And gods call the story of millions of years.

Millions, millions—did I say millions?
　Billions and trillions are more like the fact!
Millions, billions, trillions, quadrillions,
　Make the long sum of creation exact!

Confusion and Chaos, with wavering pinion,
　First swayed o'er the weltering ferment of things,
When all over all held alternate dominion,
　And the slaves of to-day were to-morrow the kings.
　　Chaos, Chaos, infinite wonder!
　　　Wheeling and reeling on wavering wings;
　　Whence issued the world, which some think a
　　　blunder,
　　　A rumble and tumble and jumble of things!

The minim of being, the dot of creation,
　The germ of Sire Adam, of you and of me,
In the folds of the gneiss in Laurentian station,
　Far west from the roots of Cape Wrath you may
　　　see.
　　Minims of being, budding and bursting,
　　　All on the floor of the measureless sea!
　　Small, but for mighty development thirsting,
　　　With throbs of the future, like you, Sir, and
　　　me!

The waters, now big with a novel sensation,
　Brought corals and buckies and bivalves to view,
Who dwell in shell houses, a soft-bodied nation;
　But fishes with fins were yet none in the blue.

Buckies and bivalves, a numberless nation!
  Buckies, and bivalves, and trilobites too!
These you will find in Silurian station, ,
  When Ramsay and Murchison sharpen your
    view.

Then fins were invented; when Queen Amphitrite
  Stirred up her force from Devonian beds,
The race of the fishes in ocean grew mighty,
  Queer-looking fishes with bucklers for heads.
    Fishes, fishes—small greedy fishes!
      With wings on their shoulders and horns on
        their heads,
      With scales bright and shiny, that shoot through
        the briny
      Cerulean halls on Devonian beds!

God bless the fishes!—but now on the dry land,
  In days when the sun shone benign on the poles,
Forests of ferns in the low and the high land
  Spread their huge fans, soon to change into coals!
    Forests of ferns—a wonderful verity!
      Rising like palm trees beneath the North
        Pole;
      And all to prepare for the golden prosperity
      Of John Bull reposing on iron and coal.

Now Nature the eye of the gazer entrances
  With wonder on wonder from teeming abodes; `
From the gills of the fish to true lungs she advances,
  And bursts into blossoms of tadpoles and toads.

Strange Batrachian people, Triassic all,
  Like hippopotamus huge on the roads !
You may call them ungainly, uncouth, and
    unclassical,
  But great in the reign of the Trias were Toads

Behold, a strange monster our wonder engages,
  If dolphin or lizard your wit may defy,
Some thirty feet long on the shore of Lyme-Regis,
  With a saw for a jaw, and a big staring eye.
    A fish or a lizard? an ichthyosaurus,
      With a big goggle eye, and a very small brain,
    And paddles like mill-wheels in clattering chorus,
      Smiting tremendous the dread-sounding main !

And here comes another ! can shape more absurb be,
  The strangest and oddest of vertebrate things?
Who knows if this creature a beast or a bird be,
  A fowl without feathers, a serpent with wings?
    A beast or a bird—an equivocal monster!
      A crow or a crocodile, who can declare ?
    A greedy, voracious, long-necked monster,
      Skimming the billow, and ploughing the air.

Next rises to view the great four-footed nation,
  Hyenas and tapirs, a singular race,
You may pick up their wreck from the great Paris
    basin,
  At the word of command every bone finds its
    place.

Palæothere, very singular creature !
    A horse or a tapir, or both can you say ?
Showing his grave pachydermatous feature,
    Just where the Frenchman now sips his café.

And now the life-temple grows vaster and vaster,
    Only the pediment fails to the plan ;
The winged and the wingless are waiting their
    master,
    The Mammoth is howling a welcome to Man.
      Mammoth, Mammoth ! mighty old Mammoth !
        Strike with your hatchet and cut a good slice ;
      The bones you will find, and the hide of the
        mammoth,
        Packed in stiff cakes of Siberian ice.

At last the great biped, the crown of the mammals,
    Sire Adam, majestic, comes treading the sod,
A measureless animal, free without trammels
    To swing all the space from an ape to a god.
      Wonderful biped, erect and featherless !
        Sport of two destinies, treading the sod,
      With the perilous licence, unbridled and tether-
        less,
        To sink to a devil or rise to a god.

And thus was completed—miraculous wonder !
    The world, this mighty mysterious thing ;
I believe it is more than a beautiful blunder,
    And worship, and pray, and adore, while I sing.

Wonder and miracle !—God made the wonder;
  Come, happy creatures, and worship with me !
I know it is more than a beautiful blunder,
  And I hope Tait, and Tyndall, and Huxley
    agree.

CONCERNING I AND NON-I

A METAPHYSICAL SONG

Air—' Seit Vater Noah ' *

SINCE father Noah first tapped the vine,
  And warmed his jolly old nose,
All men to drinking do much incline,
  But why, no drinker yet knows ;
    We drink and we never think how !
    And yet, in our drinking,
    The root of deep thinking
    Lies very profound,
    As I will expound
    To all who will drink with me now !

The poets, God knows, a jovial race,
  Have ever been lauding of wine ;
Of Bacchus they sing, and his rosy face,
  And the draught of the beaker divine ;

* The idea of this song is taken from Baggesen's song in
Methfessel's *Liederbuch*. In the execution I gave myself free
reins, feeling that to attempt a translation in such a peculiar
case would have been to insure failure.—J. S. B.

Yet all their fine phrases are vain ;
  They pour out the essence ..
  Of brain-effervescence,
  With rhyme and rant
  And jingling cant,
But nothing at all they explain.

But I, who quaff the thoughtful well
  Of Plato and old Aristotle,
And Kant and Fichte and Hegel can tell
  The wisdom that lies in the bottle ;
    I drink, and in drinking I know :
    With glance keen and nimble
    I pierce through the symbol,
    And seize the soul
    Of truth in the bowl,
  Behind the mere sensuous show !

Now brim your glass, and plant it well
  Beneath your nose on the table,
And you will find what philosophers tell
  Of I and non-I is no fable.
    Now, listen to wisdom, my son !
    Myself am the subject,
    This wine is the object ;
    These things are two,
    But I'll prove to you
  That subject and object are one.

I take this glass in my hand, and stand
  Upon my legs if I can,
And look and smile benign and bland,
  And feel that I am a man.

Now stretch all the strength of your brains !
    I drink—and the object
    Is lost in the subject,
    Making one entity,
    In the identity
Of me, and the wine in my veins !

And now if Hamilton, Fraser, or Mill
    This point can better explain,
You may learn from them, with method and skill,
    To plumb the abyss of your brain ;
      But this simple faith I avow,
        The root of true thinking
        Lies just in deep drinking,
        As I have shown
        In a way of my own,
    To this jolly good company now.

SONG OF A BACHELOR IN DIVINITY

Air—' Seit Vater Noah in Becher goss '

I'VE stood my trials, I've left the school,
    I'm capped with a learned B.D.,
Of Latin and Greek and Hebrew I'm full,
    Old Wisdom dwelleth with me ;
      And now, if you'll list to my rhymes,
        I'll flap my young pinions
        In my new dominions,
        And vent what I may
        In a delicate way ;
For stone walls have ears sometimes.

I'm a Protestant good ; I hate the Pope,
  In every shape and degree,
The Popish Pope, and the Presbyter Pope,
  And all the Popes that be ;
    For this above all things I prize,
      To have free admission,
      With no man's permission,
      Both early and late,
      Through the gracious gate,
    To the prayer-hearing God in the skies.

I hate the Pope ; and in God's own book
  I read the message of grace,
And I claim a freeman's right to look
  The Master I serve in the face ;
    And I speak this out plainly, because
      If you swear to a lesson
      From human confession,
      You're a muff and a spoon,
      And a blinking poltroon,
    And a traitor to Protestant laws.

Some preach a god so savage and grim,
  When he snorts in his terrible wrath,
They crouch and cower and fawn to him,
  And lick the dust in his path ;
    But against this I flatly rebel,
      And boldly deny it,
      That such a stern fiat
      Was forged above
      By the Father of love,
    To swamp half His children in hell.

Some say that through their chosen veins
  There creeps a magical virtue,
To charm away all sorrows and pains
  That issue of Adam is heir to ;
    But this is not Gospel at all ;
        Not narrowly creeping,
        But liberal sweeping,
        On sinful race
        Came God's free grace,
    By the preaching of Peter and Paul.

Some preach a religion of dainty air,
  They come with candle and bell,
And cassock and cope and surplice fair,
  And might of miraculous spell ;
    But this I declare to you all,
        That by dresses and laces,
        And bows and grimaces,
        A man should strive
        His soul to shrive,
    Stands not in the gospel of Paul.

And now I think you will understand,
  Of crotchet, and whim, and conceit,
We can boast enough in this Christian land,
  To turn into bitter our sweet ;
    Then take my advice sans offence ;
        To make harmless the potion,
        Of each darling notion,
        Just temper the draught,
        Before it is quaffed,
    With a few drops of plain common sense !

You've heard my song; if you think it long,
  I'll give you the gist in a line,
'Tis the letter that kills, in sermon or song,
  The Spirit alone is divine;
    God's grace comes to me and to you,
      Not by counting of beads well,
      Or conning of creeds well,
      But by resolute will
      To struggle with ill,
    And by faith that can dare and can do !

YOUNG MAN, BE WISE !

Air—' One there is above all others '

WOULD'ST thou reap life's golden treasure,
  Young man, be wise !
Cease to follow where light pleasure
  Cheats blinking eyes;
Let no flattering voices win thee,
Let no vauntful echoes din thee,
But the peace of God within thee
  Seek, and be wise !

Where the fervid cup doth sparkle,
  Young man, be wise !
Where quick glances gleam and darkle,
  Danger surmise !
Where the rattling car is dashing,
Where the shallow wave is plashing,
Where the coloured foam is flashing,
  Feast not thine eyes !

Rocking on a lazy billow
  With roaming eyes,
Cushioned on a dreamy pillow,
  Thou art not wise ;
Wake the power within thee sleeping,
Trim the plot that's in thy keeping ;
Thou wilt bless the task when reaping
  Sweet labour's prize.

Since the green earth had beginning,
  Land, sea, and skies,
Toil their rounds with sleepless spinning,
  Suns sink and rise ;
God, who with His image crowned us,
Works within, above, around us ;
Let us, where His will hath bound us,
  Work and be wise !

All the great, that won before thee
  Stout labour's prize,
Wave their conquering banners o'er thee ;
  Up, and be wise !
Wilt thou from their sweat inherit,
Fruits of peace, and stars of merit,
While their sword, when thou should'st wear it,
  Rust-eaten lies ?

Work and wait, a sturdy liver ;
  (Life fleetly flies !)
Work, and pray, and sing, and ever
  Lift hopeful eyes ;

Let no blaring folly din thee !
Wisdom, when her charm may win thee,
Flows a well of life within thee ;
 Young man, be wise !

MY LOVES

Air—' Shall I wasting in despair ? '

(Suggested by Anæcreon's ' εἰ φύλλα, κ.τ.λ.')

NAME the leaves on all the trees,
Name the waves on all the seas,
Name the notes of all the groves,
Thus thou namest all my loves.

I do love the dark, the fair,
Golden ringlets, raven hair,
Eye that swims in sunny light,
Glance that shoots like lightning bright.

I do love the stately dame
And the sportive girl the same ;
Every changeful phase between
Blooming cheek and brow serene.

I do love the young, the old,
Maiden modest, virgin bold,
Tiny beauties, and the tall ;
Earth has room enough for all.

K

Which is better, who can say,
Lucy grave or Mary gay?
She who half her charms conceals,
She who flashes while she feels?

Why should I my love confine?
Why should fair be mine or thine?
If I praise a tulip, why
Should I pass a primrose by?

Paris was a pedant fool
Meting beauty by a rule,
Pallas? Juno? Venus?—he
Should have chosen all the three.

I am wise life's every bliss
Thankful tasting; and a kiss
Is a sweet thing, I declare,
From a dark maid or a fair!

BONNIE STRATHNAVER

(Sutherlandshire)

(SONG)

BONNIE STRATHNAVER! Sutherland's pride,
With thy stream softly flowing, and mead spreading
 wide;
Bonnie Strathnaver, where now are the men
Who peopled with gladness thy green-mantled glen?
      Bonnie Strathnaver!

Bonnie Strathnaver! Sutherland's pride,
Sweet is the breath of the birks on thy side ;
But where is the blue smoke that curled from the glen,
When thy lone hills were dappled with dwellings of
    men?
                          Bonnie Strathnaver !

Bonnie Strathnaver! O tearful to tell
Are the harsh deeds once done in thy bonnie green
    dell,
When to rocks of the cold blastful ocean were driven
The men on thy green turfy wilds who had thriven,
                          Bonnie Strathnaver !

When the lusty-thewed lad, and the light-tripping maid,
Looked their last on the hills where their infancy
    strayed,
When the grey, drooping sire, and the old hirpling
    dame
Were chased from their hearths by the fierce-spreading
    flame,
                          Bonnie Strathnaver !

Bonnie Strathnaver! Sutherland's pride,
Wide is the ruin that's spread on thy side ;
The bramble now climbs o'er the old ruined wall,
And the green fern is rank in the tenantless hall,
                          Bonnie Strathnaver !

Bonnie Strathnaver! Sutherland's pride,
Loud is the baa of the sheep on thy side,

But the pipe and the song, and the dance are no more,
And gone the brave clansmen who trod thy green floor.
                              Bonnie Strathnaver !

Bonnie Strathnaver ! Sutherland's pride,
Vain are the tears which I weep on thy side ;
The praise of the bard is the meed of the glen,
But where is the charm that can bring back the men
                              To Bonnie Strathnaver ?

BURRA FIORD

(Shetland)

(SONG)

Come hither all ye Norsemen brave
    That ply the limber oar,
We'll have a jolly pull to-day
    With you on the Shetland shore !
Landlubbers we, and strange to boats ;
    But, if you'll bear a hand,
We'll shake the dust from off our coats
    On the breezy Shetland strand.

Chorus—Pull away, pull away, ye jolly Norsemen !
Where the sea-mew floats, and the kittiwake cries,
And the dark-winged guillemots plunge and rise ;
        Pull away, pull away, pull away !

Come Jamieson, Johnson, and Sandison,
    Come Josie that well may brag
How he plucked the eagle by the throat
    From the face of the white sea-crag.

O Josie, Josie! break-neck loon,
    Where thy strong arms prevail
We'll take the Fuggla by the crown,
    The Uytstack by the tail!
        Chorus—Pull away! etc.

Now lightly 'neath the toppling rock,
    Ye jolly sailors brave,
With bounding prow, we plough the deep
    And skim the sheeny wave;
While o'er our heads, a gamesome troop,
    The fowls that fish the sea,
With plumy plunge and wavy swoop
    Come drifting merrily!
        Chorus—Pull away! etc.

Now gently, gently dip your oars,
    Ye jolly sailors brave,
While 'neath the rocky arch we pass,
    And through the hollow cave,
Where the puffins stand, a staring band,
    And wonder who we be
That dare invade the fortress made
    For them on Shetland sea!
        Chorus—Pull away! etc.

Now turn the helm, and with strong arm
    The sounding billows smite,
And cross to Fuggla's jagged rock,
    That shows the saviour-light,

And bear us bravely o'er the bay
　Where the huge wave swells with pride,
And cut your way through foam and spray
　Of the big Atlantic tide !
　　Chorus—Pull away ! etc.

Now land, and scale the height which bears
　The sailor's radiant mark,
The tower, by daring builders reared
　To guide the labouring bark,
Where the tempest stalks with Titan stride,
　And the wave with thundering shock
Lashes the grim rock's furrowed side,
　And shakes the mighty block ;
　　Chorus—Pull away ! etc.

Now on the top we stand ; and now
　Our share we proudly claim
In this extremest horn of land
　That knows Victoria's name.
God save the Queen !—her praise be told
　On Shetland's Northmost isle,
With His, the Master-Builder bold
　Who raised this stable pile.

Chorus—Sing hurrah-rah-rah ! ye jolly Norsemen,
Where the wild blasts blow, and the big waves roll,
And the strong tower stands with its front to the pole ;
　　Sing hurrah, sing hurrah, sing hurrah !

Now fare ye well, ye warders wise,
　Who watch this storm-vext shore !

Backward we plough the heaving flood,
    And ply the limber oar.
Landlubbers we, and strange to boats,
    But, while we lift an arm,
We'll keep a heart beneath our coats
    To Shetland seamen warm.

Chorus—Pull away, pull away, ye jolly Norsemen,
Where the big tides roll, and the strong winds blow;
For the white fog comes, and we must go;
      Pull away, pull away, pull away!

AWAY, AWAY ADOWN THE STREAM

(A SONG OF LIFE)

THE world drives on, and we drive with it,
    And none its course may stay;
Where the swarm alights we must hive with it,
    And with it we must away.
In vain does son of man conceive
    His little self so great;
No art of mortal can deceive
    The measured chart of Fate.
        Then away, away adown the stream,
          With others let us go,
        As brothers born to share with them
          Their cup of weal and woe.

Where shines the sun, and where falls the rain,
    His plough the cottar guides;

Where blows the wind, and where rolls the main,
　　The sailor grandly rides:
The heart is glad and the heart is sad,
　　As time and chance allow;
And happy never will he be
　　Who is not happy now.
　　　　Then away, away, etc.

In vain, in vain, our sight we strain
　　Into the vasty void;
The thing that is to be God veils
　　From ken of human pride.
He gave thine eye to see His light,
　　He gave thy blood to flow;
He gave thine arms to work with might
　　The work of life below.
　　　　Then away, away, etc.

'Tis now a race, and now a march,
　　Now quick, and now 'tis slow,
Beneath a proud triumphal arch,
　　Or 'neath a portal low.
But still where it drives, we must drive with it—
　　Its course we may not stay;
Where the swarm alights we must hive with it,
　　And with it we must away.
　　　　Then away, away adown the stream,
　　　　　　With others let us go,
　　　　And hope and bear, and do and dare,
　　　　　　As time and chance may show!

THE WOOD SORREL

FAIR flower, beneath the dark fir tree
Shaded in delicate pudency,
I'll make a little rhyme to thee
   (Some years I owe it):
Pansies and lilies have their praises,
Small celandines and broad-faced daisies;
But thou sweet sorrel of the woods,
The tenderest grace of solitudes,
     I do not know it,
If thou hast stirred the deeper moods
     Of any poet.

Thou'rt like a maiden in the bud,
Bashful, ere life's full-swelling flood
Hath shot into the outer blood
     A bolder feeling.
Thy trefoil shield thou spread'st before thee,
That I to find thy flower bend o'er thee,
And wonder how so lowly there
Was set a gem so pure, so fair,
     Such charms concealing:
For why should God create the fair
     But for revealing?

Yet have I seen both fair and good
I' the perfect bloom of womanhood,
Who, like thyself, the light eschewed,
     Thou wood nymph fairest!

And wept to think how foplings shallow,
Left such deep quiet virtue fallow,
To feed vain gaze on flaunting show
Of painted things, in formal row,
      The coldest, barest;
While thou, low-veiled, and nodding low,
      Wert blushing rarest.

And God, who planted thee, was wise,
I' the shade—no vulgar-vended prize
For men, whose love is in their eyes,
      And goes no deeper:
Better for thee, and such as thou art,
To be the forest-nun thou now art,
Than yoked to some loose-dangling mate
Whom thou canst neither love nor hate,
      Thy body's keeper,
But to thy sweet soul's estimate
      Blind, or a sleeper.

Me may the God who sways the heart
Wean more from each false flaring art,
And still some modest truth impart
      Through thy revealing !
As, yearly, sooty crowds eschewing,
The fragrant first May-breezes wooing,
My footed pilgrimage I make
Through wood and wold, and passive take
      Each vagrant feeling,
Which thou, and such as thou, can wake
      With balmy healing.

MAY SONG

On Ettrick bank the primrose grows
　Where the stream is winding clearly O !
Though the ash be grey, the birch is green,
　And the birds are chanting cheerily O !
Thou weary heart, why nurse the smart
　Of a fruitless grief so drearily?
What should thee stay, to greet the May,
　Like a bird on the wing, so cheerily?
　　　Cuckoo, cuckoo, far in the wood !
　　　　Sweet mavis on gowany lea !
　　　O show me the trick of thy blithe May mood,
　　　　And teach me to sing with thee !

Blow, softly, softly breezes blow !
　For the wound is rankling greenly yet ;
And for him who is gone, whom I fear to name,
　The smart doth cut me keenly yet !
I laid him low, when in March the snow
　O'er the sod was drifting drearily,
And how shall I sing, like a bird on the wing,
　When the bright May sun shines cheerily ?
　　　Cuckoo, cuckoo, far in the wood !
　　　　Sweet mavis on gowany lea !
　　　I love the sweet trick of thy blythe May
　　　　　mood,
　　　　But grief still dwells with me !

LOVE'S LULLABY

YE waters, wildly pouring,
With hollow murmurs roaring,
Plunging o'er the rocky steep
With a furious foamy sweep,
In the cavern'd caldron boiling,
Turning, tumbling, twisting, toiling,
Sounding from the glen's dark throat
Old hymns of deep and drowsy note ;
　　Ye waters, hollow-roaring,
Lull ye, lull my love asleep !

Ye forests, dark-surrounding,
With hollow whispers sounding,
Breath that stirs the horrid woods,
Voice of vasty solitudes,
Like the sea, with murmurs swelling,
Solemn, sacred, awe-compelling,
Speaking to the pious ear
Like God's guardian presence near ;
　　Ye forests, hollow-sounding,
Lull ye, lull my love asleep !

POOR CROW

As I came through the garden ground,
　I met a little crow,
With short-clipt wing, in narrow bound,
　Hobbling, hobbling low.

Who clipt thy wing, thou little crow?
  I wish that wight may die!
'Tis seemly when worms creeping go,
  But birds were made to fly,
          Poor Crow!

Who's like to thee?—A bard, whose thought
  Once spanned the welkin wide,
But now he drags a heavy boat,
  Against life's muddy tide.
Who's like to thee?—A king high-thron'd,
  Who ruled from sea to sea,
But homeless now, an outcast thing,
  He creeps o'er Earth like thee,
          Poor Crow!

Then take my pity for thy plight,
  Thou poor misfortuned thing,
And love me, while I hate the wight
  Who clipt thy venturous wing.
So long thou hoppest on my rood,
  Thou hast a friend in me,
And while I feed on mortal food,
  I'll keep a crumb for thee,
          Poor Crow!

SONG OF THE WINDS

Blow! blow! blow!
By the eagles' rocky dwelling,
From Fairfield to Helvellyn,
    Blow! blow!
O'er the tempest's leafless track,
From Helvellyn to Saddleback,
    Blow! blow!

Blow! blow! blow!
Where the thunder loud is pealing,
Round the shepherd's lonely shieling,
    Blow! blow!
Where the torrent wildly dashing,
With white flail the rock is lashing,
    Blow! blow!

Blow! blow! blow!
O'er the grey and rocky ruin,
Where black cloud is cloud pursuing,
    Blow! blow!
Like demons, with sharp yell,
When they hunt a soul to hell,
    Blow! blow!

Blow! blow! blow!
Where the traveller on the hill
Wanders blindly without skill,
    Blow! blow!

Whom suddenly a blast
Down the sheer black wall shall cast,
    Blow! blow!

    Blow! blow! blow!
Where the sapless leaves are whirling,
Where the ruddy floods are swirling,
    Blow! blow!
Where the farmer's yellow store,
Floats to sea with rush and roar,
    Blow! blow!

    Blow! blow! blow!
Where the drowning man is calling,
Through the storm's relentless brawling,
    Blow! blow!
Where with planks and drifted dead
Wide the wreathèd sands are spread,
    Blow! blow!

    Blow! blow! blow!
With mist, and rain, and rack,
From Scawfell to Saddleback,
    Blow! blow!
Who shall check you in the hour,
When God arms your wings with power?
    Blow! blow!

SAM'EL SUMPH

Air—'Ha, ha, the wooing o't!'

SAM'EL SUMPH here cam' for Greek,
　Ha, ha, the Greeking o't!
Frae Dunnet Head he cam' for Greek,
　Ha, ha, the Greeking o't!
Brains he had na unco much,
His schooling was a crazy crutch,
But like the crab he had a clutch,
　Ha, ha, the Greeking o't!

Latin Syntax vexed him sore,
　When he tried the Greeking o't,
For Cæsar stands at Homer's door
　When folks try the Greeking o't.
Quod and *ut* he understood,
At 'speech direct' they called him good,
But *qui* with the subjunctive mood
　Was the crook in the lot at the Greeking o't!

One thing truth commands to tell,
　Ha, ha, the Greeking o't!
English he could hardly spell,
　But what's that to the Greeking o't?
English fits the vulgar clan,
The buying and the selling man,
But for the learn'd the only plan
　Is a close grip at the Greeking o't.

How he wandered through the verb,
　　It pains my tongue the speaking o't,
He said it was a bitter herb,
　　When he tried the Greeking o't.
Wi' mony a wrench and mony a screw,
At last he warstled bravely through,
All except a tense or two,
　　When he tried the Greeking o't !

How he fared with ἤ and ἄν
　　When he tried the Greeking o't.
Δὴ and γς, and all their clan,
　　It's weel worth the speaking o't.
These feckless dots of words, quo' he,
They are nae bigger than a flea,
We'll skip them ow'r and let them be,
　　They'll nae be missed at the Greeking o't !

A' the story for to tell,
　　Were nae end to the speaking o't,
But this thing in the end befell,
　　When he tried the Greeking o't ;
Though his heart was free frae vice
(Men are sometimes trapped like mice),
They plucked him ance, they plucked him twice
　　When he tried the Greeking o't !

Sair cast doun was learned Sam
　　At this end of the Greeking o't ;
He could dae nae mair wi' cram
　　At this stage o' the Greeking o't.

But he was teugh as ony Scot,
He was plucked, but yield would not,
Sooner would he hang and rot,
　　Than thus be balked at the Greeking o't.

At the door he made a din,
　　Rap, rap, for the Greeking o't!
Is the Greek Professor in?
　　Yes, yes, for the Greeking o't!
Sam his plea wi' tears would win,
He fleeched and grat his een quite blin',
To pluck him twice was just a sin,
　　For a sma' fault at the Greeking o't!

Professor was a kindly man,
　　Ha, ha, the Greeking o't!
Felt for a' the student clan
　　That swat sair at the Greeking o't,
'Though you're nae just in the van,
My heart is wae your worth to ban,
Ye hae done the best ye can,
　　So ye may pass at the Greeking o't.'

Sam'el Sumph is now M.A.,
　　Ha, ha, for the Greeking o't!
He can preach and he can pray,
　　That's the fruit of the Greeking o't.
He can thunder loud and fell,
An awfu' power in him doth dwell,
To ope and shut the gates of hell,
　　That's the prize o' the Greeking o't.

Wait a year and ye will see,
    Ha, ha, the Greeking o't !
High upon the tap o' the tree,
    Sam perch'd by the Greeking o't !
In the Kirk Assembly he
Sits as big as big can be,
Moderator Sam, D.D.,
That's the crown o' the Greeking o't !

A PSALM OF BEN MORE

How beautiful upon the mountains, Lord,
Is Earth, thy world, how beautiful and grand !
Ofttimes with firm unwearied foot I clomb
The old grey Ben, whose peak serene look'd down
In glory on the light careering clouds
That swept the nearer heights ; but never fill'd
My wondering eye such pomp of various view
As now, from thy storm-shatter'd brow, Ben More.
How fearful from this high sharp-riven rim
To look down thy precipitous forehead seam'd
With scars from countless storms, whence to the plain
In long grim lines the livid ruin falls,
And think how with a touch the involving blast
From the rude North might seize such thing as I,
And whirl me into dust in that black glen,
Sown with destruction ! But such danger now
Touches not me, when in her gentle mood
Nature, all robed in light, and shod with peace,
Upon the old foundations of her strength
Sits like a queen. How glorious in the West

The sheen of ocean lies, the boundless breadth
Of gleaming waves that girdle in the globe
With their untainted virtue, strangely cut
By rocky terraces projecting far
In measured tiers, and long-drawn sprawling arms
Of huge-slabbed granite huddled into knobs,
And studded, far as the rapt eye can reach,
With isle and islet sown in sportive strength,
Even as the sky with stars—the sandy Coll,
Tiree-tway-parted, and the nearer group
Of Ulva, Gometra, and Lunga's isle,
And the flat Pladda, and the steep Cairnburg,
Where erst the Norseman, monarch of the main,
His sea-girt castle kept; and stout Maclean
Cromwell's harsh might defied, and planted proud
The flag of Charles, and on the ill-starred clans
Brought loss and harm, and crown'd authority's
Retributive mace.   But chiefly, thy dark mass
Enchains my view, in pillared beauty rare,
World-famous Staffa, by the dædal hand
Of Titan Nature piled in rhythmic state,
A fane for gods, and with the memory wreathed
Of Fingal, and the ancient hero-kings
Whom Ossian sang to the wild ringing notes
Of his old Celtic harp, when Celtic songs
Were mighty in the land, and stirred the soul
Of generous clanship in the men who strode
Their native hills with pride, a prosperous race,
Now few and poor by Saxon lords controlled,
Shorn of their glens, and dwindling fast away
Into a name.   Nor less thy old grey line,
Iona, holds my gaze, where late I trod

The grave of kings, and by the figured cross
Stood reverent, raised by grateful piety
To the adventurous Saint, who launched his bark
From Erin's clerkly shore, nor looked behind,
Till he had made that harsh grey rock a school
For gentleness and tenderness and truth,
And Gospel charms to tame mistempered souls
Through all the savage. North. Hence veering round
Southward, Cantire's long arm, and Islay's heights
And lofty Jura's towering tops stand out
Majestic, and the quaint green-vested knolls
Of sheep-cropped Lorn, and Oban's quiet bay
Beloved of boats. And with more distant sweep
Eastward the strong sky-cleaving Grampians rise
From Arroquhar's heights to Cruachan's shapely peaks
And Buchaill's fair green cone, and thy huge bulk
Broad-breasted Nevis, and the mighty host
Of granite battlements that look sternly out
On savage Skye, and with her stiffly bear
The cuffs and buffets of the strong-armed blast
From the still-vexed Atlantic, mother of rains.
These be thy ramparts, Scotland, these the fence
Which Nature raised, to keep thy children free
From the invading Roman, and the pride
Of power aggressive. O ! how lovely sleeps
The sun upon each soft green-mantled glen,
By those grim bulwarks shielded, where the smoke
From lonely hut in odorous birchen bower
Signs the abode of men, the healthful home
Whence breezy Scotland sends her hardy sons
Far-venturing o'er the globe, to win much gold,
And fair approval, and high-throned command,

And all that Earth, a willing tribute, yields
To patient thought, strong will, prompt hand, and
    grasp
Tenacious.   Nor the fervid spirit here
Fails, that beneath a cool impassive front
Nurses the sacred flame, which bursts with power
From Caledonian pulpits, strong to wake
The sting of conscience in lethargic souls
Long drugged to drowsy dulness, or enthralled
By base convention.
                But I feel the keen
Uncustomed temper of the thin clear air
On this dry peak, where no hot streams are bred,
Creep with a gradual chillness through my frame;
And I must leave thy tale, thou mighty Ben,
Half sung: nor mine, in sooth, the learned skill
To chronicle the story of thy birth
Portentous, then when God's high call redeemed
The elements from chaos, and made Earth
Start from the seas, and bade the mountains rise
With giant fronts star-threatening, and deep glens
Sundered from glens, and mighty plains from plains
Remotely cast, abode with skill prepared
By toilsome Nature's patient alchemy
For man, proud flower and fruitage of her growth.
These grey-blue rocks in shattered fragments strewn
Upon thy aged crown, if they could speak,
Would tell a tale that science tempts in vain
With many a lofty guess, and name the hour
When the same chemic fire that smelts the bowels
Of hot Vesuvius, 'neath her rocky ribs
Mother of fertile ashes, heaved thy cones

From the tremendous depths of boiling seas
With subterranean thunders terrible,
And tremulous quakings of the tortured Earth
In her primeval throes; and say what tribes
Of monsters then first crawled in slimy beds
Unshapely, or with hideous flapping vans
Clove the thick air, and glared with great round eyes
Through the gross mists, that from the labouring
     Earth
Rose feverous.   Thus stirred by Titan force
Sprang proud Ben More to being, what long space
Of centuried ages, ere sire Adam first
Greeted with glad surprise the genial day
I know not, nor much reck.   Enough that here,
Last product of the slow-creating years,
Victors we stand, upon so vast a stage
Where human work well linked to work divine
Creates new wonders daily; I'm content.
Let others probe the immense of Possibles
With proud conjectures, stamping with the seal
Of sacred truth each darling notion bred
Of green conceit, and plumed with windy pride;
Such fair fantastic triumphs I forego,
Sober to seek, and diligent to do
My human work in this my human plot
Of God's vast garden, all my joy to pluck
The noisome weeds, and rear the fragrant rose,
Not quarrelling with its thorn.—Now fare thee well
Thou far-viewed Ben! and may the memoried pomp
Of thy great grandeur make my smallness great,
That in the strait and choking times of life
I still may wear thy presence in my soul,

And walk as in a kingly hall, hung round
With living pictures from the proud Ben More
Monarch of Mull, the fairest isle that spreads
Its green folds to the Sun in Celtic seas.

SONNETS

BEN MUICDUIBHE

O'ER broad Muicduibhe sweeps the keen cold blast,
  Far whirrs the snow-bred, white-winged ptarmigan,
  Sheer sink the cliffs to dark Loch Etagan,
And all the hill with shattered rock lies waste.
Here brew ship-foundering storms their force divine,
  Here gush the fountains of wild-flooding rivers ;
  Here the strong thunder frames the bolt that
      shivers
The giant strength of the old twisted pine.
Yet, even here, on the bare waterless brow
  Of granite ruin, I found a purple flower,
A delicate flower, as fair as aught, I trow,
  That toys with zephyrs in my lady's bower.
So Nature blends her powers ; and he is wise
Who to his strength no gentlest grace denies.

———

LOCH RANNOCH MOOR

In the lone glen the silver lake doth sleep ;
Sleeps the white cloud upon the sheer black hill :
All moorland sounds a solemn silence keep ;
I only hear the tiny trickling rill
'Neath the red moss.   Athwart the dim grey pall
That veils the day, a dusky fowl may fly ;
But, on this bleak brown moor, if thou shalt call
For men, a spirit will sooner make reply.
Come hither, thou whose agile tongue doth flit
From theme to theme with change of wordy war ;
Converse with men makes sharp the glittering wit,
But Wisdom whispers truth, when crowds are far.
Come, sit thee down upon this old grey stone ;
Men learn to think, and feel, and pray, alone.

THE LORD'S DAY IN IONA

Pure worshipper, who on this holy day
    Would'st shake thee free from soul-encrusting cares,
And to the great Creator homage pay
    In some high fane most worthy of thy prayers,
Go not where sculptured tower or pictured dome
    Invites the reeking city's jaded throngs,
Some hoar old shrine of Rhine-land or of Rome,
    Where the dim aisle the languid hymn prolongs ;
Here rather follow me, and take thy stand
    By the grey cairn that crowns the lone Dun Ee,

And let thy breezy worship be the grand
  Old Bens, and old grey knolls that compass thee,
The sky-blue waters, and the snow-white sand,
  And the quaint isles far-sown upon the sea.

THE BUCHAILL ETIVE

(Argyleshire)

THOU lofty shepherd of dark Etive glen,
  Tall Titan warder of the grim Glencoe,
  I clomb thy starward peak not long ago,
And call thee mine, and love thee much since then.
Oft have I marvelled, if mine eye had been
  Strange witness to Creation's natal hour,
How wondrous then had showed the flaming scene
  When out of seething depths thy cone with power
Was shot from God.   But now upon thy steep
  Fair greenness sleeps on old secure foundations,
And on thee browse the innocent-bleating sheep
  And timorous troops of the high-antlered nations;
And I am here, Time's latest product, Man,
To work Thy will, O Lord, and serve Thy stately plan.

MOONLIGHT AT KING'S HOUSE

(Argyleshire)

O FOR the touch that smote the psalmist's lyre,
  When the great beauty of the world he saw,
  And sang His praise, instinct with holy awe,
Who rides the whirlwind, and who reins the fire !

But not alone proud Lebanon's fulgent face
  Hath power the eye of trancèd seer to draw;
  Here, too, in Grampian land God rules by law,
Which clothes the awfullest forms in loveliest grace.
The placid moon, the huge sky-cleaving Ben,
  The moor loch glancing in the argent ray,
The long white mist low-trailing up the glen,
  The hum of mighty waters far away,
All make me wish that worthy words would come;
But all I find is—worship, and be dumb!

CHINESE GORDON

SOME men live near to God, as my right arm
  Is near to me; and thus they walk about
Mailed in full proof of faith, and bear a charm
  That mocks at fear, and bars the door on doubt,
And dares the impossible. So, Gordon, thou,
  Through the hot stir of this distracted time,
Dost hold thy course, a flaming witness how,
  To do and dare, and make our lives sublime
As God's campaigners. What live we for but this,
  Into the sour to breathe the soul of sweetness,
  The stunted growth to rear to fair completeness,
Drown sneers in smiles, kill hatred with a kiss,
  And to the sandy waste bequeath the fame
  That the grass grew behind us where we came!

———

SYDNEY DOBELL

(On hearing of his death)

AND thou too gone! One more bright soul away
　To swell the mighty sleepers 'neath the sod.
One less to honour and to love, and say,
　Who lives with thee doth live half-way to God.
My chaste-souled Sydney! Thou wert carved too fine
　For coarse observance of the general eye:
But who might look into thy soul's fair shrine
　Saw bright gods there, and felt their presence nigh.
Oh, if we owe warm thanks to Heaven, 'tis when
　In the slow progress of the struggling years
Our touch is blessed to feel the pulse of men
　Who walk in love and light above their peers
White-robed, and forward point with guiding hand,
Breathing a heaven around them where they stand.

BALLADS, LEGENDS AND NARRRATIVE POEMS

THE LAY OF THE BRAVE CAMERON

AT Quatre Bras, when the fight ran high,
Stout Cameron stood with wakeful eye,
Eager to leap, as a mettlesome hound,
Into the fray with a plunge and a bound.
But Wellington, lord of the cool command,
Held the reins with a steady hand,
Saying, 'Cameron, wait, you'll soon have enough,
Giving the Frenchman a taste of your stuff,
    When the Cameron men are wanted.'

Now hotter and hotter the battle grew,
With tramp, and rattle, and wild halloo,
And the Frenchmen poured, like a fiery flood,
Right on the ditch where Cameron stood.
Then Wellington flashed from his steadfast stance
On his captain brave a lightning glance,
Saying, 'Cameron, now have at them, boy,
Take care of the road to Charleroi,
    Where the Cameron men are wanted!'

Brave Cameron shot like a shaft from a bow
Into the midst of the plunging foe,
And with him the lads whom he loved, like a torrent
Sweeping the rocks in its foamy current;
And he fell the first in the fervid fray,
Where a deathful shot had shore its way,
But his men pushed on where the work was rough,
Giving the Frenchman a taste of their stuff,
　　　Where the Cameron men were wanted.

Brave Cameron then, from the battle's roar,
His foster-brother stoutly bore,
His foster-brother, with service true,
Back to the village of Waterloo.
And they laid him on the soft green sod,
And he breathed his spirit there to God,
But not till he heard the loud hurrah
Of victory billowed from Quatre Bras,
　　　Where the Cameron men were wanted.

By the road to Ghent they buried him then,
This noble chief of the Cameron men,
And not an eye was tearless seen
That day beside the alley green:
Wellington wept, the iron man;
And from every man in the Cameron clan
The big round drop in bitterness fell,
As with the pipes he loved so well
　　　His funeral wail they chanted.

And now he sleeps (for they bore him home,
When the war was done, across the foam)

Beneath the shadow of Nevis Ben,
With his sires, the pride of the Cameron men.
Three thousand Highlandmen stood round,
As they laid him to rest in his native ground,
The Cameron brave, whose eye never quailed,
Whose heart never sank, and whose hand never failed,
    Where a Cameron man was wanted.

THE VOYAGE OF COLUMBA

I

'Son of Brendan, I have willed it
    I will leave this land and go
To a land of savage mountains,
    Where the Borean breezes blow ;
To a land of rainy torrents,
    And of barren, treeless isles,
Where the winter frowns are lavish,
    And the summer scantly smiles ;
I will leave this land of bloodshed,
    Where fierce brawls and battles sway,
And will preach God's peaceful Gospel
    In a grey land, far away.'
Beathan spake, the son of Brendan—
    'Son of Phelim art thou wise ?
Wilt thou change the smiling Erin,
    For the scowling Pictish skies ?
Thou, the lealest son of Erin,
    Thou, a prince of royal line,
Sprung by right descent from mighty
    Neill, whose hostages were nine ?

Wilt thou seek the glens of Albyn
　　For repose from loveless strife?
Glens, where feuds, from sire to grandson,
　　Fan the wasteful flame of life?
Wilt thou leave a land of learning,
　　Home of ancient holy lore,
To converse with uncouth people,
　　Fishing on a shelvy shore?
Wilt thou leave the homes of Gartan,
　　Where thou suck'd the milky food
From the mother-breast of Aithne,
　　Daughter of Lagenian blood?
Wilt thou leave the oaks of Derry,
　　Where each leaf is dear to thee,
Wandering, in a storm-tost wherry,
　　O'er the wide, unpastured sea?
Son of Phelim, Beathan loves thee,
　　Be thou zealous, but be wise!
There be heathens here in Erin;
　　Preach to them 'neath kindly skies.'
Then the noble son of Phelim,
　　With the big tear in his eye,
To the blameless son of Brendan
　　Firmly thus made swift reply—
'Son of Brendan, I have heard thee,
　　Heard thee with a bleeding heart;
For I love the oaks of Derry,
　　And to leave them gives me smart;
But the ban of God is on me,
　　Not my will commands the way;
Molaise priest of Innishmurry
　　Hights me go, and I obey.

M

For their death is heavy on me
  Whom I slew in vengeful mood,
At the battle of Culdremhne,
  In the hotness of my blood.
For the lord that rules at Tara,
  In some brawl that grew from wine,
Slew young Carnan, branch of promise,
  And a kinsman of my line;
And the human blood within me
  Mounted, and my hand did slay,
For the fault of one offender,
  Many on that tearful day;
And I soil'd the snow-white vestment
  With which Etchen, holy man,
Clonfad's mitred elder, clad me
  When I join'd the priestly clan;
And my soul was rent with anguish
  And my sorrows were increased,
And I went to Innishmurry,
  Seeking solace from the priest.
And the saintly Molaise told me—
  "For the blood that thou hast spilt,
God hath shown me one atonement
  To make clear thy soul from guilt;
Count the hundreds of the Christians
  Whom thy sword slew to thy blame,
Even so many souls of heathens
  Must thy word with power reclaim;
Souls of rough and rude sea-rovers,
  Used to evil, strange to good,
Picts beyond the ridge of Albyn,
  In the Pagan realm of Brude."

Thou hast heard me, son of Brendan ;
   I have will'd it ; and this know,
Thou with me, or I without thee,
   On this holy hest will go ! '
Beathan heard, with meek agreement,
   For he knew that Colum's will, ·
Like a rock against the ocean,
   Still was fixed for good or ill.
' Son of Phelim, I have heard thee ;
   I and Cobhtach both will go,
Past the wintry ridge of Albyn,
   O'er the great sea's foamy flow ;
Far from the green oaks of Derry,
   Where the cukoo sings in May,
From the land of falling waters
   Far, and clover's green display ;
Where Columba leads we follow,
   Fear with him I may not know,
Where the God thou servest calls thee,
   Son of Phelim, I will go.'

II

' Son of Brendan, I am ready :
   Is the boat all staunch and trim ?
' Light our osier craft and steady,
   Like an ocean gull to swim ?
I have cast all doubt behind me,
   Seal'd with prayer my holy vow,
And the God who heard me answers
   With assuring presence now.'
And the son of Brendan answer'd—
   ' Son of Phelim, thou shalt be

Like God's angel-guidance to us
　　As we plough the misty sea.
We are ready, I and Cobhtach,
　　Diarmid in thy service true,
Rus and Fechno, sons of Rodain,
　　Scandal, son of Bresail, too ;
Ernan, Luguid Mocatheimne,
　　Echoid, and Tochannu brave,
Grillan and the son of Branduh,
　　Brush with thee the briny wave.'
Thus spake he.　Columba lifted
　　High his hand to bless the wherry,
And they oar'd with gentle oarage
　　From the dear-loved oaks of Derry ;
Loath to leave each grassy headland,
　　Shiny beach and pebbly bay,
Thymy slope and woody covert,
　　Where the cuckoo hymn'd the May ;
Loath from some familiar cabin's
　　Wreathy smoke to rend their eye,
Where a godly widow harbour'd
　　Laughing girl or roguish boy.
On they oar'd, and soon behind them
　　Left thy narrow pool, Loch Foyle,
And the grey sea spread before them
　　Many a broad unmeasured mile.
Swiftly now on bounding billow
　　On they run before the gale,
For a strong south-wester blowing
　　Strained the bosom of their sail.
On they dash : the Rhinns of Islay
　　Soon they reach, and soon they pass ;

Cliff and bay, and bluffy foreland,
    Flit as in a magic glass.
What is this before them rising
    Northward from the foamy spray?
Land, I wis—an island lorded
    By the wise Macneil to-day,
Then a brown and barren country,
    Cinctured by the ocean grey.*
On they scud ; and there they landed,
    And they mounted on a hill,
Whence the far-viewd son of Brendan
    Look'd, and saw green Erin still.
' Say'st thou so, thou son of Brendan ? '
    Quoth Columba ; ' then not here
May we rest from tossing billow
    With light heart and conscience clear,
Lest our eyes should pine a-hunger
    For the land we hold so dear,
And our coward keel returning
    Stint the vow that brought us here.'
So they rose and trimmed their wherry,
    And their course right on they hold
Northward, where the wind from Greenland
    Blows on Albyn clear and cold ;
When, behold, a cloud came darkling
    From the west, with gusty blore,
And the horrent waves rose booming
    Eastward, with ill-omened roar ;

---

* The Island of Colonsay, south of Mull, from which the late
Lord Colonsay took his title. The verses were written before
his death.

And the night came down upon them,
    And the sea with yeasty sweep
Hiss'd around them, as the wherry
    Stagger'd through the fretted deep.
Eastward, eastward, back they hurried,
    For to face the flood was vain,
Every rib of their light wherry
    Creaking to the tempest's strain;
Eastward, eastward, till the morning
    Glimmer'd through the pitchy storm,
And reveal'd the frowning Scarba,
    And huge Jura's cones enorm.
'Blessed God,' cried now Columba,
    'Here, indeed, may danger be
From the mighty whirl and bubble
    Of the cauldron of the sea;
Here it was that noble Breacan
    Perish'd in the gulfing wave—
Here we, too, shall surely perish,
    If not God be quick to save!'
Spake: and with his hand he lifted
    High the cross above the brine;
And he cried, 'Now, God, I thank Thee
    Thou hast sent the wished-for sign!
For, behold, thou son of Brendan,
    There upon the topmost wave,
Sent from God, a sign to save us,
    Float the bones of Breacan brave!
And his soul this self-same moment,
    From the girth of purging fire,
Leaps redeem'd, as we are 'scaping
    From the huge sea-cauldron dire.'

Spake : and to the name of Breacan
   Droop'd the fretful-crested spray ;
And full soon a mild south-easter
   Blew the surly storm away.*

III

Little now remains to tell ye,
   Gentles, of great Phelim's son ;
How he clave the yielding billow
   Till Iona's strand he won.
Back they steer'd, still westward, westward ;
   Past the land where high Ben More
Nods above the isles that quaintly
   Fringe its steep and terraced shore.
On they cut—still westward ! westward !
   On with favouring wind and tide,
Past the pillar'd crags of Carsaig
   Fencing Mull's sun-fronting side,
Pass the narrow Ross, far-stretching
   Where the rough and ruddy rocks
Rudely rise in jumbled hummocks,
   Of primeval granite blocks ;
Till they come to where Iona
   Rears her front of hoary crags,
Fenced by many a stack and skerry
   Full of rifts, and full of jags ;

---

* The legend about the bones of Breacan is of course taken from the old Latin book, otherwise it had no title to be here. In Gaelic, the first element of the compound word *corryvreckan* means a *cauldron*, and the other element *breac* means *spotted* : so that etymologically the name seems only to mean the whirl or cauldron of the sea spotted with foam.

And behind a small black islet
    Through an inlet's narrow space,
Sail'd into a bay white bosom'd,
    In the island's southward face.
Then with eager step they mounted
    To the high rock's beetling brow—
'Canst thou see, thou far-view'd Beathan,
    Trace of lovely Erin now?'
'No! thou son of Phelim, only
    Mighty Jura's Paps I see,
These and Isla's Rhynns, but Erin
    Southward lies in mist from me.'
'Thank thee, God!' then cried Columba;
    'Here our vows are paid, and here
We may rest from tossing billow,
    With light heart and conscience clear.'
Downward then their way they wended
    To the pure and pebbly bay,
And with holy cross uplifted,
    Thus did saintly Colum say—
'In the sand we now will bury
    This trim craft that brought us here, ·
Lest we think on oaks of Derry,
    And the land we hold so dear;'
Then they dug a trench and sank it
    In the sand, to seal their vow,
With keel upwards, as who travels
    In the sand may see it now.

———

THE DEATH OF COLUMBA

SAXON stranger, thou did'st wisely,
 Sunder'd for a little space
From that motley stream of people
 Drifting by this holy place;
With the furnace and the funnel
 Through the long sea's glancing arm,
Let them hurry back to Oban,
 Where the tourist loves to swarm.
Here, upon this hump of granite,
 Sit with me a quiet while,
And I'll tell thee how Columba
 Died upon this old grey isle.

I

'Twas in May, a breezy morning,
 When the sky was fresh and bright,
And the broad blue ocean shimmer'd
 With a thousand gems of light.
On the green and grassy Machar,
 Where the fields are spredden wide,
. And the crags in quaint confusion
 Jut into the Western tide:
Here his troop of godly people,
 In stout labour's garb array'd,
Blithe their fruitful task were plying
 With the hoe and with the spade.
'I will go and bless my people,'
 Quoth the father, 'ere I die,

But the strength is slow to follow
   Where the wish is swift to fly;
I am old and feeble, Diarmid,
   Yoke the oxen, be not slow,
I will go and bless my people,
   Ere from earth my spirit go.'
On his ox-drawn wain he mounted,
   Faithful Diarmid by his side;
Soon they reach'd the grassy Machar,
   Soft and smooth, Iona's pride:
'I am come to bless my people,
   Faithful fraters, ere I die;
I had wish'd to die at Easter,
   But I would not mar your joy,
Now the Master plainly calls me,
   Gladly I obey His call;
I am ripe, I feel the sickle,
   Take my blessing, ere I fall.'
But they heard his words with weeping,
   And their tears fell on the dew,
And their eyes were dimmed with sorrow,
   For they knew his words were true.
Then he stood up on the waggon,
   And his prayerful hands he hove,
And he spake and bless'd the people
   With the blessing of his love:
'God be with you, faithful fraters,
   With you now, and evermore;
Keep you from the touch of evil,
   On your souls His Spirit pour;
God be with you, fellow workmen,
   And from loved Iona's shore

Keep the blighting breath of demons,
   Keep the viper's venom'd store !'
Thus he spake, and turn'd the oxen
   Townwards; sad they went, and slow,
And the people, fix'd in sorrow,
   Stood, and saw the father go.

II

List me further, Saxon stranger,
Note it nicely, by the causeway
   On the left hand, where thou came
With the motley tourist people,
   Stands a cross of figured fame.
Even now thine eye may see it,
   Near the nunnery, slim and grey ;—
From the waggon there Columba
   Lighted on that tearful day,
And he sat beneath the shadow
   Of that cross, upon a stone,
Brooding on his speedy passage
   To the land where grief is none ;
When, behold, the mare, the white one
   That was wont the milk to bear
From the dairy to the cloister,
   Stood before him meekly there,
Stood, and softly came up to him,
   And with move of gentlest grace
O'er the shoulder of Columba
   Thrust her piteous-pleading face,
Look'd upon him as a friend looks
   On a friend that goes away,

Sunder'd from the land that loves him
  By wide seas of briny spray:
'Fie upon thee for thy manners!'
  Diarmid cried with lifted rod,
'Wilt thou with untimely fondness
  Vex the prayerful man of God?'
'Not so, Diarmid,' cried Columba;
  'Dost thou see the speechful eyne
Of the fond and faithful creature
  Sorrow'd with the swelling brine?
God hath taught the mute unreasoning
  What thou fail'st to understand,
That this day I pass for ever
  From Iona's shelly strand.
Have my blessing, gentle creature,
  God doth bless both man and beast;
From hard yoke, when I shall leave thee,
  Be thy faithful neck released.'
Thus he spoke, and quickly rising
  With what feeble strength remain'd,
Leaning on stout Diarmid's shoulder,
  A green hillock's top he gained.
There, or here where we are sitting,
  Whence his eye might measure well
Both the cloister and the chapel,
  And his pure and prayerful cell.
There he stood, and high uplifting
  Hands whence flowed a healing grace,
Breathed his latest voice of blessing
  To protect the sacred place,—
Spake such words as prophets utter
  When the veil of flesh is rent,

And the present fades from vision,
 On the germing future bent:
'God thee bless, thou loved Iona,
 Though thou art a little spot,
Though thy rocks are grey and treeless,
 Thine shalt be a boastful lot;
Thou shalt be a sign for nations;
 Nurtured on thy sacred breast,
Thou shalt send on holy mission
 Men to teach both East and West;
Peers and potentates shall own thee,
 Monarchs of wide-sceptre'd sway
Dying shall beseech the honour
 To be tomb'd beneath thy clay;
God's dear saints shall love to name thee,
 And from many a storied land
Men of clerkly fame shall pilgrim
 To Iona's little strand.'

III

Thus the old man spake his blessing;
 Then, where most he loved to dwell,
Through the well-known porch he enter'd
 To his pure and prayerful cell;
And then took the holy psalter—
 'Twas his wont when he would pray—
Bound with three stout clasps of silver,
 From the casket where it lay;
There he read with fixed devoutness,
 And with craft full fair and fine,
On the smooth and polish'd vellum
 Copied forth the sacred line,

Till he came to where the kingly
　　Singer sings in faithful mood,
How the younglings of the lion
　　Oft may roam in vain for food,
But who fear the Lord shall never
　　Live and lack their proper good.*
Here he stopped, and said, ' My latest
　　Now is written ; what remains
I bequeath to faithful Beathan
　　To complete with pious pains.'
Then he rose, and in the chapel
　　Conned the pious vesper song
Inly to himself, for feeble
　　Now the voice that once was strong ;
Hence with silent step returning
　　To his pure and prayerful cell,
On the round smooth stone he laid him
　　Which for pallet served him well.
Here some while he lay ; then rising,
　　To a trusty brother said :
' Brother, take my parting message,
　　Be my last words wisely weigh'd
'Tis an age of brawl and battle ;
　　Men who seek not God to please,
With wild sweep of lawless passion
　　Waste the land and scourge the seas.
Not like them be ye ; be loving,
　　Peaceful, patient, truthful, bold,
But in service of your Master
　　Use no steel and seek no gold.'

* Psalm xxxiv. 10.

Thus he spake; but now there sounded
   Through the night the holy bell
That to Lord's Day matins gather'd
   Every monk from every cell.
Eager at the sound, Columba
   In the way foresped the rest,
And before the altar kneeling,
   Pray'd with hands on holy breast.
Diarmid followed; but a marvel
   Flow'd upon his wondering eyne,—
All the windows shone with glorious
   Light of angels in the shrine.
Diarmid enter'd; all was darkness.
   'Father!' But no answer came.
'Father! art thou here, Columba?'
   Nothing answer'd to the name.
Soon the troop of monks came hurrying,
   Each man with a wandering light,
For great fear had come upon them,
   And a sense of strange affright.
'Diarmid! Diarmid, is the father
   With thee? Art thou here alone?'
And they turn'd their lights and found him
   On the pavement lying prone.
And with gentle hands they raised him,
   And he mildly look'd around,
And he raised his arm to bless them,
   But it dropped upon the ground;
And his breathless body rested
   On the arms that held him dear,
And his dead face look'd upon them
   With a light serene and clear;

And they said that holy angels
  Surely hover'd round his head,
For alive no loveliest ever
  Look'd so lovely as this dead.

Stranger, thou hast heard my story,
  Thank thee for thy patient ear ;
We are pleased to stir the sleeping
  Memory of old greatness here.
I have used no gloss, no varnish,
  To make fair things fairer look ;
As the record stands, I give it,
  In the old monk's Latin book.
Keep it in thy heart, and love it,
  Where a good thing loves to dwell ;
It may help thee in thy dying,
  If thou care to use it well.

GLENCOE

A HISTORICAL BALLAD

1

THE snow is white on the Pap of Glencoe,
  And all is bleak and dreary,
But gladness reigns in the vale below,
  Where life is blithe and cheery,
Where the old Macdonald, stout and true,
Sits in the hall which his fathers knew,
Sits, with the sword which his fathers drew
  On the old wall glancing clearly,

Where the dry logs blaze on the huge old hearth,
And the old wine flows that fans the mirth
  Of the friends that love him dearly.
Heavily, heavily lies the snow
  On the old grey ash and the old blue pine,
And the cold winds drearily drearily blow
  Down the glen with a moan and a whine;
But little reck they how the storm may bray,
  Or the linn may roar in the glen,
Where the bright cups flow, and the light jests play,
  And Macdonald is master of men,
Where Macdonald is king of the feast to-night,
And sways the hour with a landlord's right,
And broadens his smile, and opens his breast,
As a host may do to a dear-loved guest;
And many a stirring tale he told
  Of battle, and war, and chase,
And heroes that sleep beneath the mould,
  The pride of his lordly race;
And many a headlong venture grim,
  With the hounds that track the deer,
By the rifted chasm's hanging rim
  And the red-scaured mountain sheer.
And many a song did the harper sing
  Of Ossian blind and hoary,
That made the old oak rafter ring
  With the pulse of Celtic story;
And the piper blew a gamesome reel
  That the young blood hotly stirred,
And they beat the ground with lightsome heel
  Till the midnight bell was heard.
And then to rest they laid them down,

N

And soon the strong sleep bound them,
While the winds without kept whistling rout,
And the thick snows drifted round them.

II

But one there was whose eyes that night
    No peaceful slumber knew,
Or, if he slept, he dreamt of blood,
And woke by Coe's far-sounding flood,
    To make his dreaming true.
A Campbell was he, of a hated clan,
    —God's curse be on his name!—
Who to Macdonald's goodly glen
    On traitor's errand came.
He had the old man's niece to wife,
(A love that should have buried strife,)
And shook his hand for faithful proof,
And slept beneath his friendly roof;
And he that night had shared the mirth
Around the old man's friendly hearth,
    And, wise in devil's art,
Had laughed and quaffed, and danced and sung,
And talked with honey on his tongue,
    And murder in his heart.
And now, to buy a grace from power
And men the slaves of the venal hour,
Or with the gust of blood to sate
A heart whose luxury was hate,
His hand was on the whetted knife
That thirsts to drink the old man's life;
    And soon the blood shall flow,
    From which the curse shall grow,

That since the world to sin began
Pursues the lawless-handed man ;
And false Glen Lyon's traitor name
Shall live, a blazing badge of shame,
While memory links the crimson crime,
The basest in the book of Time,
    With Campbell and Glencoe.

III

'Tis five o'clock i' the morn ; of light
    No glimmering ray is seen,
And the snow that drifted through the night
    Shrouds every spot of green.
Not yet the cock hath blown his horn,
    But the base red-coated crew
Creep through the silence of the morn
    With butcher-work to do.
And now to the old man's house they came,
Where he lived in the strength of his proud old
        name
    A brave unguarded life ;
And now they enter the old oak room,
Where he lay, all witless of his doom,
    In the arms of his faithful wife ;
And through the grace of his hoary head,
As he turned him starting from his bed,
They shot the deadly-missioned lead,
    And reaved his purple life ;
Then from the lady, where she lay
With outstretched arms in blank dismay,
They rove the vest, and in deray
    They flung her on the floor ;

And from her quivering fingers tore
With their teeth the rare old rings she wore ;
Then haled her down the oaken stair
Into the cold, unkindly air,
And in the snow they left her there,
    Where not a friend was nigh,
With many a curse, and never a tear,
    Like an outcast beast to die.

IV

And now the butcher-work went on
Hotly, hotly up the glen ;
For the order was given full sharply then
The lion to slay with the cubs in his den,
    And never a male to spare ;
And the king's own hand had signed the ban,
To glut the hate of the Campbell clan,
    And the spite of the Master of Stair.
From every clachan in long Glencoe
The shriek went up, and the blood did flow
Reeking and red on the wreathèd snow.
    Every captain had his station
On the banks of the roaring water,
    Watching o'er the butchered nation
Like the demons of the slaughter.
Lindsay raged at Invercoe,
And laid his breathless twenty low ;
At Inveruggen, Campbell grim
Made the floor with gore to swim—
Nine he counted in a row
Brothered in a bloody show,

And one who oft for him had spread
The pillow 'neath his traitor head,
   To woo the kindly rest.
At Auchnachoin stern Barker pressed
The pitiless work with savage zest,
And on the broad mead by the water
Heaped ten souls in huddled slaughter.
The young man blooming in his pride,
   The old man with crack'd breath,
The bridegroom severed from his bride,
And son with father side by side,
   Lie swathed in one red death ;
And Fire made league with Murder fell,
Where flung by many a raging hand,
From house to house the flaming brand
Contagious flew ; and crackling spar
And crashing beam, make hideous jar,
   And pitchy volumes swell.
What horror stalked the glen that day,
What ghastly fear and grim dismay,
   No tongue of man may tell ;
What shame to Orange William's sway,
When Murder throve with honours decked,
   And every traitor stood erect,
   And every true man fell !

V

'Tis twelve o'clock at noon ; and still
Heavily, heavily on the hill
The storm outwreaks his wintry will,
   And flouts the blinded sun ;

And now the base red-coated crew,
And the fiends in hell delight to view
   The sanguine slaughter done.
But where be they, the helpless troop,
Spared by red murder's ruthless swoop—
The feeble woman, the maiden mild,
The mother with her sucking child,
And all who fled with timely haste
From hissing shot, and sword uncased?
Hurrying from the reeking glen,
   They are fled, some here, some there ;
Some have scrambled up the Ben
   And crossed the granite ridges bare,
And found kind word and helping hand
On Appin's green and friendly strand ;
Some in the huts of lone Glenure
Found kindly care and shelter sure,
And some in face of the tempest's roar,
Behind the shelving Buchailmore,
With stumbling foot did onward press
To thy Ben-girdled nook, Dalness ;
And some huge Cruachan's peak behind
Found a broad shield from drift and wind,
And warmed their frozen frames at fires
Kindled by friendly Macintyres,
But most—O Heaven !—a feeble nation,
Crept slowly from the mountain station ;
The old, the sickly, and the frail,
Went blindly on with staggering trail,
The little tender-footed maid,
The little boy that loved to wade
In the clear waters of the Coe,

Ere blood had stained their amber flow—
On them, ere half their way was made,
The night came down, and they were laid
Some on the scaurs of the jaggèd Bens,
Some in black bogs and stony glens,
Faint and worn, till kindly Death
Numbed their limbs, and froze their breath,
And wound them in the snow.
And there they lay with none to know,
And none with pious kind concern
To honour with a cross or cairn
The remnant of Glencoe.
And on the hills a curse doth lie
That will not die with years;
And oft-times 'neath a scowling sky,
Through the black rent, where the torrent grim
Leaps 'neath the huge crag's frowning rim,
The wind comes down with a moan and a sigh;
And a voice, like the voice of a wail and a cry,
The lonely traveller hears,
A voice, like the voice of Albyn weeping
For the sorrow and the shame
That stained the British soldier's name,
When kingship was in butcher's keeping,
And power was honour's foe;
Weeping for scutcheons rudely torn,
And worth disowned and glory shorn,
And for the valiant-hearted men
That once were mighty in the glen
Of lonely, bleak Glencoe.

ANCRUM MOOR

A HISTORICAL BALLAD

KING HENRY was a rampant loon,
  No Turk more bold than he
To tread the land with iron shoon
  And tramp with royal glee.

God made him king of England; there
  His royal lust had scope
Tightly to hold beneath his thumb
  People and peer and Pope.

And bishops' craft and lawyers' craft
  Were cobwebs light to him,
And law and right were blown like chaff
  Before his lordly whim.

And many a head of saint and sage
  In ghastly death lay low,
That never a man on English ground
  Might say King Henry no.

Now he would swallow Scotland too
  To glut his kingly maw,
And sent his ships, two hundred sail,
  Bewest North Berwick Law.

And he hath sworn by force to weld
  Two kingdoms into one,
When Scotland's Queen with Scotland rights,
  Is wed to England's son.

And he hath heaped the quay of Leith
   With devastation dire,
And swept fair Embro's stately town
   Three days with raging fire.

And he hath hired two red-cross loons,*
   False Lennox and Glencairn,
From royal Henry's graceless grace
   A traitor's wage to earn.

And he hath said to the warders twain—
   Sir Ralph and stout Sir Bryan—
' Ride north, and closely pare the claws
   Of that rude Scottish lion.

' And all the land benorth Carlisle
   That your good sword secures,
Teviotdale and Lauderdale,
   And the Merse with all its moors,
Land of the Douglas, Ker, and Scott,
   My seal hath made it yours.'

And they have crossed from Carter Fell,
   And laid the fields all bare ;
And they have harried Jeddart town, ·
   And spoiled the abbey there.

---

* The Border clans who had been induced to side with Henry
wore the red cross of St George as a badge to distinguish them
from the patriotic party.

And they have ravaged hearth and hall,
  With steel untaught to spare
Or tottering eld, or screaming babe,
  Or tearful lady fair.

And they have come with snorting speed,
  Plashing through mire and mud,
And plunged with hot and haughty hoof
  Through Teviot's silver flood.

And past the stronghold of the Ker *
  Like rattling hail they pour,
Right in the face of Penilheugh,
  And up to Ancrum Moor.

'Where be these caitiff Scots ?' outcries
  Layton, with hasty fume.
'There !' cries Sir Eure ; 'the cowards crouch
  Behind the waving broom.

' Have at them, boys ! they may not stand
  Before our strong-hoofed mass ;
Like clouds they come, and like the drift
  Of rainless clouds they pass !'

' Not so, Sir Eure ! ye do not well
  Thus with light word to scorn
The Douglas blood, the strong right arm
  Of Bruce at Bannockburn.

  * Ancrum House, now the residence of Sir William Scott of
Ancrum, but at the date of the ballad possessed by a branch of
the noble race of the Kers.

'Lo! where they rise behind the broom
  And stand in bristling pride,
Sharp as the jag of a grey sea-crag
  That flouts the billowy tide.

'With six-foot lances sharply set
  They stand in serried lines,
Like Macedonian phalanx old,
  Or rows of horrid pines.'

Sir Eure was hot: he might not hear,
  Nor pause to weigh the chances,
But spurred his steed in mid career
Upon the frieze of lances.

Madly they plunge with foaming speed
  On that sharp fence of steel,
And on the ground with bleeding flanks,
  They tumble, toss, and reel.

Charge upon charge; but all in vain
  The red-cross troop advances—
Rider and horse, high heaped in death,
  Lay sprawling 'neath the lances.

But what is this that now I see?
  In battailous array
Matrons and maids from Ancrum town
  Are mingled in the fray.

A goodly band; not Sparta bred
  More valiant-hearted maids
Than these that front the fight to-day.
  With pitchforks and with spades.

And as they come, 'Broomhouse!' they cry;
    These butcher loons shall rue
Their damnèd force on that fair dame
    Whom at Broomhouse they slew.*

And there stands one, and leads the van,—
    A Maxton † maid, not tall,
But with heroic soul supreme
    She soars above them all.

With giant stroke she flails about,
    And heaps a score of dead,
That bring—oh, woe! a vengeful troop
    Upon her single head.

With swoop of trenchant blades they come,
    And cut her legs away,
And look that she shall straightway fall
    On ground and bite the clay.

Say, is it by St Bothan's power,
    Or by St Boswell's grace,
That still she fights, and swings her arms,
    And stoutly holds her place?

I know not; but true men were there,
    Who saw her stand a while
Fighting, till streams of her brave blood
    Gave riches to the soil;

* In one of their savage raids the troops of the warder had
burnt the tower of Broomhouse, and in it its lady, a noble and
aged matron, with her whole family.—TYTLER.
    † A village on the Tweed, about two miles north of Ancrum
Moor, once very populous, and still marked by an old cross.

And then she fell ; and true men there,
   Upon the blood-stained moor
Upraised a stone to tell her fame,
   That ever shall endure.

All praise to Humes, and Kers, and Scotts !
   But fair Maid Lilliard's deed
Shall in green honour keep this spot,
   While Teviot runs to Tweed !

IPHIGENIA

Λιτὰς δε καὶ κληδόνας πατρῴους
παρ' ουδὲν αἰῶνα παρθένειόν τ'
ἔθεντο φιλόμαχοι βραβῆς
φράσεν δ' ἀόζοις πατὴρ μετ' εὐχὰν
δίκαν χιμάιρας ὕπερθε βωμοῦ
πέπλοισι περιπετῆ
παντὶ θυμῷ προνωπῆ
λαβεῖν ἀέρδην στόματός τε καλλιπρώρου φυλακὰν κάτασχειυ
φθόγγον ἀραῖον οἴκοις.—ÆSCHYLUS.

THE ships are gathered in the bay,
   A thousand-masted army,
All eager for the Trojan fray,
   But the sky looks black and stormy.
From Strymon's shore, with surly roar,
   The Thracian blasts are blowing ;
With fretted breast, and foamy crest,
   The adverse tide is flowing.

And Aulis' shore, so bright before,
  Is bleak, and grey, and dreary ;
With dull delay, from day to day,
  The seamen's hearts are weary.
Dire omen to their ears the roar
  Of Jove's loud-rattling thunder ;
The shivered sail, the shattered oar,
  The cable snapt in sunder.

What man is he that stands apart,
  In priestly guise long-vested,
Communing deep with his own heart,
  By sombre thoughts infested ?
He hath a laurel in his hand,
  And on the dark storm gazing,
He broods, as he would understand
  The secret of its raising.

'Tis Calchas, whose divining mind
  The secret thought can follow
Of Jove, who shows to human kind
  His counsel by Apollo.
And they who trust in prophet's skill,
  On the lone rock have found him,
And throng, to learn the Supreme will,
  In eager crowds around him.

He stands ; he looks, and reads the ground ;
  He will nor see nor hear them ;
But still they press, with swelling sound
  Of blameful murmurs, near him.

He goes ; against a host in vain
   He plants his single freedom ;
And to the tent o' the king of men
   With fretful force they lead him.

The Atridan stood without his tent,
   And scanned the welkin curiously,
If that the storm at length had spent
   Its gusty burden furiously.
Small help got he from cloud or sky,
   From sad thoughts that oppressed him ;
But blithe was his eye, when the seer came nigh,
   And thus the king addressed him :—

' O son of Thestor ! thou art wise,
   Thou see'st what wintry weather
Scowls on our bright-faced enterprise,
   And with a close-drawn tether
Holds us bound here against our will ;
   What cause doth so delay us ?
Speak, sith thou hast a prophet's skill,
   To me and Menelaus.'

The seer was dumb ; his fixed eye read
   The insensate sand demurely ;
' Nay, speak the truth,' the Atridan said,
   ' For thou dost know it surely.
Thou need'st not fear the strong man's arm,
   The king of men doth swear it,
Even by this kingly staff—no harm
   Shall touch thee, while I bear it !'

The seer was dumb ; the king was wroth :
  'Thou sellest dear thy prayers,
Thou sour-faced priest, and by my troth,
  Like thee are all soothsayers.
A mouthing and a mumping crew,
  With all things they will meddle ;
And when they have made much ado,
  They speak a two-faced riddle ! '

The seer was dumb.   ' Nay, not for me,
  Stiff priest, for love of Hellas,
If Jove hath shown the truth to thee,
  Untie thy tongue and tell us.
If, in our sacred things, a vice
  Some god hath sore offended,
Declare, and, at a tenfold price,
  I vow it shall be mended.

' If fault there be in me or mine,
  Or in the chiefs the highest,
I will not swerve, but so incline
  As Jove shall point, unbiassed.
My crown, my wealth, my blood, my all,
  Myself and Menelaus,
Will give, if so we may recall
  The blasts that now delay us.'

Then spake the prophet : ' King, not well
  Apollo's priest thou chidest ;
But I the unwelcome truth will tell,
  And follow where thou guidest.

The best loved stag of Dian thou
 Hast slain with evil arrow;
Therefore this vengeful tempest now
 Consumes the Argive marrow.

'And thou, even thou, whose was the guilt,
 Must work the just atoning;
When blood for blood is freely spilt,
 To joy will turn thy moaning.
If thou wilt ferry thee and thine
 Safe o'er the smooth-faced water,
Thou to the goddess must resign
 Blood of thy blood, thy daughter.'

The monarch stood, and with his staff
 He smote the ground in sorrow;
Nor spake: the cup that he must quaff
 Is fire that burns his marrow.
No aid Laertes' son supplied,
 Nestor, or Menelaus;
For we must stay the winds, they cried,
 From Thrace, that so delay us.

And they have choked the father's prayer;
 And this their general will is,
To bring the maid, with promise fair
 To wed her to Achilles.
And they have sent a courier far
 To Argos steed-delighting,
And Clytemnestra reins the car,
 To answer their inviting.

o

And they have come in trim array,
　The mother and the daughter,
As hasting to a bridal gay
　Beside the briny water.
But, when they reach the Aulian strand,
　No sight of gladness meets them ;
Hushed lies the camp ; with outstretched hand
　No forward father greets them.

And she is led, the daughter fair,
　By will that may not falter,
Where priests a sacrifice prepare
　For Dian's gloomy altar ;
Where Calchas stands with folded hands,
　And dense beholders gather ;
And with grief bent, on a plane-tree leant
　With backward gaze, her father.

Ah, woe is me ! and can it be,
　That, with sharp knife, thou darest
Strike such a neck, and forceful break
　This flower thy first and fairest ?
Will he not hear, her father dear,
　When her shrill plaint she poureth ;
Nor Jove above look down in love,
　When guiltless youth imploreth ?

She stretched her hands to the standers by,
　And tenderly besought them ;
With shafts of pity from her eye,
　The lovely maiden smote them.

O ! like a picture to be seen
  Was she, so chaste and beautiful,
And to her father's will had been
  In all so meek and dutiful.

How often, at his kingly board,
  With filial heart devoted,
To grace the banquet, she had poured
  The mellow lay clear-throated !
But now that voice shall sing no more ;
  They gag her mouth, lest, dying,
A curse on Argos she should pour,
  With evil-omened crying.

And, as stern Calchas gives behest,
  They with a cord have bound her ;
And she hath wrapt her saffron vest
  In decent folds around her.
And as a kid supine is laid,
  They on the altar lay her ;
As bleeds a kid, so bleeds the maid
  To the knife o' the priestly slayer.

But a weight is rolled from the heart of Greece
  And the clouds from the sky are driven,
And the sun looks down with an eye of peace
  From the fresh blue face of heaven.
The westering breeze the seamen hailed,
  That smoothed the Ægean water ;
But with sad heart the monarch sailed,
  For he had lost a daughter.

ARIADNE

Χρυσοκόμης δε Διάνυσος ξανθὴν 'Αριάδνην
κούρην Μίνωος, θαλερὴν ποιήσατ' ἄκοιτιν
τὴν τέ οἱ ἀθάνατον καὶ ἀγήρω θῆκε Κρονίων.—HESIOD.

 ' Protinus adspicies venienti nocte coronam
   Gnossida ; Theseo crimine facta dea est.'—OVID.

I

ARIADNE, Ariadne,
Thou art left alone, alone !
And the son of Attic Aegeus,
Faithless Theseus, he is flown.
Ariadne, Ariadne,
In a sea-cave left she sleepeth ;
In her dreams her bosom heaveth,
Through her dreams the maiden weepeth.
With an ugly dream she struggles ;
In the bright and sunny weather,
O'er the meadows green and flowery,
She and Theseus walk together.
Suddenly there sweeps a change ;
O'er a moor of hard brown heather,
O'er a bare and treeless waste,
She and Theseus walk together.
Cold and loveless is the air,
Huge white mists are trailing near her :
And the fitful swelling blast
Pipes with shrill note clear and clearer.
By an old grey tower she stands,
Where the ruin starts and crumbles ;

Wandering by a lone black lake,
On a cold grey stone she stumbles.
'Theseus! Theseus!'—to his arms
Close she clings; but like a trailing
Mist he flees; and o'er the waste
Laughter answers to her wailing.
Dim confusion blinds her eye,
Through her veins the chilly horror
Shoots: she stands; she looks; she runs
O'er the moor with mazy error.
And she screams, with rending cries,
'Save me, Jove, save Ariadne!
Theseus, Theseus, in the waste
Hast thou left thy Ariadne?'
And the Spirits of the storm
Shout around her—'Ariadne!
Thou art left alone, alone,
In the waste, O Ariadne!'

II

From the painful dream she wakes,
Starts, and looks, and feels for Theseus;
On the cold rock-floor her hand
Falls, and feels in vain for Theseus.
'Theseus, Theseus!'—he is gone;
Dost thou see that full sail swelling?
There he hies, with rapid keel,
Soon to find his Attic dwelling.
'Theseus! Theseus!'—she doth beat
The breasted wave with idle screaming.

Like a white sea-bird so small,
Now his distant sail is gleaming:
Now 'tis vanished.   O'er the isle
Hurries vagrant Ariadne;
None she sees, and, when she calls,
Answers none to Ariadne.
'Neath a high-arched rock she rests,
Weary, and, with meek behaviour,
Stretched upon a stony floor,
Plains her prayer to Jove the Saviour :—

Mighty Jove, strong to destroy,
    Stronger to save,
Hear ; nor in vain may Minos' daughter
    Thy mercy crave!
Weak is a maiden's wit : I saw
    The galliard stranger,
And, with wise clue, I brought him through
    The mazy danger.
My father's halls I left; I gave
    My heart's surrender ;
He loved the flower, and plucked the fruit,
    With hand untender.
Mighty Jove, the suppliant's friend,
    My supplication
Hear thou, and touch my prostrate woe
    With restoration !
She spake ; and, on the stony floor,
Stretched she lay in tearful sorrow ;
Slumber, sent from Saviour Jove,
Bound her gently till the morrow.

III

Wake, Ariadne!
Wake from thy slumbers;
Wake with new heart,
With no sorrow encumbers!
Black night is away now,
And glorious Day now
   Reddens apace.
The white mists are fleeing,
And o'er the Ægean,
His shining steeds follow
The call of Apollo,
   And snort for the race.
Hark! through thy slumbers,
Undulant numbers
   Quicken the air!
O'er the Ægean
Swells the loud pæan
   With melody rare;
The clear-throated flute,
And the sweet-sounding lute,
The cymbal's shrill jangle,
And tinkling triangle, .
   And tambour, are there.
Wake, Ariadne!
Look through thy slumbers!
The Mænads, to meet thee,
Marshal their numbers.
Down, from the sky
Dionysus has sent them;
Rosiest beauty

Venus has lent them.
Hovering nigh,
Their thin robes floating,
With balm in their eye,
Thy wounds they are noting,
   O Ariadne !
Blest be the bride
(So echoes their song)
That shall sleep by the side
Of the wine-god strong,
   Fair Ariadne !
Daughter of Minos,
A mortal betrays thee,
But a god for his bride
To Olympus shall raise thee !
Like a gem thou shalt shine
'Mid the bright starry glory ;
A name shall be thine
With the famous in story.
Wake, Ariadne,
From Earth's heavy slumbers ;
Wake to new life,
Which no sorrow encumbers !

IV

Ariadne from her slumber
Woke and rose, and smiled benignly,
Radiant from the rapturous dreams
That stirred her inmost soul divinely.
Round her stood the Mænad maids,
Round her swelled their tuneful chorus

Round her wheeled their floating dance,
To a piping reed sonorous.
With them wheeled a prick-eared crew,
Hairy-limbed, with goatish features;
Pans and Satyrs strange to view,
Forest-haunting, freakish creatures.
Old Silenus, bald and broad,
Stood beside, his bright face showing
Ploughed with laughter; his full eye
Brimmed with mirth to overflowing.
Strange; but Ariadne saw,
With broad eyes, a sight yet stranger;
Troops of shaggy forest whelps
Thronged around, and brought no danger.
Bearded goat, and tusky boar,
Fox that feasts on stealthy slaughter,
Tawny lion, tiger fierce,
Harmless looked on Minos' daughter
Lo! a spotted pard appears
At the feet of Ariadne;
Comes, and, like a prayerful child,
Kneels before thee, Ariadne.
Pleased the savage brute she sees
Stretch its brindled length demurely;
Mounts the offered seat, and rides
On the panther's back securely.
Forward now the spotted pard
Moves with measured pace and wary;
Then aloft (O wonder strange!)
Paws the heavenward pathway airy.
Fear thee not, thou Gnossian maid
Gods are with thee where thou fliest;

Dionysus waits for thee,
Near the throne of Jove the Highest.
In Olympus' azure dells,
Waits the god in ivy bowers,
Where for the immortal Hebe
Twines the amaranthine flowers ;
Where the purple bowl of joy
Brims for thee ; where bitter sorrow
Grows not ; where to-day's keen thrill
Leaves no languid throb to-morrow.
Flourish there, immortal bride,
In sculptor's stone and minstrel's story ;
Shine, to sorrowing hearts a sign,
High amid the starry glory !

MARATHON

Λειμῶνα τόν ἐρόεντα Μαραθῶνος.—ARISTOPHANES

I

FROM Pentelicus' pine-clad height
  A voice of warning came,
That shook the silent autumn night
  With fear to Media's name.
Pan from his Marathonian cave
  Sent screams of midnight terror,
And darkling horror curled the wave
  On the broad sea's moonlit mirror.
      Woe, Persia, woe ! thou liest low, low !
        Let the golden palaces groan !
      Ye mothers weep for sons that shall sleep
        In gore on Marathon !

II

Where Indus and Hydaspes roll,
  Where treeless deserts glow,
Where Scythians roam beneath the pole,
  O'er fields of hardened snow,
The great Darius rules ; and now,
  Thou little Greece, to thee
He comes ; thou thin-soiled Athens, how
    Shalt thou dare to be free ?
      There is a God that wields the rod
        Above : by Him alone
      The Greek shall be free, when the Mede
          shall flee
        In shame from Marathon.

III

He comes ; and o'er the bright Ægean,
  Where his masted army came,
The subject-isles uplift the pæan
  Of glory to his name.
Strong Naxos, strong Eretria yield ;
  His captains near the shore
Of Marathon's fair and fateful field,
    Where a tyrant marched before.
      And a traitor guide, the sea beside,
        Now marks the land for his own,
      Where the marshes red shall soon be the bed
        Of the Mede in Marathon.

IV

Who shall number the host of the Mede ?
  Their high-tiered galleys ride,

Like locust-bands with darkening speed,
  Across the groaning tide.
Who shall tell the many-hoofed tramp
  That shakes the dusty plain?
Where the pride of his horse is the strength of his
      camp,
    Shall the Mede forget to gain?
        Oh fair is the pride of those turms as they
            ride,
          To the eye of the morning shown!
        But a god in the sky hath doomed them to lie
          In dust, on Marathon.

v

Dauntless beside the sounding sea
  The Athenian men reveal
Their steady strength.   That they are free
  They know; and inly feel
Their high election, on that day,
  In foremost fight to stand,
And dash the enslaving yoke away,
  From all the Grecian land.
        Their praise shall sound the world around,
          Who shook the Persian throne,
        When the shout of the free travelled over the
            sea,
          From famous Marathon.

vi

From dark Cithæron's sacred slope,
  The small Platæan band

Bring hearts, that swell with patriot hope,
  To wield a common brand
With Theseus' sons, at danger's gates;
  While spell-bound Sparta stands,
And for the pale moon's changes waits
  With stiff unkindly hands;
      And hath no share in the glory rare,
        That Athens shall make her own,
      When the long-haired Mede with fearful
        speed
      Falls back from Marathon.

VII

'On, sons of the Greeks!' the war-cry rolls;
  'The land that gave you birth,
Your wives, and all the dearest souls
  That circle round each hearth;
The shrines upon a thousand hills,
  The memory of your sires,
Nerve now with brass your resolute wills,
  And fan your valorous fires!'
      And on like a wave came the rush of the
        brave—
        'Ye sons of the Greeks, on, on!'
      And the Mede stept back from the eager
        attack
      Of the Greek, in Marathon.

VIII

Hear'st thou the rattling of spears on the right?
  Seest thou the gleam in the sky?

The gods come to aid the Greeks in the fight,
  And the favouring heroes are nigh.
The lion's hide I see in the sky,
  And the knotted club so fell,
And kingly Theseus' conquering eye,
  And Macaria, nymph of the well.
      Purely, purely the fount did flow,
        When the morn's first radiance shone ;
      But eve shall know the crimson flow
        Of its wave, by Marathon.

IX

On, son of Cimon, bravely on !
  And Aristides just !
Your names have made the field your own,
  Your foes are in the dust !
The Lydian satrap spurs his steed,
  The Persian's bow is broken ;
His purple pales ; the vanquished Mede
  Beholds the angry token
      Of thundering Jove who rules above ;
        And the bubbling marshes moan
      With the trampled dead that have found
        their bed
      In gore, at Marathon.

X

The ships have sailed from Marathon,
  On swift disaster's wings ;
And an evil dream hath fetched a groan
  From the heart of the king of kings.

An eagle he saw, in the shades of night,
　With a dove that bloodily strove;
And the weak hath vanquished the strong in fight,
　The eagle hath fled from the dove.
　　　Great Jove, that reigns in the starry plains,
　　　　To the heart of the king hath shown,
　　　That the boastful parade of his pride was laid
　　　　In dust, at Marathon.

XI

But through Pentelicus' winding vales
　The hymn triumphal runs,
And high-shrined Athens proudly hails
　Her free-returning sons.
And Pallas, from her ancient rock,
　With her shield's refulgent round,
Blazes; her frequent worshippers flock,
　And high the pæans sound,
　　　How in deathless glory the famous story
　　　　Shall on the winds be blown,
　　　That the long-haired Mede was driven with
　　　　　speed
　　　　By the Greeks, from Marathon.

XII

And Greece shall be a hallowed name,
　While the sun shall climb the pole,
And Marathon fan strong freedom's flame
　In many a pilgrim soul.
And o'er that mound where heroes sleep,
　By the waste and reedy shore,

Full many a patriot eye shall weep,
  Till Time shall be no more.
      And the bard shall brim with a holier hymn
      When he stands by that mound alone,
      And feel no shrine on earth more divine
      Than the dust of Marathon.

SALAMIS

Ὦ κλεινὰ Σαλαμὶς σὺ μέν του
ναίεις ἁλίπλαγκτος, εὐδαίμων
πᾶσιν περίφαντος ἀεί.—SOPHOCLES.

SEEST thou where, sublimely seated on a silver-footed
    throne,
With a high tiara crested, belted with a jewelled zone,
Sits the king of kings, and, looking from the rocky
    mountain-side,
Scans with masted armies studded far the fair Saronic
    tide?
Looks he not with high hope beaming? looks he not
    with pride elate?
Seems he not a god, the Thunderer? and his words
    are winged with fate.
He hath come from far Euphrates, and from Tigris'
    rushing tide,
To subdue the strength of Athens, to chastise the
    Spartan's pride:
He hath come with countless armies, gathered
    slowly from afar,
From the plain, and from the mountain, marshalled
    ranks of motley war;

From the land, and from the ocean, that the
  burdened billows groan,
That the air is choked with banners, which great
  Xerxes calls his own.
Soothly he hath nobly ridden, o'er the fair fields,
  o'er the waste,
As the Earth might bear the burden, with a
  weighty-footed haste;
He hath cut in twain the mountain, he hath bridged
  the rolling main,
He hath lashed the flood of Helle, bound the billow
  with a chain;
And the rivers shrink before him, and the sheeted
  lakes are dry,
From his burden-bearing oxen, and his hordes of
  cavalry;
And the gates of Greece stand open; Ossa and
  Olympus fail;
And the mountain-girt Æmonia spreads the many-
  watered vale;
And her troops of famous horse, before the puissant
  Persian's nod,
Flee; the death-defying Spartans prostrate lie be-
  neath his rod,
Where with fleshy breast they walled thy famous
  pass, Thermopylæ.
And the god that shakes Cithæron feared to block
  his forceful way;
And the blue-eyed maid of Athens shook not then
  her heavenly spear,
Rock-perched Pallas, when the tread of the high-
  clambering foe was near;

P

And the sacred snake, huge-twining guardian of the
    virgin shrine,
Where the honeyed cake was waiting, tasted not the
    food divine;
Stood nor man nor god before him; he hath scoured
    the Attic land,
Chased the valiant sons of Athens to a barren
    island's strand;
He hath hedged them round with triremes, lines on
    lines of bristling war;
He hath doomed the prey for capture; he hath
    spread his meshes far;
And he sits sublimely seated on a throne with pride
    elate,
To behold the victim fall beneath the sudden-
    swooping Fate.

Who may stand against his might?—with thy thin
    slip of rocky coast,
Athens, wilt thou tell thy fifties 'gainst the thou-
    sands of his host?
All the might of all the Orient, from the Ganges-
    watered Ind
To the isles that fringe the Ægean, 'gainst thy
    little state combined;
Turbaned Persians, with gay panoply from the gold
    of distant mines,
Host immortal with their wives, and troops of
    spangled concubines;
Mitred Cissians, high-capped Sacae, and the As-
    syrian brazen-crested;

The high-booted Paphlagonian; the swart Indian
  cotton-vested;
Shaggy warriors, goatskin-mantled, from the dreary
  Caspian strand,
And the camel-mounted riders from the incense-
  bearing land,
Thracians fierce, with shouts Bacchantic, and more
  savage war-halloo;
Sacred Tmolus' sons, and Lydia's soft and silken-
  vested crew;
And the sons of hoariest Thebes, and sacerdotal
  Memphis, where
Gods, in brutish incarnation, bellow through the
  sacred air;
And the sun-scorched, painted Ethiop, with his
  huge-spanned bow of war,
And the woolly-headed Libyan, driving swift the
  scythèd car;
And the boatmen of the lowland, that, with fre-
  quent-beating oar,
Plough the pools where floats the lotus, by the fat
  Nile's peopled shore:
Such a crew he drives against thee. 'Neath the
  dusky-vested Night,
He hath ranged them to entrap thee.

            Now behold the glorious light,
Beaming broadly from the chariot of the silver-
  steeded day,
Shows revealed the triple barrier of his ships in
  close array,

Girdling in the coast of Ajax. Yet no wavering
    fear is there;
Firmly stands the line of Athens.

            Hark! their loud shouts split the air.
Not the expected note of terror, not the wild cry
    of despair;
Foolish Xerxes! 'tis the exultant power that swells
    strong manhood's breast;
'Tis the broadly-billowed pæan from the freemen of
    the West.

'Sons of the Greeks! now save your country!
    save your wives and children dear!
Save the sepulchres of your fathers! save the
    shrines of gods that hear
When the patriot prays! This day makes us free
    or slaves for ever!'
On they sail, with steady helming, sworn to die or
    to deliver.
Now they meet. Now beak on beak is furious
    dashed; and Sidon old
Drives her brazen-breasted triremes 'gainst the ships
    of Athens bold.
A moment equal; but the Athenian, in the des-
    perate-handed strife,
Wields, as patriots well may wield, a surer sword
    and sharper knife.
On he presses—close and closer; cloven booms
    and shattered sails,
And the frequent-crashing oarage, mark the track
    where he prevails.

Ocean seethes beneath his fury; and the hostile-
fretted flood

Yawns to drink the reeling Tyrian, and the floun-
dering Cyprian's blood.

Sobs the wave with drowned and drowning:
where the narrow channels flow,

Vain the strife with death two-handed, here the
water, there the foe.

Ship on ship is rudely clashed; for in the narrow
strait confined,

Room is none to use their numbers; and, with
strivings vain and blind,

Where they move they clog the movements of the
friend they hoped to aid,

Where they fight they help the battle of the foe
they should have stayed.

Vainly, with her Carian triremes, o'er the terror-
tangled scene

Artemisia rides the battle like an Amazonian
queen;

All is reasonless confusion. O'er the purple-stream-
ing tide,

Helmless ships and shipless pilots struggle with the
billows' pride

Vainly—for the west wind rising with harsh wing
and savage roar

Drives the foundered and the drowning countless
on the Colian shore.

And to crown such wreck and carnage, when the
hottest fight was o'er,

Rode the Athenian galleys proudly to a rocky
islet's shore,

Near to Salamis — there the king, to top the sure
    deemed victory,
Susa's chiefest bloom had stationed ; and in waiting
    there they lie
To help their conquering friends, and swell the
    hoped-for triumph.   Them the foe
Circle round with bristling beaks, and, where the
    billowy waters flow,
Blast them with the arrowy tempest, crush them
    with the huge-heaved rock,
Mow them down in rows defenceless, like the butch-
    ered bleating flock.
From his throne the monarch sees it, heap on heap
    of helpless slaughter,
With the life of Persia crimsoned far the fair
    Saronic water.
Rend thy robes, thou foolish Xerxes, rend the air
    with piteous cries !
On the rocky coast of Hellas gashed the pride of
    Persia lies !

Wake thee ! wake thee ! blinded Xerxes ! God hath
    found thee out at last ;
Snaps thy pride beneath His judgment, as the tree
    beneath the blast.
Haste thee ! haste thee ! speed thy couriers—Persian
    couriers travel lightly—
To declare thy stranded navy, and by cruel death
    unsightly
Dimmed thy glory. Hie thee ! hie thee ! hence
    e'en by what way thou camest,

Dwarfed to whoso saw thee mightiest, and where
    thou wert fiercest, tamest!
Hide thee, where blank Fear shall hunt thee, and,
    more surely to undo thee,
Thirst and hunger where thou goest, brothered
    demons, shall pursue thee.
Where Cithæron dear to Bromius nods his horror-
    crested wood,
To the Phocian, to the Dorian, where Spercheius
    rolls his flood,
Through Æmonia steed-delighting, by Magnesia's
    wave-lashed strand,
Through the hardy Macedonian's, through the
    fierce-souled Thracian's land,
By the reedy Bolbe's waters, by the steep Pangæan
    height,
By the stream of holy Strymon thou shalt spur
    thy sleepless flight.
Frost and Fire shall league together, wrathful
    Heaven to Earth respond,
Strong Poseidon with his trident break thy im-
    pious vaunted bond;
Where he passed, with mouths uncounted eating
    up the famished land,
Now a slender skiff shall ferry Xerxes to the Asian
    strand
Haste thee! haste thee! they are waiting by the
    palace gates for thee,
By the golden gates of Susa eager mourners wait
    for thee;
Haste thee, where the guardian elders wait, a
    hoary-bearded train;

They shall see their king, but never see the sons
    they loved again.
Where thy weeping mother waits thee, queen
    Atossa waits to see
Dire fulfilment of her troublous vision-haunted sleep
    in thee.
She hath dreamt, and she shall see it, how an
    · Eagle cowed with awe
Gave his kingly crest to pluck before a puny
    Falcon's claw.
Haste thee! where the mighty shade of great
    Darius through the gloom
Rises dread, to teach thee wisdom, couldst thou
    learn it, from the tomb.
There begin the sad rehearsal, and, while streaming
    tears are shed,
To the thousand tongues that ask thee, tell the
    myriads of the dead!
Blame the god that so deceived thee—for the
    mighty men that died
Blame all gods that be, but chiefly blame thyself,
    and thine own pride!
Drown thy sorrow with much wailing! beat thy
    breast, thy vesture rend,
Tear thy hair, and pluck thy beard—weep till
    thou hast no tears to spend;
Call the mourning women to thee! while they lift
    the Mysian wail,
Thou to Susa's sonless mothers pour the sorrow-
    streaming tale!

POLEMO

Ἀμὴν ἀμὴν λέγω σοι, ἐὰν μή τις γεννηθῇ ἄνωθεν, οὐ δύναται
ἰδεῖν τὴν βασιλείαν τοῦ Θεοῦ.—JOHN iii. 3.

Peregrinatus est hic in nequitiá, non habitavit
VALERIUS MAXIMUS

'Tis morn.   On Parnes, nurse of hardy pines,
  Gleams the new-started day,
And on Ægina's briny water shines
  The clear far-shimmering ray.

'Neath the old Attic rock white vapours creep
  And on the dusty road,
O'er the meek army of his bleating sheep
  The shepherd wields his goad.

The city sleeps ; save where the market shows
  The first green-furnished stalls,
And from his lair of shelterless repose
  The squalid beggar crawls.

Who bursts into the peaceful street, with sound
  Of brawl, and wrangling fray,
Rushing with blushless stare and staggering bound,
  To greet the modest day ?

A band of revellers, with torn chaplets crowned ;
  And at their head I know
The rich man's son, for shameless vice renowned,
  Licentious Polemo

Onward they reel, as whim may point the way ;
    But he, with firmer pace,
Who hath a will strong to assert its sway
    Even in the drunkard's place.

And whither now ?   Sometimes God leads a fool
    To knock at wisdom's door ;
And so the reveller rushes to the school
    Where Plato's holy lore

Is taught by sage severe Xenocrates,
    Who, at that early hour,
Mingled wise disputation with the breeze
    That stirred the learnèd bower.

Amid the listening scholars Polemo
    Sate down ; and, from his place,
With impudent stare his strong contempt did show,
    In the mild lecturer's face.

The teacher saw, nor stirred his soul serene,
    That reveller to reprove,
But changed his theme, and, with unaltered mien,
    More apt discourse he wove

Of temperance, purity, high self-control,
    Ideal harmonies fine,
And all that lifts man's doubtful-swaying soul
    From bestial to divine.

The scoffer heard ; but soon, with softened stare
    And flinching look, confessed
How deep the preacher probed his heart ; for there
    He felt a strange unrest.

And as the wise man, with the waxing theme,
    More grave and weighty grew,
With swelling doubts he felt his bosom teem,
    His flushed cheek paled its hue.

And from his head he plucked the violets blue;
    And, as the speaker woke
More fretful tempest in his breast, he drew
    His hand beneath his cloak;

And rose; and stood as one that fronts a foe;
    Then, with a sudden turn,
Sank; in a gushing flood the salt tears flow;
    And, with wild thoughts that burn,

He from the audience rushed.   But not his soul
    From the new awe that found him
Might rush; but, with a tyrannous strong control,
    Missioned from God, it bound him,

And with his mutinous temper wrestled long,
    Till, like a lamb, he lay;
Then rose, like one with a new nature strong,
    To a new life that day;

And by the chaste and blue-eyed goddess sware
    That, from that sacred hour,
He the philosopher's sober garb should wear,
    And walk in learnèd bower:

And, as he sware, so lived, that not a breath
    Might his pure fame besmirch;
And taught by word, and mightier deed, till death;
    A saint in Plato's church.

PROMETHEUS

Πᾶσας τέχνας βροτοῖσιν ἐκ Προμηθέως.—ÆSCHYLUS

I

BLOW blustering winds; loud thunders roll!
Swift lightnings rend the fervid pole
With frequent flash! his hurtling hail
Let Jove down-fling! hoarse Neptune flail
The stubborn rock, and give free reins
To his dark steeds with foamy manes
That paw the strand!—such wrathful fray
Touches not me, who, even as they,
Immortal tread this lowly sod,
    Born of the gods a god.

II

Jove rules above; Fate willed it so.
'Tis well; Prometheus rules below.
Their gusty game let wild winds play,
And clouds on clouds in thick array
Muster dark armies in the sky;
Be mine a harsher trade to ply,
This solid Earth, this rocky frame
To mould, to conquer, and to tame;
And to achieve the toilsome plan,
    My workman shall be MAN.

III

The Earth is young.   Even with these eyes
I saw the molten mountains rise

From out the seething deep, while Earth
Shook at the portent of their birth.
I saw from out the primal mud
The reptiles crawl of dull cold blood,
While wingèd lizards with broad stare
Peered through the raw and misty air.
Where then was Cretan Jove? where then
    This king of gods and men?

IV

When naked from his mother Earth,
Weak and defenceless, man crept forth,
And on mis-tempered solitude
Of unploughed field and unclipt wood
Gazed rudely; when with brutes he fed
On acorns, and his stony bed
In dark unwholesome caverns found;
No skill was then to till the ground,
No help came then from him above,
    This tyrannous-blustering Jove.

V

The Earth is young.   Her latest birth,
This weakling man, my craft shall girth
With cunning strength.   Him I will take,
And in stern arts my scholar make.
This smoking reed, in which I hold
The empyrean spark, shall mould
Rock and hard steel to use of man;
He shall be as a god to plan
And forge all things to his desire
    By alchemy of fire.

VI

These jagged cliffs that flout the air,
Harsh granite block so rudely bare,
Wise Vulcan's art and mine shall own,
To piles of shapeliest beauty grown.
The steam that snorts vain strength away
Shall serve the workman's curious sway
Like a wise child; as clouds that sail
White winged before the summer gale,
The smoking chariot o'er the land
    Shall roll, at his command.

Blow, winds, and crack your cheeks! my home
Stands firm beneath Jove's thundering dome,
This stable Earth.   Here let me work!
The busy spirits, that eager lurk
Within a thousand labouring breasts,
Here let me rouse; and whoso rests
From labour let him rest from life.
To live 's to strive; and in the strife
To move the rock, and stir the clod,
    Man makes himself a god.

THE NAMING OF ATHENS

Παρθένοι ὀμβροφόροι
ἔλθωμεν λιπαράν χθόνα Πάλλαδος, εὔανδρον γᾶν
Κέκροπος ὀψόμεναι πολυήρατον.—ARISTOPHANES.

ON the rock of Erectheus the ancient, the hoary,
  That rises sublime from the far-stretching plain,

Sate Cecrops, the first in Athenian story
  Who guided the fierce by the peace-loving rein.
Eastward away by the flowery Hymettus,
  Westward where Salamis gleams in the bay,
Northward, beneath the high-peaked Lycabettus,
  He numbered the towns that rejoiced in his
    sway.
Pleased with his eye with the muster, but rested
  At length where he sate with an anxious love,
When he thought on the strife of the mighty broad-
    breasted
  Poseidon, with Pallas, the daughter of Jove ;
For the god of the earth-shaking ocean had sworn it,
  The city of Cecrops should own him supreme,
Or the land and the people should ruefully mourn it,
  Swamped by the swell of the broad ocean-stream.
Lo ! from the North, as he doubtfully ponders,
  A light shoots far-streaming ; the welkin it fills ;
Southward from Parnes bright-bearded it wanders,
  Swift as the courier-fires from the hills.
Far on the flood of the winding Cephissus,
  There gleams like the shape of a serpentine rod,
Shimmers the tide of the gentle Ilissus
  With radiance from Hermes the messenger-god.
Twas he : on the Earth with light touch he de-
    scended,
  And struck the grey rock with his gold-gleaming
    rod,
While Cecrops with low-hushed devotion attended,
  And reverent awe to the voice of the god.
' Noble autochthon ! a message I bear thee,
  From Jove in Olympus who regally sways ;

Wise is the god the dark trouble to spare thee,—
  Blest is the heart that believes and obeys.
On the peaks of Olympus, the bright snowy-crested,
  The gods are assembled in council to-day ;
The wrath of Poseidon, the mighty broad-breasted,
  'Gainst Pallas, the spear-shaking maid, to allay ;
And thus they decree—that Poseidon offended,
  And Pallas shall bring forth a gift to the place ;
On the hill of Erectheus the strife shall be ended,
  When she with her spear, and the god with his
    mace,
  Shall strike the quick rock ; and the gods shall
    deliver
  The sentence as Justice shall order ; and thou
Shalt see thy loved city established for ever
  With Jove for a judge, and the Styx for a vow.'
He spake ; and, while Cecrops devoutly was
    bending,
  To worship the knees of the herald of Jove,
Shone from the pole, in full glory descending,
  The cloud-car that bore the bright gods from
    above,
Beautiful, glowing with many-hued splendour.
  O what a kinship of godhead was there !
Juno the stately, full-eyed ; and the tender
  Bland-beaming Venus, so rosily fair ;
Dian the huntress, with arrow and quiver,
  And airily tripping with light-footed grace ;
Apollo, with radiance poured like a river
  Diffusive o'er Earth, from his joy-giving face ;
Bacchus the rubicund ; and with fair tresses,
  The bright-fruited Ceres, and Vesta the chaste ;

And the god that delights in fair Venus' caresses,
    Stout Mars, in his mail adamantine encased.
Then, while wild thunders innocuous gather
    Round his brow, diademed green with the oak,
On the rock of Erectheus descended the Father,
    And thus to good Cecrops serenely he spoke :
' Kingly autochthon ! the sorrow deep-rooted
    ' That gnaweth thy heart, the Olympians know ;
Too long with Poseidon hath Pallas disputed,—
    This day shall be peace, or great Jove is their foe.'
He spake ; and a sound like the rushing of ocean,
    From smooth-grained Pentelicus, seizes their ears ;
From his home in Euboea, with haughty commotion,
    To the place of the judgment, the sea-monarch
        nears.
On the waves of the wind his blue car travelled
        proudly,
    Proudly his locks to the breeze floated free,
Snorted his mane-tossing coursers, and loudly
    Blew from the tortuous conch of the sea
Shrill Tritons the clear-throated blast undisputed,
    That curleth the wild wave, and cresteth the main
While Nereids around him, the fleet foamy-footed,
    Floated, as floated his undulant rein.
Thus on the rock of Erectheus alighted
    The god of the sea, and the rock with his mace
Smote ; for he knew that the gods were invited
    To judge of the gift that he gave to the place.
Lo ! at the touch of his trident a wonder !
    Virtue to Earth from his deity flows :
From the rift of the flinty rock cloven asunder,
    A dark-watered fountain ebullient rose.

Q

Inly elastic with airiest lightness
    It leapt, till it cheated the eyesight; and, lo!
It showed in the sun, with a various brightness,
    The fine-woven hues of the rain-loving bow.
'WATER IS BEST!' cried the mighty, broad-breasted
    Poseidon; 'O Cecrops, I offer to thee
To ride on the back of the steeds foamy-crested,
    That toss their wild manes on the huge-heaving
        sea.
The globe thou shalt mete on the path of the waters,
    To thy ships shall the ports of far ocean be free;
The isles of the sea shall be counted thy daughters,
    The pearls of the East shall be treasured for
        thee!'
He spake; and the gods, with a high-sounding
        pæan,
    Applauded; but Jove hushed the many-voiced
        tide;
'For now, with the lord of the briny Ægean,
    Athena shall strive for the city,' he cried.
'See, where she comes!'—and she came, like
        Apollo,
    Serene with the beauty ripe wisdom confers;
The clear-scanning eye, and the sure hand to follow
    The mark of the far-sighted purpose, was hers.
Strong in the mail of her father she standeth,
    And firmly she holds the strong spear in her
        hand;
But the wild hounds of war with calm power she
        commandeth,
    And fights but to pledge surer peace to the land.
Chastely the blue-eyed approached, and, surveying

The council of wise-judging gods without fear,
The nod of her lofty-throned father obeying,
   She struck the grey rock with her nice-tempered
      spear.
Lo! from the touch of the virgin a wonder!
   Virtue to Earth from her deity flows:
From the rift of the flinty rock cloven asunder,
   An olive-tree greenly luxuriant rose—
Green, but yet pale, like an eye-drooping maiden,
   Gentle, from full-blooded lustihood far;
No broad-staring hues for rude pride to parade in,
   No crimson to blazon the banners of war.
Mutely the gods, with a calm consultation,
   Pondered the fountain, and pondered the tree;
And the heart of Poseidon, with high expectation,
   Throbbed, till great Jove thus pronounced the
      decree:
'Son of my father, thou mighty, broad-breasted
   Poseidon, the doom that I utter is true;
Great is the might of thy waves foamy-crested,
   When they beat the white halls of the screaming
      sea-mew:
Great is the pride of the keel when it danceth,
   Laden with wealth, o'er the light-heaving wave;
When the East to the West, gaily floated, advanceth,
   With a word from the wise, and a help from the
      brave.
But Earth, solid Earth, is the home of the mortal,
   That toileth to live, and that liveth to toil;
And the green olive-tree twines the wreath of his
      portal,
   Who peacefully wins his sure bread from the soil.'

Thus Jove; and aloft the great council celestial
  Rose, and the sea-god rolled back to the sea;
But Athena gave Athens her name, and terrestrial
  Joy, from the oil of the green olive-tree.

JOHN FRAZER

John Frazer was a pious man,
  Who dwelt in lone Dalquhairn,
Where huge hills feed the founts of Ken,
  'Twixt Sanquhar and Carsphairn.

King Charles he was a despot fell;
  With harlots and buffoons
He filled his court, and scoured the hills
  With troopers and dragoons.

For he hated all the godly men,
  When, free on heather braes,
Their hearts would brim with an holy hymn
  To their great Maker's praise.

And he hated good John Frazer,
  And he bade his troopers ride
Up dale and dell, by crag and fell,
  And snow-wreathed mountain side.

One night in bleak December,
  When the snow was drifting down,
John Frazer sate by his ingle-side
  With his good wife Marion.

And they spake as godly folk will speak,
  O' the kirk, and the kirk's concerns,
Of hair-breadth 'scapes in thousand shapes,
  And they spake o' their bonnie bairns.

Tramp, tramp! Who's there? 'Tis they, O Heaven!
  The Devil's own errand loons!
They've lifted the latch, and there they stand,
  Six striding stark dragoons!

'Too late, too late, thou crop-eared Whig!
  Too late to turn and flee!
To-morrow thou'lt dance thy latest jig,
  High on a gallows-tree!'

They bound his arms and legs with thongs,
  As hard as they were able;
Then took him where their horses stood,
  And locked him in the stable.

Then back to the house they came, and bade
  The sorrowful gudewife pour
The stout brown ale—for well they knew
  She kept a goodly store.

The gudewife was a prudent dame;
  The stout brown ale brought she;
They filled and quaffed, and quaffed and filled,
  And talked with boisterous glee.

And many a ribald song they sang,
  And told in jeering strain
How God's dear saints were seized and bound,
  And hounded o'er the main.

And many an ugly oath they swore,
    That made the gudewife turn pale ;
But she smoothed her face with a decent grace,
    And still she poured the ale.

And still they drank, and still they sang,
    And still they cursed and swore ;
The clock struck twelve ! the clock struck one
    And still they cried for more.

The gudewife was a prudent dame,
    She broached her ripest store :
The clock struck two ! the clock struck three !
    And still the gudewife did pour.

Then up and spake the first dragoon,
    ' Now mount and grip the reins, boys !
It suits not well that a bold dragoon
    Should drink away his brains, boys. '

Then up they rose, and, with an oath,
    Went reeling to the stable ;
Their steeds bestrode, and off they rode
    As fast as they were able.

With lamp in hand the gudewife rose
    And to the stable ran,
And looked, and looked, till in a nook
    She found her own gudeman !

Now, God be praised ! he's fresh and hale !
    A mighty work this day
The Lord hath done !   The stout brown ale
    Hath stol'n their wits away.

Eftsoons she brought a huge sharp knife
  And cut the thongs in tway ;
Now, run gudeman, and save thy life !
  They'll be back by break o' day !

And off he ran, like a practised man—
  For oft for his life ran he—
And lurked in the hills, till God cast down
  King Charles and his company.

And lived to tell, when over the wave
  Went James with his Popish loons,
How God by stout brown ale did save
  His life from the drunk dragoons.

THE TWO MEEK MARGARETS

It fell on a day in the blooming month of May,
  When the trees were greenly growing,
That a captain grim went down to the brim
  O' the sea, when the tide was flowing.

Twa maidens he led, that captain grim,
  Wi' his red-coat loons behind him,
Twa meek-faced maids, and he sware that he
  In the salt sea-swell should bind them.

And a' the burghers o' Wigton town
  Came down, full sad and cheerless,
To see that ruthless captain drown
  These maidens meek, but fearless.

O what had they done, these maidens meek,
  What crime all crimes excelling,
That they should be staked on the ribbed sea-sand,
  And drowned, where the tide was swelling?

O wae's me, wae! but the truth I maun say!
  Their crime was the crime of believing
Not man, but God, when the last false Stuart
  His Popish plot was weaving.

O spare them! spare them! thou captain grim!
  No! no!—to a stake he hath bound them,
Where the floods as they flow, and the waves as they
    grow,
  Shall soon be deepening around them.

The one had threescore years and three;
  Far out on the sand they bound her,
Where the first dark flow of the waves as they grow
  Is quickly swirling round her.

The other was a maiden fresh and fair;
  More near to the land they bound her,
That she might see by slow degree
  The grim waves creeping round her.

O captain, spare that maiden grey,
  She's deep in the deepening water!
No! no! she's lifted her hands to pray,
  And the choking billow caught her!

'See, see, young maid,' cried the captain grim,
'The wave shall soon ride o'er thee !
She's swamped in the brine whose sin was like
thine,
See that same fate before thee ! '

' I see the Christ who hung on a tree
When His life for sins he offered ;   .
I'm one of His members, even He
With that meek maid hath suffered.'

' O, captain, save a meek young maid ;
She's a loyal farmer's daughter !'
'Well, well ! let her swear to good King James,
And I'll hale her out from the water ! '

' I will not swear to Popish James,
But I pray for the head of the nation,
That he and all, both great and small,
May know God's great salvation ! '

She spoke ; and lifted her hands to pray,
And felt the greedy water,
Deep and more deep, around her creep,
Till the choking billow caught her !

O, Wigton, Wigton ! I'm wae to sing
The truth o' this waesome story ;
But God will sinners to judgment bring,
And His saints shall reign in glory.

VENUS ANADYOMENE

APHRODITE, Ocean daughter,
　　Once a goddess, still the same,
When I look on purest water
　　Then I spell thy mystic name.
When I see the tips of Ocean,
　　Curling, cresting in the breeze,
And the Sun with lightsome motion
　　Shimmering o'er the azure seas;
When I see the sport of shadow
　　Where the silvery wavelets sleep,
And a hue that mocks the meadow
　　Purpling o'er the various deep,—
Then I know thee, Aphrodite,
　　Queen of beauty, queen of power,
Thee the lovely, thee the mighty,
　　From life's first to latest hour.
When before my raptured eye
　　Soft thy silver shell ascending,
Borne by Triton-hands on high,
　　Wreaths of rosy Nymphs attending,
Soars, a milder feature blending
　　With the awe that clothes the sky.
Steep Olympus opes its portals;
　　Thou dost tread the starry way,
And the host of strong Immortals
　　Bends before thy gentle sway.
Pallas veils her sterner glory,
　　Wisdom wisely yields to love,

Flees the weighty cloud before thee
    From the thunder-brow of Jove.
Mars, the fierce mane-shaking lion,
    Now a lamb to greet thee falls ;
Haughty Hera, love defying,
    Lonely walks through ether's halls.
Aphrodite, Ocean daughter,
    Though I bear no heathen name,
    When I see thy fairest frame
Rising from the bright blue water,
    I may worship without blame.

THE OLD SOLDIER OF THE GARELOCH HEAD

(A SONG WRITTEN ON THE SPOT)

I'VE wander'd east and west,
    And a soldier I have been ;
The scars upon my breast
    Tell the wars that I have seen.
But now I'm old and worn,
    And my locks are thinly spread,
And I'm come to die in peace
    By the Gareloch Head.

When I was young and strong,
    Oft a wandering I would go,
By the rough shores of Loch Long,
    Up to lone Glencroe.

But now I'm fain to rest,
   And my resting-place I've made
On the green and gentle bosom
   Of the Gareloch Head.

'Twas here my Jeanie grew,
   Like a lamb amid the flocks,
With her eyes of bonnie blue,
   And her golden locks.
And here we often met,
   When with lightsome foot we sped
O'er the green and grassy knolls
   At the Gareloch Head.

'Twas here she pined and died—
   O ! the salt tear in my e'e
Forbids my heart to hide
   What Jeanie was to me !
'Twas here my Jeanie died,
   And they scoop'd her lowly bed
'Neath the green and grassy turf
   At the Gareloch Head.

Like a leaf in leafy June
   From the leafy forest torn,
She fell; and I'll fall soon,
   Like a sheaf of yellow corn ;
For I'm sere and weary now,
   And I soon shall make my bed
With my Jeanie 'neath the turf
   At the Gareloch Head.

THE MERRY BALLAD OF STOCK GEILL

Good lords and ladies, who refuse to bend before
    a log,
I'll tell you of a merry gest, that gave the Pope
    a shog;
A gest that chanced in Embro' toun, and in the
    High Street old
Where Willock taught, and stout John Knox, that
    faithful preacher bold.
        Sing hey Stock Geill! and ho Stock Geill!
        the tale I tell is true;
        We dashed his bones against the stones,
        and his stump in flinders flew!

'Twas the first day of September, and the priests were
    all agog,
All through the town, with pomp to bear the newly-
    painted log;
For the old Stock Geill, the silly god, was in the
    North Loch drowned,
And they have beaten about about, till a new one
    they have found.
        Sing hey Stock Geill! and ho Stock Geill!
        the old god and the new!
        We dashed his bones against the stones,
        and his stump in flinders flew!

There goes a stir through all the streets, a buzz
    through all the town;
With banners, flags, and crosses, they are walking up
    and down;

The Regent Queen, the wily Guise, put on her
  proudest smile,
And busked her in her brawest gown, to march with
  the young Stock Geill;
      Sing hey Stock Geill! and ho'Stock Geill!
        the old god and the new!
      We'll dash his bones against the stones, and
        shame the shaveling crew!

A marmoset! a marmoset! the devil work them
  sorrow!
They've brought him from the Grey Friars, and
  nailed him to a barrow!
Then on their heads they lift him, and with sounding pomp they come,
With Latin rant, and snivelling chant, and pipe, and
  fife, and drum.
      Sing hey Stock Geill! and ho Stock Geill!
        this day the priests shall rue!
      Against the stones we'll dash the bones o'
        the idol painted new!

A marmoset! a marmoset! the puppet-god to show
West about, and east about, and round about they go;
Along the Luckenbooths they trail, and down to
  Big Jack's Close,
And the bone of his arm, to work a charm, they kiss
  at the Abbey Cross!
      Sing hey Stock Geill! and ho Stock Geill!
        this kissing ye shall rue!
      We'll dash your bones against the stones,
        though you're painted fresh and new!

Now hold your god, ye shaveling loons! for the
    Queen she's gone to dine,
Full weary from the march, I ween, with Sandy
    Carpentine;
There brews a storm betwixt the Bows—the crowd
    looks black and grim!
They rush!—they spring!—hold fast your god!
    they'll tear him limb from limb!
        Sing hey Stock Geill! and ho Stock Geill!
          this dainty godling new!
        They mass their bands, and with strong
          hands they'll do! they'll do! they'll do!

They rived the nails, they seized him by the feet—
    I tell thee true,
They dashed his head against the stones—his stump
    in flinders flew.
Thou young Stock Geill, and wilt thou die, poor imp,
    and give no token?
Thy father had a stouter skull, was not so lightly
    broken!
        Sing hey Stock Geill! and ho Stock Geill!
          the silly godling new!
        We dashed his bones against the stones,
          and his stump in flinders flew!

Then hurly burly! light as straw the priests were
    blown asunder;
They puffed and blew, they panted hot, they gaped
    with foolish wonder;
Down go their crosses! up their skirts! their caps fly
    in the air;

Their surplice flaps; they run as fast as them their
    legs can bear!
        Like crows at pop of gun, the grey and
            black-stoled friars flew,
        'Mid curse and sneer, and gibe and jeer,
            and merry, wild halloo!

And so this gest was bravely done that gave the Pope
    a shog,
That now no stout Scotch knee might bend before
    a painted log!
The Devil's lumber-room we swept—for thus John
    Knox did say;
' *Pull down the rookery, and the rooks will quickly fly*
    away! '
        We left no trappings of Stock Geill; that
            day we ne'er shall rue,
        When we dashed his bones against the
            stones, and his stump in flinders flew!

THE EMIGRANT LASSIE

As I came wandering down Glen Spean
    Where the braes are green and grassy,
With my light step I overtook
    A weary-footed lassie.

She had one bundle on her back,
    Another in her hand,
And she walked as one who was full loath
    To travel from the land.

Quoth I, 'My bonnie lass!'—for she
  Had hair of flowing gold,
And dark brown eyes, and dainty limbs,
  Right pleasant to behold—

'My bonnie lass, what aileth thee,
  On this bright summer day,
To travel sad and shoeless thus
  Upon the stony way?

'I'm fresh and strong, and stoutly shod,
  And thou art burdened so;
March lightly now, and let me bear
  The bundles as we go.'

'No, no!' she said, 'that may not be;
  What's mine is mine to bear;
Of good or ill, as God may will,
  I take my portioned share.'

'But you have two, and I have none;
  One burden give to me;
I'll take that bundle from thy back
  That heavier seems to be.'

'No, no!' she said; '*this*, if you will,
  That holds—no hand but mine
May bear its weight from dear Glen Spean
  'Cross the Atlantic brine!'

'Well, well! but tell me what may be
  Within that precious load,

R

Which thou dost bear with such fine care
　　Along the dusty road?

'Belike it is some present rare
　　From friend in parting hour;
Perhaps, as prudent maidens wont,
　　Thou tak'st with thee thy dower.'

She drooped her head, and with her hand
　　She gave a mournful wave:
'Oh, do not jest, dear sir!—it is
　　Turf from my mother's grave!'

I spoke no word: we sat and wept
　　By the road-side together;
No purer dew on that bright day
　　Was dropt upon the heather.

TRANSLATIONS FROM THE GAELIC

MARY LAGHACH

(After John MacDonald)

CHORUS

Ho ! my bonnie Mary,
My dainty love, my queen,
The fairest, rarest Mary
On earth was ever seen.
Ho ! my queenly Mary
That made me king of men,
To call thee mine own Mary
Born in the bonnie glen !

I

Young was I and Mary,
  In the windings of Glensmeoil,
When came that imp of Venus,
  And caught us with his wile,
And pierced us with his arrows
  That we thrilled in every pore,
And loved as mortals never loved
  On this green earth before.

II

Oftimes myself and Mary
   Strayed up the bonnie glen,
Our hearts as pure and innocent
   As little children then ;
Boy Cupid finely taught us
   To dally and to toy,
When the shade fell from the green tree,
   And the sun was in the sky.

III

If all the wealth of Albyn
   Were mine, and treasures rare,
What boots all gold and silver,
   If sweet love be not there ?
More dear to me than rubies
   In deepest veins that shine
Is one kiss from the lovely lips
   That rightly I call mine.

IV

Thy bosom's heaving whiteness
   With beauty overbrims,
Like swan upon the waters
   When gentliest it swims ;
Like cotton on the moorland,
   Thy skin is soft and fine,
Thy neck is like the sea-gull
   When dipping in the brine.

V

The locks about thy dainty ears
  Do richly curl and twine ;
Dame Nature rarely grew a wealth
  Of ringlets like to thine.
There needs no hand of hireling
  To twist and plait thy hair,
But where it grew it winds and falls
  In wavy beauty there !

VI

Like snow upon the mountains,
  Thy teeth are pure and white ;
Thy breath is like the cinnamon,
  Thy mouth buds with delight.
Thy cheeks are like the cherries,
  Thine eyelids soft and fair,
And smooth thy brow, untaught to frown,
  Beneath thy golden hair.

VII

The pomp of mighty kaisers
  Our state doth far surpass,
When beneath the leafy coppice
  We lie upon the grass ;
The purple flowers around us
  Outspread their rich array,
Where the lusty mountain streamlet
  Is leaping from the brae.

VIII

Nor harp, nor pipe, nor organ
   From touch of cunning men,
Made music half so eloquent
   As our hearts thrilled with then ;
When the blithe lark lightly soaring,
   And the mavis on the spray,
And the cuckoo in the greenwood,
   Sang hymns to greet the May.

MY LOVE SHE IS FAIRER

(After Ewan MacLachlan)

I

My love she is fairer
Than swan when it swims,
Or the foam of the sea
When on pebbles it brims ;
Like milk in the milk-pail
When purest its flow,
Or tips of the pine tree
New sprinkled with snow.

II

Her ringlets are floating
In golden display,
Like cloudlets that sail
O'er the blossomy brae !

Her cheeks like the roses
When freshest their hue,
And the sun on May morning
Is kissing the dew.

III

Like Venus when brightest
She looks from the sky,
Is the charm of her look
And the trick of her eye.
Her neck it is jewelled
With beauty and grace,
Like the bright silver moon
When the stars hide their face.

IV

The lark and the mavis,
In field and on spray,
Pour greeting full-throated
In praise of the May ;
But the lark has no skill,
And the mavis no glee,
When my lass thrills the air
With sweet soul-melodie !

V

When summer with daisies
Has spotted the lea,
And the home of the warbler
Is flooded with glee,

I wander alone
'Neath the green-waving tree,
And I sing of the maid
That brings summer to me !

MO CHAILINN DILIS DONN

I

MAY health and joy be with you,
My bonnie nut-brown maid,
With your dress so trim and tidy,
And your hair of bonnie braid.
Thy voice to me is music
When heavy I may be,
And it heals my heart's deep sorrow
To speak a word with thee.

II

'Tis in sadness that I'm rocking
This night upon the sea,
Right scanty is my slumber
When thy smile is far from me ;
'Tis on thee that I am thinking,
'Tis thy face that I behold,
And if I may not find thee
May I lie beneath the mould.

III

Thine eyes are like the blaeberry
Full and fresh upon the brae ;
Thy cheeks blush like the rowans
On a mellow autumn day.
If the gossips say I hate thee,
'Tis an ugly lie they tell,
Each day's a year to me since
I left my lovely Nell.

IV

They said that I did leave thee
To feed on lovelier cheer,
That I turned my back upon thee
For thy kiss was no more dear;
O never heed their tattle,
My bonnie, bonnie lass,
Thy breath to me is sweeter
Than the dew upon the grass.

V

Before we heaved our anchor
Their evil speech began,
That you no more should see me
The false and faithless man ;
Droop not thy head, my darling,
My heart is all thine own,
No power from thee can part me
But cruel death alone.

VI

There are story-telling people
In the world, great and small,
Their heart it swells with poison,
And their mouth it droppeth gall ;
Ev'n let them spin their lies now,
They'll see the thing that's true,
When the minister shall speak the word
That maketh one of two.

VII

The knot of love that binds us
Is tied full sure and tight ;
What matters if they wrong me,
When I know that I am right ?
There's many a rich curmudgeon
Frets his heart with bitter spleen ;
But I can live, and love, and laugh,
Although my purse be lean.

BEN DORAIN

(After Duncan Ban)

I

Honour be to Ben Dorain
    Above all Bens that be !
Beneath the sun mine eyes beheld
    No lovelier Ben than he ;

With his long smooth stretch of moor,
And his nooks remote and sure
  For the deer,
When he smiles in the face of day,
And the breeze sweeps o'er the brae
  Keen and clear;
With his greenly-waving woods,
And his grassy solitudes,
And the stately herds that fare
  Feeding there;
And the troop with white behind,
When they scent the common foe,
Then wheel to sudden flight
  In a row,
Proudly snuffing at the wind
  As they go.

Right mettlesome is he,
The stag with lightsome glee;
  Who like him,
When he paces on the side
Of the Ben, with healthy pride,
So gallant and so gay,
In the fashion of the brae,
  Neat and trim?
No cause hath he to fear
The wearing of his gear
  With the time,
When with mantle of the red,
Round his shoulders bravely spread,
  He doth climb.
And a youth doth walk behind,

With his face against the wind,
And with danger in his mind
    To the deer.
His hand is firm and steady,
And his eight-grooved gun is ready
    With its gear,
With its flint full sharp and keen,
And its trigger close and clean
    To the hand;
When the hammer right and tight
On the pan's smooth lid shall smite
It will bring a deadly light
    At command;
With a bore of honest fame,
And a stock that none may blame,
From a gun of goodly shape
No deer may find escape
    In the land.
For the hunter hath a skill
That will work his wary will
Though the quarry on the hill
    Flee like wind;
And should Donald with his men,
Stoutly striding through the glen,
Mark his prey with cunning ken
    From behind,
O the bullets then will fly
Like lightning from the sky
    On thy head,
And the hind that walks the Ben
In her gory garment then
    Will lie dead!

II

'Tis a nimble little hind,
Giddy-headed like her kind,
That goes sniffing up the wind
     In her scorning;
With her nostrils sharp and keen,
Somewhat petulant I ween,
'Neath the crag's rim she is seen
    . In the morning;
For she feareth to come down
From the broad and breezy crown
     Of Ben Dorain,
Lest the hunter's cruel shot
In the low encircled spot
     Should be pouring.
She hath breath in breast at will
As she scampers o'er the hill
     Without panting,—
Ruddy wealth of healthy blood
From the lusty fatherhood
Of Ben Dorain's antlered brood
     Finely vaunting;
And I stand with charmèd ear
     As I go,
If the echo I may hear
     Of her low.
And she seeketh round about
For the stag I little doubt,
When the season of the year
Brings hot passion to the deer:

The stag she seeks to please
In the flaunting of the breeze,
When he lifts his haughty head,
With his horns so grandly spread
        Loudly roaring ;
And right well knoweth he
All the leafy nooks that be
        In Ben Dorain.
Though in sooth it passeth me
All the antlered troops to tell
That sweep through dale and dell
        In Ben Dorain,
The hind I know full well,
With her slender shapely limb
So fashioned and so trim,
When she leads her dappled brood
Through the rough and tangled wood
        Up the pass ;
You will never with your ken
Mark her flitting paces when
With lightsome tread she trips
O'er the light unbroken tips
        Of the grass ;
Not in all the islands three,
Nor wide Europe, may it be
That a step so light and clean
        Hath been seen,
When she sniffs the mountain breeze
And goes wandering at her ease,
Or sports as she may please
        On the green ;
Not she will ever feel

Fret or evil humour when
She makes a sudden wheel,
And flies with rapid heel
    O'er the Ben;
With her fine and frisking ways
She steals sorrow from her days,
Nor shall old age ever press
On her head with sore distress
    In the glen.
And surely she doth wear
A dress both rich and rare
In firm flesh and healthy looks
    Much excelling,
With the green and grassy nooks
Of the forest fresh and fair
    For her dwelling.
And for choice food in sooth
She hath a dainty tooth
When she wanders at her will
Through the green depths of the hill,
    Richly storing
For her fawns sweet milk that flows
From soft mountain grass that grows
    On Ben Dorain;
Stout nurslings of the hill,
Whom the cold blasts may not chill
    Of the mountain,
As they foot it to and fro,
Drinking vigour as they go,
From the pure untainted flow
    Of the fountain;
With no sorrow in their heart,

As from glen to glen they dart
    On the mountain.
Nor need they fear the snow,
    Nor the swelling
Of the storm, nor winds that blow
    Sharply yelling,
Though no shapely house their own
Of the well-compacted stone
    They can show;
Yet with prudent haste they hurry
To their refuge in the corrie
    Which they know,
'Neath the hollows of the rocks,
'Mid the rugged stumps and stocks
'Neath the boulders and the blocks
    Lying low.

III

My delight it was to rise
With the early morning skies,
    All aglow,
And to brush the dewy height
Where the deer in airy state
    Wont to go;
At least a hundred brace
Of the lofty antlered race,
When they left their sleeping-place,
    Light and gay;
When they stood in trim array,
And with low deep-breasted cry,
Flung their breath into the sky,
    From the brae:

When the hind, the pretty fool,
Would be rolling in the pool
    At her will;
Or the stag in gallant pride,
Would be strutting at the side
Of his haughty-headed bride,
    On the hill.
And sweeter to my ear
Is the concert of the deer
    In their roaring,
Than when Erin from her lyre
Warmest strains of Celtic fire
    May be pouring;
And no organ sends a roll
So delightsome to my soul,
As the branchy-crested race,
When they quicken their proud pace
And bellow in the face
    Of Ben Dorain.
O what joy to view the stag
When he rises 'neath the crag,
And from depth of hollow chest
Sends his bell across the waste,
While he tosses high his crest,
    Proudly scorning.
And from milder throat the hind,
Lows an answer to his mind,
With the younglings of her kind
    In the morning;
With her vivid swelling eye,
While her antlered lord is nigh,
She sweeps both earth and sky,

S

Far away;
And beneath her eyebrow grey
Lifts her lid to greet the day,
And to guide her turfy way
    O'er the brae.
O how lightsome is her tread,
When she gaily goes ahead
O'er the green and mossy bed
    Of the rills;
When she leaps with such a grace
You will own her pretty pace
Ne'er was hindmost in the race,
    When she wills;
Or when with sudden start
She defies the hunter's art,
And is vanished like a dart
    O'er the hills !
And her food full well she knows,
In the forest where she goes,
Where the rough old pasture grows
    To her mind.
Stiff grass of virtue rare,
Glossy fatness to prepare,
'Neath her coat of shining hair,
    To the hind;
And for drink she hath the well,
Where the water-cresses dwell,
Far sweeter to her taste,
In the freshness of the waste,
    Than sweet wine;
The blushing daisy-tips
Are a dainty to her lips,

As the nodding grass she clips,
     Very fine;
St John's wort too she knows,
And where the sweet primrose
And the spotted orchis grows,
     She will dine.
With such food and drink, I ween,
You will never find them lean,
But girt with pith and power,
To stand stoutly in the hour
     Of distress;
And though laden on the back
With weighty fat no lack,
With well-compacted limb
They will wear it light and trim,
     Like a dress.
O how pleasant 'twas to see
How happy they would be,
When they gathered all together
To their home upon the heather,
     In the gloaming!
At the bottom of the hill
They were safe from touch of ill,
In their nook of shelter tight,
When they rested for the night
     From their roaming.
What though the nights were long,
And the winds were sharp and strong
     In their roaring,
Wrapt in thick fur of the red,
Where the moor is widely spread,
Here they make their turfy bed,

And their sleep was sweet and sound,
With no wish beyond the bound
    Of Ben Dorain.

IV

For Ben Dorain lifts his head
    In the air,
That no Ben was ever seen
With his grassy mantle spread,
And rich swell of leafy green,
    May compare;
And 'tis passing strange to me
When his sloping side I see
    That so grand
And beautiful a Ben
Should not flourish among men,
In the scutcheon and the ken
    Of the land.
'Tis plenished o'er and o'er,
With rich gifts a fruitful store,
You will seek and far explore
    Ere you find;
Not a single spot is bare,
From the jewelled greenness there,
And blossoms waving fair
    In the wind;
Where the cock, the prideful-breasted,
    Swells his crow,
And the birds, the gentle-nested,
    Pour the flow
Of their voicing and rejoicing,
    As they go;

There the roebuck too is seen,
So nimble on the green
    Of the brae,
When he runs and never tumbles,
When he climbs and never stumbles,
    All the way;
With sharp horn upon his head,
And stout tramping hoof to tread,
With a soul of joyous brightness,
And long limbs of limber lightness,
And a tidy tripping tightness,
    He will climb,
Through the brushwood and the fern,
With brave dash of unconcern,
On the low and lushy meadow,
'Neath the mighty mountain shadow,
Or high upon the jag
Of the mist-engirdled crag,
    All sublime.
When the heat is in his blood,
He will dart from out the wood,
    Nothing slow;
He will gather up his might,
Like an arrow drawn for flight
    From the bow;
And then spring with lightsome skill
To the nook behind the hill,
Where he pleasures at his will
    With the doe.
And in sooth it suits her well
With her dappled brood to dwell
    In the glen,

This coquettish little doe,
That is waiting for her beau
  From the Ben.
With an eye so keen and clear,
With an ear so quick to hear,
And rapid hoofs that clear
The long bleak moor behind
  Like the wind.
If all the mighty race
Of the Fin should give her chase,
  Or the men
Who receive the golden pay
Of King George, in red array,
She would mock their lagging way
  On the Ben.
If only free from scot,
To their powder and their shot,
  She might go,
No man of mortal kin,
Would bring sorrow to the skin
  Of the doe ;
Such a web of shifting ways,
In the windings of the braes,
  She will try ;
And though she shy the race
Of the hounds in panting chase,
Up the steepest granite face
  She will fly,
Till she triumph o'er the foe,
This tricksy little doe,
As she tosses her light head
  In the air ;

Then crouching she will lie,
With a wakeful watching eye,
And the dappled people nigh
    To her lair.

v

This is my pretty doe,
With her fine fantastic ways,
As so lightly she will go,
With her slender shapely limb,
'Neath the green and shaggy rim
    Of the braes;
Sweet leafage of the wood
And crisp heather for her food,
    She will praise:
Very light of heart, I ween,
Right sprightly is her mien,
And her frown was never seen
    On the Ben,
Though a foolish thought will flit
Through her slight unsteady wit
In a gay and giddy fit,
    Now and then;
But right modest is my doe,
And in grace is nothing scant,
When she quietly will go
To her home and hidden haunt
    In the glen;
And my vagrant little doe,
When she wanders far and free
On the rough and mottled meadow,
Where the big rock flings a shadow,

On Monday and on Sunday
    You may see;
And well she knows to find
The bushy coppice nigh,
Where in covert from the wind
    She may lie;
The screened and shaded place
Which the tempest's rapid race
And the thunder's rolling pace
    Passes by.
And when she wills to drink,
Straight she stands upon the brink
    Of the fountain
That comes gushing from a chink
    In the mountain;
And she taketh in a wealth
Of freshness and of health
    From the draught,
Such as mortal never knew
Strong ale of stiffest brew
    When he quaffed.
And when the mountain ranger
Brings glimpse of sudden danger
    To the doe,
She hath limbs of supple length
That will try the hunter's strength
    Round and round,
As he follows every fit
Of her rapid-shifting wit
    O'er the ground.
O how oft I felt the grace
Of her light-complexioned face,

And her warm coat's ruddy pride
On the healthy mountain side,
Not to mention winning ways,
And points of pretty praise
  Many mo;
In Europe far and near
She hath fleetness without peer,
And the sharpest ear to hear
  That I. know.

VI

Right pleasant was the view
Of that fleet red-mantled crew,
As with sounding hoof they trod
O'er the green and turfy sod
  Up the brae,
As they sped with lightsome hurry
Through the rock-engirded corrie,
With no lack of food, I ween,
When they cropped the banquet green
  All the way.
O grandly did they gather,
In a jocund troop together,
  In the corrie of the Fern
With light-hearted unconcern;
Or by the smooth green loan
Of Achalader were shown,
Or by the ruined station
Of the old heroic nation
  Of the Fin,
Or by the willow rock
Or the witch-tree on the knock

The branchy-crested flock
    Might be seen.
Nor will they stint the measure
Of their frolic and their pleasure
    And their play,
When with airy-footed amble
At their freakish will they ramble
    O'er the brae,
With their prancing and their dancing,
And their ramping and their stamping,
And their plashing and their washing
    In the pools,
Like lovers newly wedded,
Light-hearted, giddy-headed
    Little fools.
No thirst have they beside
The mill-brook's flowing tide
And the pure well's lucid pride
    Honey-sweet ;
A spring of lively cheer,
Sparkling cool and clear,
And filtered through the sand
    At their feet ;
'Tis a life-restoring flood
To repair the wasted blood
The cheapest and the best in all the land ;
And vainly gold will try
For the Queen's own lips to buy
    Such a treat.
From the rim it trickles down
Of the mountain's granite crown
    Clear and cool ;

Keen and eager though it go
Through your veins with lively flow,
Yet it knoweth not to reign
In the chambers of the brain
  With misrule ;
Where dark water-cresses grow
You will trace its quiet flow,
With mossy border yellow,
So mild, and soft, and mellow,
  In its pouring.
With no slimy dregs to trouble
The brightness of its bubble
As it threads its silver way
From the granite shoulders grey
  Of Ben Dorain.
Then down the sloping side
It will slip with glassy slide
  Gently welling,
Till it gather strength to leap,
With a light and foamy sweep,
To the corrie broad and deep
  Proudly swelling ;
Then bends amid the boulders,
'Neath the shadow of the shoulders
  Of the Ben,
Through a country rough and shaggy,
So jaggy and so knaggy,
Full of hummocks and of hunches,
Full of stumps and turfs and bunches,
Full of bushes and of rushes,
  In the glen,
Through rich green solitudes,

And wildly hanging woods
With blossom and with bell,
In rich redundant swell,
    And the pride
Of the mountain daisy there,
And the forest everywhere,
With the dress and with the air
    Of a bride.

VII

On the moor both broad and bare
Swept by breezy mountain air,
Where the rifted hollow goes,
And the rocks with jutting nose
    Sharply run,
There the bonnie heather corrie
Spreads forth its purple glory
    To the sun,
Where the air is sweet and mild,
Where the fawn, the mountain child,
    Comes to view,
And the dappled people wild
    Not a few.
Right snug the shelter there
Boon Nature did prepare
    For the hind
From the driving and the tearing,
And the cutting edge unsparing
    Of the wind ;
She, the sweetheart of the stag,
When he gazes down the crag,

With hoof untaught to lag
    On the Ben;
No cassocked priest they need
To make their marriage speed
    There and then.
A healthy bride is she,
Right fine and fair to see,
    Nice and sweet;
If you kissed her you would know
That the breath from her doth go
    Very sweet.
This corrie is the praise
    Of all men
Who trained in hunting ways
Ever came to feed their gaze
    On a Ben;
And 'tis here in autumn weather
That the hunters come together,
When the breeze is racing shrill
Through the big gaps of the hill
    Down the glen.
All fruitfulness is there
That springeth fresh and fair,
Where the rainy virtue rare
    Will be pouring;
All pleasantness it knows
Of the scent that largely flows
From the wild rasp and the rose
    On Ben Dorain;
With stream and streamlet too
Where fishes not a few
    Suffer scath,

When the flashing light will bribe
The thoughtless finny tribe
    To the death ;
Where a stalwarth youth shall stand
With a strong spear in his hand
    Right and tight,
And will pierce them with the pine,
Where the gleaming torches shine,
    Through the night.
Right pleasant too to watch
    At the station
Of the eddy dark and deep
Where the salmon love to rise,
And the spotted trout will leap,
    A dainty meal to catch
    With surprise
From the light and buzzing nation
    Of the flies.
Such is my corrie fine ;
    In the bound
Of the broad earth and the brine
No virtue like to thine,
Thou heather corrie fine,
    May be found.

VIII

The hind that dwelleth in this glen
    Is light of foot and airy ;
Who tracks her way upon the Ben
    Must be full wise and wary.
Softly, softly on her traces

He must steal with noiseless paces,
     Nigh and still more nigh,
Lest she turn with sudden starting,
And, like feathered arrow darting,
     Cheat his eager eye.
He must know to dodge behind
Rock and block in face of wind,
In the ditch and in the pit
Dripping lie and soaking sit,
     Stoop, and creep, and crawl,
Ever with quick eye to note
Face of earth and clouds that float
     In the azure hall.
Wisely, wisely wending round
Where she surely will be found;
     And then planted surely
Where with fixed and steady aim
He may mark the dappled game
     For his own securely;
Then his gun he well must know
How to handle 'gainst the foe,
With his firm forefinger's end
He the trigger back must bend;
New and closely locked the flint,
Smart and sharp the hammer's dint,
Stroke whence flies a spark that never
Failed to kindle flame, however
     Small the smutty grain;
Powder dry—well-seasoned stuff—
Rammed with tow both rough and tough,
That without fail both loud and large
May speed the deadly dun discharge

Of smoke and leaden rain ;
'Tis a pleasant sight, I ween,
When the lusty youth are seen
In their hunting gear
Brushing briskly through the heather,
Planted on the grass together
Watching of the deer,
With a gun that none may blame,
And a flash of sudden flame,
Winged with mortal fear ;
And the hounds, a restless crew,
Keen for bloody work to do,
Sharply nosing all the path,
Full of rapine and of wrath,
Yelping, howling at the sight,
Leaping with a wild delight ;
With their tails they lash their side
Bristling with their hair,
Their huge jaws they open wide,
With lowering brows they frown,
With forward tongue and panting breath,
Exulting in the scent of death,
They for the feast of blood prepare
When the deer is down.
And now their time is come ; they know
Full well the winding way to go,
With rapid feet and sure,
Up and down, and to and fro
Across the breezy moor ;
The mighty Ben, the rocks reply,
As with tempest speed they fly,
To the howling and the yelling,

And the deathful bustle swelling
    O'er the breezy moor.
And now behold, with cunning wending,
    They have chased her down,
To the narrow glen descending
    From the mountain's crown.
In the pool of treacherous water
She must float and she must flounder
With a ring of death around her;
Looking in the face of slaughter
    She must now abide,
With her dear life's purple tide
    Welling from her side;
For now they hold her in their grasp
    With a grip of death;
While the yelping hounds confound her
She must plash and she must flounder,
She must pant and she must gasp,
    Till she find no breath.
But I must cease to flood your ear
With all I know about the deer
    And the fine craft of stalking;
'Twould leave you deaf the half to hear,
And me drive from my senses sheer,
    With such unmeasured talking.

T

TRANSLATIONS FROM THE GERMAN

DIE WACHT AM RHEIN

(Max Schneckenburger)

A LOUD cry swells like thunder's peal,
Like roaring wave, like clashing steel :
The Rhine, the Rhine, the German Rhine !
Who'll come to watch the German Rhine ?
    Dear fatherland, no fear be thine,
      Brave hearts and true shall watch the Rhine.

From heart to heart the quick thrill flies,
And lightning leaps from countless eyes,
Where each true German, sword in hand,
Guards the old border of the land.
    Dear fatherland, etc.

And though with Death he make his bed,
No stranger foot thy bank shall tread ;
Rich, as in waves thy regal flood,
Is Deutschland in true hero-blood.
    Dear fatherland, etc.

He lifts his eye to Heaven's high crown,
Whence his high-hearted sires look down,
And swears an oath to keep thy flood
As German as his true heart's blood.
    Dear fatherland, etc.

Till the last drop shall drain our veins,
While in one arm one blade remains,
And while one fuming shot is sped,
No Frankish foot thy bank shall tread.
    Dear fatherland, etc.

The oath flies forth, the billows flow,
The forward banners flout the foe !
The Rhine, the Rhine, the German Rhine,
True Germans all, we watch the Rhine !
    Dear fatherland, no fear be thine,
    We watch, true Germans all, the Rhine !

WAS GLÄNZT DORT VOM WALDE?
LÜTZOW'S WILD CHASE

(Körner)

WHAT gleams from yon wood, in the bright sun-
    shine ?
  Hark ! nearer and nearer 'tis sounding ;
It hurries along, black line upon line,
And the shrill-voiced horns in the wild chase join,
  The soul with dark horror confounding :
And if the black troopers' name you'd know,
'Tis Lützow's wild Jäger—a-hunting they go !

From hill to hill, through the dark wood they hie,
　　And warrior to warrior is calling ;
Behind the thick bushes in ambush they lie,
The rifle is heard, and the loud war-cry,
　　In rows the Frank minions are falling :
And if the black troopers' name you'd know,
'Tis Lützow's wild Jäger—a-hunting they go !

Where the bright grapes glow, and the Rhine roll
　　wide,
　　He weened they would follow him never ;
But the pursuit came like the storm in its pride,
With sinewy arms they parted the tide,
　　And reached the far shore of the river :
And if the dark swimmers' name you'd know,
'Tis Lützow's wild Jäger—a-hunting they go !

How roars in the valley the angry fight ;
　　Hark ! how the keen swords are clashing !
High-hearted Ritter are fighting the fight,
The spark of Freedom awakens bright,
　　And in crimson flames it is flashing :
And if the dark Ritter's name you'd know,
'Tis Lützow's wild Jäger—a-hunting they go !

Who gurgle in death, 'mid the groans of the foe,
　　No more the bright sunlight seeing ?
The writhings of death on their face they show,
But no terror the hearts of the freemen know,
　　For the Frantzmen are routed and fleeing :
And if the dark heroes' name you'd know,
'Tis Lützow's wild Jäger—a-hunting they go !

The chase of the German, the chase of the free,
   In hounding the tyrant we strained it !
Ye friends, that love us, look up with glee !
The night is scattered, the dawn we see,
   Though we with our life's-blood have gained it !
And from sire to son the tale shall go :
'Twas Lützow's wild Jäger that routed the foe !

WAS BLASEN DIE TROMPETEN

Why blare loud the trumpets ? — to horse, ye
   hussars !
'Tis the gallant old field-marshal that rides to the
   wars !
So cheerily rides he his own good steed,
So brightly his sword flashes time to his speed ;
     Sound fife, trump, and drum ! for the Germans
       are come !
     Hurrah for right and liberty, the Germans are
       come !

O see how his blue eye, so clear and so kind,
Is beaming, and wave his white locks to the wind !
Like a stout old wine, so mellow and so fine,
O he's the man to marshal the sons of the Rhine !
     Sound, etc.

O he is the man, when all was dark and dim,
Who waved his sword in Heaven's eye—'twas all
   bright to him !

He swore by his true steel to teach them yet aright—
He swore an angry oath—how the Germans can fight.
       Sound, etc.

His good oath he kept : when the war-cry rang,
On his horse, with a bound, bold Blücher sprang ;
And his clear blue eye shot fire to wash the shame
Of Auerstadt and Jena from the German name.
       Sound, etc.

At Lützen, impatient, he headed the van,
Like a strong young lion, the old veteran :
There the Teut first taught the hot Frenchman to
       bleed,
By the altar of freedom, the stone of the Swede.
       Sound, etc.

The Katzbach was red with the fierce-drifting rain,
But eve saw it redder with the blood of the slain !
' Fare-thee-well, fare-thee-well ! and fairly may'st thou
       sail,
And find a grave, false Frantzmann, with the Baltic
       whale.'
       Sound, etc.

Then forward, my brave boys, begun's half done :
We'll teach the nimble Corsican to run, boys, run !
O'er the Elbe, o'er the Elbe, now Preuss and Swede
       advance,
And the fleet Don Cossack with his long, long lance !
       Sound, etc.

On the red field of Leipzig he laid the French pride
    low ;
He blew the blast of freedom loud at Leipzig, Oho !
They fell, there they fell, ne'er to rise from their fall ;
And we cheered old Blücher there—Long live the
    Field-marshal !
      Sound, etc.

Then blow loud, ye trumpets, and tramp, ye hussars !
'Tis our old Field-marshal that rides to the wars :
To the Rhine, to the Rhine, and beyond the Rhine's
    the way,
Thou doughty old Field-marshal, and God be with
    thee aye !
      Sound, etc.

VATER ICH RUFE DICH

KÖRNER'S BATTLE PRAYER

FATHER, I call on Thee !
Clouds from the thunder-voiced cannon enveil me,
Lightnings are flashing, death's thick darts assail me ;
    Ruler of Battles, I call on Thee !
    Father, O lead Thou me !

Father, O lead Thou me !
Lead me to victory, or to death lead me ;
With joy I accept what Thou has decreed me.
    God, as Thou wilt, so lead Thou me !
    God, I acknowledge Thee !

God, I acknowledge Thee !
Where, in still autumn, the sear leaf is falling,
Where peals the battle its thunder appalling ;
Fount of all Grace, I acknowledge Thee !
Father, O bless Thou me !

Father, O bless Thou me !   .
Into Thy hand my soul I resign, Lord ;
Deal, as Thou wilt, with the life that is Thine, Lord.
Living or dying, O bless Thou me !
Father, I praise Thy name !

Father, I praise Thy name !
Not for earth's wealth or dominion contend we ;
The holiest rights of the freeman defend we.
Victor or vanquished, praise I Thee !
God, in Thy name I trust !

God, in Thy name I trust !
When in loud thunder my death-note is knelling,
When from my veins the red blood is welling,
God, in Thy holy name I trust !
Father, I call on Thee !

DU SCHWERDT AN MEINER LINKEN

THE SWORD SONG OF KÖRNER

THOU sword so cheerly shining,
What are thy gleams divining ?
Look'st like a friend on me,
Triumphs my soul in thee.
          Hurrah ! hurrah ! hurrah !

'I love my brave knight dearly,
Therefore I shine so cheerly.
Borne by a gallant knight,
Triumphs the sword so bright.'
        Hurrah ! etc.

Yes, trusty sword, I love thee ;
A true knight thou shalt prove me.
Thee, my beloved, my bride,
I'll lead thee forth in pride.
        Hurrah ! etc.

'My iron-life, clear raying,
I gave it to thy swaying.
Oh, come, and fetch thy bride !
Lead, lead me forth in pride !
        Hurrah ! etc.

The festal trump is blaring,
The bridal dance preparing.
When cannon shakes the glen,
I'll come and fetch thee then.
        Hurrah ! etc.

' Oh, blest embrace that frees me !
My hope impatient sees thee.
Come, bridegroom, fetch thou me ;
Waits the bright wreath for thee ? '
        Hurrah ! etc.

Why in thy sheath art ringing,
Thou iron-soul, fire-flinging ?

So wild with battle's glee,
Why ray'st thou eagerly?
    Hurrah! etc.

'I in my sheath am ringing;
I from my sheath am springing;
Wild, wild with battle's glee,
Ray I so eagerly.'
    Hurrah! etc.

Remain, remain within, love;
Why court the dust and din, love?
Wait in thy chamber small,
Wait till thy true knight call.
    Hurrah! etc.

'Then, speed thee, true knight, speed thee!
To love's fair garden lead me;
Show me the roses red,
Death's crimson-blooming bed.'
    Hurrah! etc.

Then, from thy sheath come free thee!
Come, feed mine eye to see thee!
Come, come, my sword, my bride,
I lead thee forth in pride!
    Hurrah! etc.

'How glorious is the free air!
How whirls the dance with glee there!
Glorious, in sun arrayed,
Gleams, bridal-bright, the blade.'
    Hurrah! etc.

Then up, true Ritter German !
Ye gallant sons of Hermann !
Beats the knight's heart so warm,
With's true love in his arm ;
  Hurrah ! etc.

With stolen looks divining,
Thou, on my left, wert shining.
Now on my right, my bride,
God leads thee forth in pride.
  Hurrah ! etc.

'Then press a kiss of fire on
The bridal mouth of iron.
Woe now or weal betide,
Cursed whoso leaves his bride !
  Hurrah ! etc.

'Then break thou forth in singing,
Thou iron-bride, fire-flinging !
Walk forth in joy and pride !
Hurrah ! thou iron-bride !
  Hurrah ! hurrah ! hurrah !

ADDENDUM

THE POETICAL WORKS OF JOHN STUART BLACKIE

Translations, etc.

1834. Faust, Goethe. (Macmillan & Co.).
1850. Lyrical Dramas of Aeschylus. (Parker).
1866. Homer and the Iliad. (Douglas).
1870. War Songs of the Germans. (Douglas).
1876. The Language and Literature of the Scottish Highlands. (Douglas).
1882. Altavona. (Douglas).
1883. The Wisdom of Goethe. (Blackwood).

Original Verse

1857. Lays and Legends of Ancient Greece. (Sutherland & Knox).
1860. Lyrical Poems. (Sutherland & Knox).
1869. Musa Burschicosa. (Douglas).
1872. Lays of the Highlands and Islands. (Walter Scott).
1876. Songs of Religion and Life. (Douglas).

1877. The Wise Men of Greece.   (Macmillan).
1886. Messis Vitae.   (Macmillan).
1890. A Song of heroes.   (Blackwood).

Numerous poems (uncollected) in 'The Scottish Students' Song Book,' 'The Scotsman,' 'The Pall Mall Gazette,' 'The People's Friend,' 'The Student,' 'The Contemporary Review,' 'Blackwood's Magazine,' 'Cassells' Magazine,' 'The Scot's Magazine,' 'Tait's Magazine,' 'Fraser's Magazine,' 'Alma Mater,' etc., etc., etc.

THE END

Colston & Company, Limited, Printers, Edinburgh

HASTINGS HOUSE,
NORFOLK STREET, STRAND,
January 1897.

Mr. John Macqueen's List.

Works in the Press.

Summer Days for Winter Evenings.

A Series of Nature Idylls. By J. H. CRAWFORD, F.L.S., Author of "The Wild Life of Scotland." Illustrations by JOHN W LLIAMSON. Handsomely bound, in uniform with "The Wild Life of Scotland." Large crown 8vo, 8s. 6d. net.
[*January.*

The Love-Philtre, and Other Poems.

By HELEN F. SCHWEITZER. Royal 8vo, 5s. net.
[*Shortly.*

A Flirtation with Truth.

By CURTIS YORKE, Author of "A Record of Discords," etc. Crown 8vo, 6s. [*End February.*

A Russian Wild Flower.

By E. A. BRAYLEY HODGETTS, Author of "Round about Armenia," etc. Crown 8vo, 6s. [*March.*

L'Abbé Constantin.

By LUDOVIC HALÈVY. Translated from the French by THÉRÈSE BATHEDAT. Crown 8vo.

The Wooing of Avis Grayle.

By CHARLES HANNAN, Author of "Chin Chin Wa," etc. etc. Crown 8vo, 6s.

The Wild Flowers of Scotland.

By J. H. CRAWFORD, F.L.S., Author of "The Wild Life of Scotland," etc. Illustrations by JOHN WILLIAMSON. Handsomely bound, in uniform with Mr. Crawford's other Works. Large crown 8vo, 8s. 6d. net. [*April.*

The Wild Life of Scotland.

By J. H. CRAWFORD, F.L.S.   Illustrations by JOHN WILLIAMSON.   Handsomely bound.   Large crown 8vo, 8s. 6d. net.

Spring Bird Life—Early Burn Fishing—On the Moor—Gulls and Divers—The North Sea—Marine Mammals and Predatory Fishes—Baits and Sea Fishing—Shetland—Loch Leven and Loch Tay—By the Loch-side—The Stag—Among the Border Streams—Feathered Game—Vermin—Autumn Bird Life—Wild Fowl in an Estuary—Winter.

The Times says : " Mr. Crawford's skill in depicting various phases of nature and animal life ought to send his readers forth into the country with eyes ready to note and appreciate many things to which they have, perhaps, hitherto been totally blind. To read papers like ' Gulls and Divers' or ' The North Sea ' on a July day in London is almost the next best thing to being in reality within sound of the waves."

The Spectator says : " This is a very delightful as well as informing book, which, in respect of style, recalls Thoreau rather than either Jefferies or Burroughes. . . . Altogether this book, which belongs to the rare order that can be taken up at any moment and easily read in instalments, is by far the best and most convenient hand-book to Scottish Natural History—in the most comprehensive sense of the word—that has ever been published."

The Saturday Review says : "' Wild Life of Scotland ' is one of those delightful books which one places on the shelf with the Colquhouns and the St. Johns, nor is it possible to give it higher praise. . . . But we might go on indefinitely with our comments on a book which is a wellspring of enjoyment and a mine of information."

The Daily Mail says : " The book is thoroughly enjoyable and exhilarating. Its contents have a wide range of interest. . . . Something worth one's attentive reading is to be found on every page."

The Sketch says : " One of the latest and best works on Natural History and Sport."

The Publisher's Circular says : " The entire contents reach a high level of merit, and those observantly fond of Nature will derive much pleasure from its pages."

The Glasgow Herald says : " This book partakes of the nature of an ' edition de luxe,' and it is one in which the naturalist may well delight, and add to the art corner of his library."

Rod and Gun says : " The illustrations, by Mr. John Williamson, are a graceful addition to this charming volume, which will be duly appreciated, we doubt not, by all good sportsmen."

The Globe says : " This is the very book for the holiday-maker who cares for nature."

Black and White says : " The holiday-maker in Scotland could have no more entertaining volume."

Nature says : " This collection of papers, which represent the result of his (Mr. Crawford's) observations and meditations, are typical of the forms of life in the woods and waters of Scotland ; they are pleasantly written and attractively illustrated, and will interest all country naturalists."

The Scotsman says : " To naturalists and sportsmen, and to all who love and study the ways of birds and fish and four-footed beasts in their own haunts, Mr. Crawford's ' Wild Life of Scotland ' will be a most welcome find. . . . Few have written upon these favourite subjects with greater charm and knowledge."

Mr. Macqueen's New 6s. Novels.

The Sign of the Cross.

A Novel founded on the theme of the famous Play of the same name. By WILSON BARRETT. With a Preface by the Bishop of Truro. Crown 8vo. First Edition of 20,000 Copies exhausted.   [*Second Edition now ready*.

Daily News says : " Few will read unmoved the concluding chapter of a story that has running through it something of the sense of haunting, overmastering fate that impresses one so terribly in Greek tragedy, while it inspires at the same time sympathy for the noblest ideals of humanity."

Christian World says : " The book, as well as the play, is a phenomenon of our time, the significance of which, we believe, is wholly for good.'

Her Ladyship's Income.

By LORIN KAYE. Crown 8vo.   [*Third Edition*.

The Times says : " One of the best novels of the day. The author has more wit, reading, and intellect than the best advertised of the risky school, and she has much less affectation and *préciosité*. Her skill is most remarkable. . . . Her ability is incontestable."

The Daily Chronicle says : " The brightness and smartness of the style is perfectly captivating, and yet withal, when a deeper note is struck, there is discovered a thoughtfulness and grasp which show that the writer has something very much more than a superficial knowledge of men and things."

Truth says : " A brilliant novel."

The Gentlewoman says : " Many parts of the story are realistically truthful, and nowhere is the satire exaggerated. It is a book everybody should read."

The Daily Telegraph says : " A brilliantly-written story . . . teems with bright, cynical, up-to-date dialogue."

Denys D'Auvrillac.

A Story of French Life. By HANNAH LYNCH, Author of " Daughters of Men," etc. Crown 8vo.

Vanity Fair says : " ' Denys D'Auvrillac' is a new character in English-written literature . . . the importance of this book is indubitable . . . the distinguished style gives this novel the air of a classic—a classic which must stand quite by itself in English literature."

The Glasgow Herald says : " Miss Lynch shows a power which is as welcome as it is unusual. . . . One of the most original novels we have read for some time."

Athenæum says : " ' Denys D'Auvrillac' may be honourably distinguished from the rank and file of current fiction."

Pall Mall Gazette says : " It is by intrinsic quality of a superior order that this book excels."

Mr. Macqueen's New 6s. Novels—continued.

The Radical's Wife.

By H. G. M'KERLIE, Author of "Priests and People." Crown 8vo.

The Athenæum says : "'The Radical's Wife' has interest—an interest that mostly centres in Katherine Burns herself. In spite of her dual position as politician and heroine (difficult parts to sustain in fiction and out of it), she remains a fresh and attractive person."

The Birmingham Post says : "A singular compound of love and Socialism, written with great ability, and bears the unmistakable stamp of originality. . . . An excellent novel."

The Daily Telegraph says : "The book is decidedly clever."

At the Sign of the Cross Keys.

A Romance. By PAUL CRESWICK. Crown 8vo, cloth.

The Pall Mall Gazette says : "The writer tells his story in a fresh and spirited manner."

The Dundee Courier says : "Mr. Creswick is to be congratulated on the exquisite romance he has given us.

The Glasgow Herald says : "A well-told and stirring story."

The Dover Chronicle says : "We have rarely seen a novel indicating greater promise. . . . Mr. Creswick is worthy to rank with Stanley Weyman and Gilbert Parker in the matter of style and distinction of literary speech."

Miss Cherry-Blossom of Tôkyô.

A Japanese Novel. By JOHN LUTHER LONG. Crown 8vo.

Saturday Review says : "Miss Cherry-Blossom is the first view of Madame Chrysanthème as the New Woman, educated in Boston, and revolutionising Japanese immemorial custom by her love-making with a young Englishman . . . she is charming. The graceful end to the romance comes all too soon."

Daily Chronicle says : Smart and pretty, and sets forth in a very charming way the joy of life in the land of the art-loving Jap."

Literary World says : "A really Japanese novel. . . . A fresh, artistic, love story, full of human interest."

The Bristol Mercury says : "The book is most cleverly written, and the character of Cherry-Blossom is very wonderfully drawn, and is a most entrancing one."

The Mighty Toltec.

A Story of Adventure. By S. J. ADAIR FITZ-GERALD and S. O. LLOYD. Frontispiece. Crown 8vo.

The Manchester Courier says : "This is one of the best books of adventure that the book season has brought forth.

A Flirtation with Truth.

By CURTIS YORKE, Author of "A Record of Discords," etc. Crown 8vo, 6s.   [*In the Press.*

A Russian Wild Flower.

By E. A. BRAYLEY HODGETTS, Author of "Round about Armenia," etc. Crown 8vo.   [*In the Press.*

Mr. Macqueen's New 3s. 6d. Novels.

My Dear Grenadier.

A Novel. By SYBIL BEATRICE REED, Author of "Sweet Peas." Crown 8vo, 3s. 6d.

The Daily Telegraph says: "A charmingly sprightly story. We do not propose to disclose the dénouement of this pretty story, which is well worthy of perusal, being delicately and felicitously informed with the element of surprise. We sincerely congratulate Miss Reed upon having produced a work of fiction which more than fulfils the promise of her previous romance, 'Sweet Peas.'"

The Glasgow Herald says: "Beatrice Faithful Damer is a charming 'Grenadier.' . . . The book is very pleasantly written and entirely wholesome."

The Spectator says: "There is fun and pathos in the tale, and it is wholesome."

The Dover Telegraph says: "We have seen few novels of late so bright and fresh and charming as 'My Dear Grenadier.'"

A Dream's Fulfilment.

A Sporting Novel. By H. CUMBERLAND BENTLEY. Crown 8vo, 3s. 6d. Second Edition.

The Times says: "To say that 'A Dream's Fulfilment' may be reckoned an unusually excellent work in its *genre*, a wholesome unpretentious book which may be read 'for human pleasure,' is no exaggeration. . . . The book will undoubtedly be regarded as 'ripping.'"

Worthy.

A Novel dealing with the Franco-Prussian War. By Mrs. CADELL. Crown 8vo, 3s. 6d.

The Literary World says: "Is worthy of the ingenuity of that popular favourite, Mr. Stanley Weyman."

You never Know your Luck.

By THEO. IRVING. Crown 8vo, 3s. 6d.

The Daily Telegraph says: "A *fin-de-siècle* society novel of considerably more than average merit, smartly written, replete with interest."

A Cardinal Sin.

By HUGH CONWAY, Author of "Called Back," etc. etc. Eighth Thousand. Crown 8vo, 3s. 6d. Uniform with his other works.

The Westminster Review says: "A capital novel—better far than 'Called Back.' The plot is ingeniously complicated and cleverly unravelled."

Bound Together.

By HUGH CONWAY, Author of "Called Back." Ninth Thousand. Crown 8vo, 3s. 6d. Uniform with his other works.

The Saturday Review says: "Clever, amusing, thrilling, packed full of interest."

Works by Clement Scott.

From "The Bells" to "King Arthur."

A Volume of Dramatic Criticism, dealing exclusively with the Irving Productions at the Lyceum, and containing the Casts of all the most important Revivals at that Theatre since 1871. By CLEMENT SCOTT. Demy 8vo, fully illustrated, 7s. 6d.

Truth says: "All playgoers, especially the enthusiastic Irvingites among them, will welcome the appearance of Mr. Clement Scott's handsome volume."

The Daily News says: "The book will be invaluable to those who are concerned with the history of the contemporary stage."

Pictures of the World.

Pencilled by CLEMENT SCOTT. Crown 8vo, cloth, illustrated, 3s. 6d. Second Edition.

Black and White says: "There is not a dull page in Mr. Scott's volume."

Daily Chronicle says: "Mr. Scott's book is a very joyous record."

Court Journal says: "Mr. Scott is to be congratulated upon a most charming book of travel."

Globe says: "His pen is that of the ready writer, and in these 'pictures' his style is as light and bright as the matter is pleasantly instructive."

Publisher's Circular says: "A distinctly bright and entertaining volume."

Among the Apple Orchards.

By CLEMENT SCOTT. Fcap. 8vo, 1s. 6d.

The Athenæum says: "This is a little volume which no student of late Victorian style can fail to peruse with the deepest interest."

Indifference in Matters of Religion.

By the ABBÉ F. DE LAMENNAIS. Translated from the French, with a Preface by LORD STANLEY of Alderley. Demy 8vo, 12s.

The Spectator says: "The questions with which it deals still burn, perhaps with a greater heat than they did in 1817, when first the volume was published. It is impossible for an Anglican to accept all De Lamennais' statements, but he will feel, we venture to say, more in than out of harmony with him. The translation reads well."

The Catholic Herald says: "A thoroughly good and conscientious translation. The acute penetration, close reasoning, and lofty eloquence which characterise the best French writers, are to be found here in a high degree."

The National Observer says: "This well-executed translation deserves to be read."

Works by Dorothea Gerard.

A Queen of Curds and Cream.

Crown 8vo, cloth, 3s. 6d. Fourth Edition.

Etelka's Vow.

Crown 8vo, cloth, 3s. 6d. Third Edition.

On the Way Through.

Crown 8vo, cloth, 3s. 6d. Second Edition.

Orthodox.

Crown 8vo, cloth, 3s. 6d. Third Edition, ready.

The Standard says: "It would be difficult for the author of 'Lady Baby' to write anything but a clever novel."

The Morning Post says: "Miss Gerard is a novelist who has made a place for herself, in which she stands alone. An excellent delineator of character, she has a charmingly fresh style, and a knowledge of cosmopolitan life in all its phases which is hardly equalled by any other English writer."

Gordon in China and the Soudan.

By A. G. EGMONT HAKE. New Edition. Large crown 8vo, 6s.

The Scotsman says: "The new edition will be especially welcome as bringing the work within reach of a large class of readers, to whom in its original shape it was practically inaccessible."

The Gentlewoman says: "It is a book of pathetic interest, and gives a most sympathetic presentment of a truly great man."

A Manual of Italian Literature.

By F. H. CLIFFE. Crown 8vo, 6s.

The Glasgow Herald says: "Judged as a whole the book is a useful one. . . The merits of the volume are by no means inconsiderable."

The Scotsman says: "Mr. Cliffe approves himself a thoughtful and well-informed guide . . . should give both zest and aid to the study of Italian letters."

WILLIAM LE QUEUX in *The Literary World* says: "Considerable thought and pains have been bestowed upon this book, for the critical estimates are, for the most part, sound, the examples of style are generally well chosen, and the biographical detail obtained from the best available sources. Mr. Cliffe gives a little too much prominence perhaps to his pet writer Leopardi; nevertheless the work has few faults, and those of a trivial character. It is useful and may be relied upon, as well as being interesting."

A Narrative of the Boer War.

By T. F. CARTER. Demy 8vo, 10s. 6d.

The Sheffield Telegraph says: "This great work is history, exhaustive, impartial, and realistic."

The Pall Mall Gazette says: "The best book on the subject."

The African Critic says: "The book is generally recognised as a standard work on the subject."

South Africa says: "The best work of its class."

Lesser Questions.

A Book dealing with the Principal Social Questions of the Day. By LADY JEUNE. Crown 8vo, cloth, 6s.

The Times says: "Not only are these great questions in themselves, but they involve, either directly or indirectly, some of the greatest of all the great questions of our time—nothing less than the social welfare and prospects of the whole body politic. On these questions, Lady Jeune writes from direct experience and often with excellent judgment, with full sympathy, and yet not with unregulated enthusiasm."

Daily Telegraph says: "Lady Jeune, in these papers, blends grave and gay in a manner to engage all readers, and to instruct not a few."

Gunner Jingo's Jubilee.

By Major-General TOM BLAND STRANGE (late R.A.). With 15 full-page Illustrations, Plans, Maps, and numerous Thumbnail Sketches. Demy 8vo, 5s. Third Edition.

The Times says: "His reminiscences are full of stirring incident, told in a very lively, at times almost a boisterous fashion, which recalls the rollicking style of Lever in his earlier days."

Saturday Review says: "An entertaining, clever, if somewhat eccentric book, which we are glad to see has reached a second edition."

The Selected Poems of John Stuart Blackie.

With a Portrait after the Painting by J. H. LORIMER, A.R.S.A. Edited, with an Appreciation, by his Nephew, ARCHIBALD STODART WALKER. Crown 8vo, 5s.

The Scotsman says: "A fairly representative selection, with an introduction delightful to read. . . . The book will be welcome to many."

The Daily News says: "This book will abide, or should abide, for the sake of its introduction."

Cheer, Boys, Cheer!

Memories of Men and Music. Portrait. By HENRY RUSSELL. Crown 8vo, 3s. 6d.

The Daily Chronicle says: "There is ample store of anecdotes in this cheap and handsome volume."

Catalogue of Publications

Albert Chevalier.
A Record by Himself and BRYAN DALY. Illustrated. Crown 8vo, 6s.

Among the Apple Orchards.
By CLEMENT SCOTT. Fcap. 8vo, 1s. 6d.

At the Sign of the Cross Keys.
A last Century Romance. By PAUL CRESWICK. Crown 8vo, 6s.

Banshee's Warning, The.
By Mrs. J. H. RIDDELL, Author of "The Head of the Firm." Crown 8vo, 6s.

Blackie, John Stuart, Selected Poems of.
Portrait. Edited, with an Appreciation, by his Nephew, ARCHIBALD STODART WALKER. Crown 8vo, 5s.

Boer War, A Narrative of the.
By T. F. CARTER. Demy 8vo, 10s. 6d. New Edition.

Bound Together.
By HUGH CONWAY, Author of "Called Back." Crown 8vo, 3s. 6d. Uniform with his other works. Ninth Thousand.

Captain Kangaroo.
A Story of Australian Life. By J. EVELYN. Crown 8vo, 7s. 6d.

Cardinal Sin, A.
By HUGH CONWAY, Author of "Called Back," etc. Crown 8vo, 3s. 6d. Eighth Thousand.

Cheer, Boys, Cheer!
Memories of Men and Music. Frontispiece. By HENRY RUSSELL. Crown 8vo, 3s. 6d.

Chesney, General F. R., Life of the late.
The Colonel Commandant Royal Artillery, D.C.L., F.R.G.S., etc. By his WIFE and DAUGHTER. Edited by STANLEY LANE-POOLE. Portrait and Map. Second Edition. Demy 8vo, 12s.

Court of England under George IV., The.
Founded on a Diary interspersed with Letters written by Queen Caroline and various other Distinguished Persons. Two Volumes, demy 8vo, 25s.

Cry of the Curlew, The.
A Bush Yarn. By GUY EDEN. Crown 8vo, cloth, 3s. 6d.

Denys D'Auvrillac.
A Story of French Life. By HANNAH LYNCH, Author of "Daughters of Men," etc. etc. Crown 8vo, 6s.

Diderot's Thoughts on Art and Style.
With some of his Shorter Essays. Selected and Translated by BEATRIX L. TOLLEMACHE (Hon. Mrs. Lionel Tollemache). Crown 8vo, 5s.

Diogenes' Sandals.
A Novel. By Mrs. ARTHUR KENNARD. Second Edition. Crown 8vo, cloth, 3s. 6d.

Double Ruin, A.
A Novel. By Mrs. A. HART (Sophie Kappey), Author of "A Modern Martyr." Crown 8vo, 3s. 6d.

Drama Birthday Book, The.
Compiled from the Works of the Dramatists of the Day. By PERCY S. PHILLIPS. Fcap. 8vo, art linen, 3s. 6d.; morocco, 10s. 6d.

Dream's Fulfilment, A.
A Sporting Novel. By H. CUMBERLAND BENTLEY. Second Edition. Crown 8vo, 3s. 6d.

Dr. Fitz-Simond's Sweethearts.
A Novel. By GERVAS WILLIAMS. Crown 8vo, 3s. 6d.

Duke Ernest of Saxe-Coburg-Gotha, Memoirs of (Brother of the late Prince Consort of England).

With Portraits of Prince Albert and Duke Ernest. Four Volumes, demy 8vo, cloth, 55s.

Early Bird, The, and other Drawing-Room Plays.

By BEATRIX L. TOLLEMACHE (Hon. Mrs. Lionel Tollemache). Crown 8vo, 2s. 6d.

Etelka's Vow.

A Novel. By DOROTHEA GERARD, Author of "On the Way Through," "Orthodox," "Lady Baby," etc. etc., and Joint-Author of "The Waters of Hercules" and "Reata." Third Edition. Crown 8vo, 3s. 6d.

For the Sake of the Family.

A Novel. By MAY CROMMELIN, Author of "Love Knots," etc. Second Edition. Crown 8vo, 3s. 6d.

Four Red Nightcaps.

By C. J. HYNE, Author of "The Honour of Thieves," etc. Crown 8vo, 3s. 6d.

From "The Bells" to "King Arthur."

By CLEMENT SCOTT. Fully Illustrated. Demy 8vo, 7s. 6d.

Gordon in China and the Soudan.

By A. EGMONT HAKE. New Edition. Crown 8vo, 6s.

Gunner Jingo's Jubilee.

By Major-General TOM BLAND STRANGE, late R.A. With Fifteen full-page Illustrations, Plans, Maps, and numerous Thumb-nail Sketches. Third Edition. Demy 8vo, cloth, 5s.

He Went Out with the Tide.

By GUY EDEN, Author of "The Cry of the Curlew." Crown 8vo, 6s.

Her Ladyship's Income.

A Society Novel. By LORIN KAYE. Third Edition. Crown 8vo, 6s.

Highland Brigade in the Crimea, The.

By Sir ANTHONY STERLING, K.C.B., a Staff Officer who was there. With Frontispiece and 18 Maps. Second Edition. Handsomely bound in cloth, demy 8vo, 7s. 6d.

Indifference in Matters of Religion.

By the ABBÉ F. DE LAMENNAIS. Translated from the French, with a Preface by LORD STANLEY of Alderley. Demy 8vo, 12s.

Infant, The.

A Novel. By FREDERICK WICKS, Author of "The Veiled Hand." Illustrations by A. MORROW. Second Edition. Large crown 8vo, 6s.

Italian Literature, A Manual of.

By F. H. CLIFFE. Crown 8vo, 6s.

Juarez, Life of, President of Mexico.

By ULICK R. BURKE. With Map and Portrait. Crown 8vo, 5s.

King's Second Marriage, A ; or, The Romance of a German Court.

Crown 8vo, 3s. 6d.

Kreutzer Sonata, The.

By COUNT LEO TOLSTOI. Translated from the Russian by H. SUTHERLAND EDWARDS. Paper covers, 1s. Thirty-seventh Thousand.

Lady's Impressions of Cyprus in 1893, A.

By Mrs. LEWIS. With Map. Crown 8vo, 5s.

Land of Ararat, The.

By A. F. MACDONALD, Author of "Too Late for Gordon." With Map and Illustrations. Demy 8vo, 6s.

Lesser Questions.

By LADY JEUNE. A Book dealing with the Principal Social Questions of the Day. Third Edition. Crown 8vo, 6s.

Lighter Life, The

A Series of Dialogues and Sketches. By WILLIAM WALLACE. Frontispiece. Crown 8vo, 3s. 6d.

Light that Lies, The

By COCKBURN HARVEY. Illustrated. Fcap. 8vo, 2s. 6d.

Literary Recollections.

By MAXIME DU CAMP, Member of the French Academy. Two Volumes, demy 8vo, 30s.

Love Knots.

A Novel. By MAY CROMMELIN, Author of "For the Sake of the Family," etc. etc. Crown 8vo, 3s. 6d.

The Love-Philtre, and Other Poems.

By HELEN F. SCHWEITZER. Royal 8vo, 5s. net.

Mapleson Memoirs, The.

Forty Years of Operatic Management, 1848–1888. By J. H. MAPLESON. With Portrait. Third Edition. Two Volumes, demy 8vo, 10s. 6d.

Mark Twain Birthday Book, The.

Cloth, gilt edges, 2s. 6d. ; morocco, 6s. 6d. Ninth Thousand.

Melbournians, The.

A Novel. By FRANCIS ADAMS, Author of "John Webb's End," etc. Crown 8vo, 3s. 6d.

Memories of the Mutiny.

By Colonel FRANCIS CORNWALLIS MAUDE, V.C., C.B., who commanded the Artillery of Havelock's Column. Two Volumes, on special paper, with Maps and Illustrations, demy 8vo, 30s.

Mighty Toltec, The.

A Story of Adventure. By S. J. ADAIR FITZ-GERALD. Crown 8vo, 6s.

Miss Cherry-Blossom of Tôkyô.

A Japanese Novel. By JOHN LUTHER LONG. Crown 8vo, 6s.

Mrs. Fenton.

A Sketch. By W. E. NORRIS. Third Edition. Crown 8vo, 2s. 6d.

My Dear Grenadier.

A Novel. By SYBIL BEATRICE REID, Author of "Sweet Peas." Crown 8vo, 3s. 6d.

New Day, The.

Sonnets. By Dr. T. GORDON HAKE. With Portrait of the Author by ROSSETTI. Crown 8vo, 5s. Rosslyn Series.

Old and New Poems.

By WALTER HERRIES POLLOCK. With a Portrait of the Author. Crown 8vo, 5s. Rosslyn Series.

On the Way Through.

By DOROTHEA GERARD, Author of "A Queen of Curds and Cream," and Joint-Author of "Reata" and "The Waters of Hercules." Crown 8vo, cloth, 3s. 6d.

Orthodox.

By DOROTHEA GERARD, Author of "Lady Baby," "On the Way Through," etc., and Joint-Author of "The Waters of Hercules" and "Reata." Third Edition. Crown 8vo, cloth, 3s. 6d.

Out Back.

A Romance of the Australian Bush. By KENNETH MACKAY, Author of "Stirrup Jingles." Third Edition. Crown 8vo, cloth, 3s. 6d.

Pictures of the World.

By CLEMENT SCOTT. Illustrated. Crown 8vo, cloth, 3s. 6d.

Poet's Walk.

An Introduction to English Poetry. Chosen and arranged by MOWBRAY MORRIS. Third Edition. Fcap. 8vo, 5s.

Queen of Curds and Cream.

A Novel. By DOROTHEA GERARD, Author of "Lady Baby," "On the Way Through," etc., and Joint-Author of "The Waters of Hercules" and "Reata." Fourth Edition. Crown 8vo, cloth, 3s. 6d.

Reminiscences of a Midshipman's Life, 1850–1856.

By Captain CECIL SLOANE-STANLEY, R.N. Second Edition. Crown 8vo, 3s. 6d.

Round the World with "A Gaiety Girl."

By GRANVILLE BANTOCK and F. G. AFLALO. Illustrated. Crown 8vo, 2s. 6d.

Shakspeare's Historical Plays: Roman and English.

With Revised Text, Introduction and Notes, Glossarial, Critical and Historical. By the late Right Rev. Bishop WORDSWORTH, D.C.L., LL.D. New Edition. Three Volumes, crown 8vo, 15s.

Shakspeare's Knowledge and Use of the Bible.

By the late Right Rev. Bishop WORDSWORTH, D.C.L., LL.D. Crown 8vo, cloth, 5s.; full calf, 8s.

Shilrick the Drummer; or, Loyal and True.

By JULIA AGNES FRASER. Three Volumes, crown 8vo, 31s. 6d.

Sin and the Woman, The.

A Novel. By DEREK VANE. Crown 8vo, 3s. 6d.

Sixty Years of Recollections.

By ERNEST LEGOUVÉ of the Académie Française. Translated with Notes by the Author of "An Englishman in Paris." Two Volumes, demy 8vo, cloth, 18s.

Something about Horses, Sport, and War.

By H. STRICKLAND CONSTABLE. Illustrated cover, crown 8vo, 3s. 6d.

Sonnets and Poems.

By the late EARL OF ROSSLYN. With Portrait of the Author. Crown 8vo, 7s. 6d. Second Edition.

Steve Brown's Bunyip.

By J. A. BARRY. With Introductory Verses by RUDYARD KIPLING. Fifth Edition. Crown 8vo, 3s. 6d.

Story of Chinese Gordon, The.

By A. EGMONT HAKE. A complete account of Gordon's Life, including his Campaigns in China and the Soudan, until his death at the Fall of Khartoum. Demy 8vo, with Portrait and Map, 15s. Vol. II. out of print.

Studies in a Mosque.

By STANLEY LANE-POOLE. Second Edition. Demy 8vo, cloth, 7s. 6d.

Summer Days for Winter Evenings.

A Series of Nature Idylls. By J. H. CRAWFORD, F.L.S., Author of " The Wild Life of Scotland." Illustrations by JOHN WILLIAMSON. Handsomely bound, in uniform with " The Wild Life of Scotland." Large crown 8vo, 8s. 6d. net.

Sweet Peas.

By SYBIL BEATRICE REID. Crown 8vo, cloth, 2s.

Thoughts of a Queen.

By CARMEN SYLVA (Elizabeth, Queen of Roumania). Translated into English, with Special Permission, by H. SUTHERLAND EDWARDS. Fcap. 8vo, cloth, 1s. 6d.

Veiled Hand, The.

By FREDERICK WICKS. With Illustrations by JEAN DE PALEOLOGUE. Fourth Edition. Crown 8vo, cloth, 3s. 6d.

Vestigia Retrorsum.

Poems by ARTHUR J. MUNBY. With Portrait of the Author. Crown 8vo, 5s. Rosslyn Series.

Wild Life of Scotland, The.

By J. H. CRAWFORD. With Illustrations by JOHN WILLIAMSON. Large crown 8vo, 8s. 6d. net.

Worthy.

The later and more exciting portion of the Tale deals with the Franco-German War. By Mrs. CADELL. Crown 8vo, 3s. 6d.

You Never Know Your Luck.

A Society Novel. By THEO. IRVING. Crown 8vo, 3s. 6d.

Standard Library of Foreign Classics.

Cheap and Popular Reprint of the Standard Foreign Authors in the Original Tongue. Handsomely bound in cloth, fcap. 8vo. Edited, with a Critical Preface, by W. H. SONLEY JOHNSTONE.

Vol. I. *THE COMEDIES OF MOLIÈRE.* 1s. 6d.

Vol. II. *MAXIMS AND REFLECTIONS OF LA ROCHE-FOUCAULD.* 1s.

LONDON:

JOHN MACQUEEN,

HASTINGS HOUSE, NORFOLK STREET, STRAND.

Agents in Scotland—

OLIVER & BOYD, EDINBURGH.

www.ingramcontent.com/pod-product-compliance
Lightning Source LLC
Chambersburg PA
CBHW030923050726
47498CB00003BA/876